tea & Comfort

#2

Tea & Comfort

ANDREA HURST

*And the day came when the risk to remain tight in a bud
was more painful than the risk it took to blossom.*
~ Anais Nin

Cover design: Lidia Vilamajo
Copy Editors/Proofreaders: Audrey Mackaman & Marie DeHaan
Developmental Editor: Cate Perry
Marketing & Publicity: 2MarketBooks

© 2015 Andrea Hurst
First edition printed April 2015
10 9 8 7 6 5 4 3 2 1

ISBN-13: 978-1511453820
ISBN-10: 1511453826

This book is a work of fiction. Names, characters, places and events are a product of the author's imagination and are used fictitiously.

table of Contents

Prologue

The Hamptons, New York
Two Years Ago

The day glistened in a way only white sand, turquoise waters, and golden sun could reflect. Thousands of tourists had besieged the peninsula for the Labor Day weekend. Luke's parents were in Europe and his brother was off jet-setting somewhere glamorous. Even though Darcy and Luke had the whole estate in East Hampton to themselves, they chose to stay in the guesthouse, which was a mini-mansion in itself and only steps from the beach. They hadn't left the house since Thursday. On the way there, a stop at a farm stand and Stuart's Fish Market had provided sweet shrimp, lavish vegetables, fresh berries, crusty bread, and assorted cheeses. With her insane work hours as a model, Darcy craved these lazy days when all she and Luke did was make love all afternoon, then supper on the sprawling deck and sip chilled chardonnay in crystal glasses.

It was a Sunday morning, the day they'd promised to go over to Luke's billionaire friend Tyler's infamous mansion for a cocktail party and art showing by the highly acclaimed artist,

Ian McPherson. Luke raved to Darcy about Ian's work, and he wanted to share it with her. And like almost everything in their whirlwind romance, Darcy wanted to share everything with him, too. Her persona as Darcy Devereux, super model, required changing from Luke's big T-shirt and into an elegant Stella McCartney summer dress before going out in public. Her gelled hair-spiking and makeup routine required time, time she resented spending these days since she'd been dating Luke. Even in the morning, when she woke all full of sleep, he told her how beautiful she was. And when she dressed up perfectly the way the world knew her, he devoured her with his eyes.

Darcy stepped into her Valentino sling-backs. She ran her fingers along the back of her calf. The bruises seemed to be getting worse. She reminded herself to call the doctor for her blood test results when she got home tomorrow.

As she walked into the living room, Luke rose from the white Bedford chair. He was a tall, lanky vision in khaki slacks and an aqua shirt setting off his bronze tan and golden hair. A devilish smile crossed his face as he whisked her into his arms.

"A woman of many charms," he whispered in her ear. His kisses trailed down her neck as he pulled her close. "Forget the party, I don't want to leave."

It took all her resolve not to melt into his arms. She gently pushed him back to catch her breath. "No, we promised we'd go and I want to see this artist's work."

Darcy brushed her lips against his full mouth. "We don't have to stay long."

Light danced behind his silver-grey eyes. His gaze made her wish he'd rip off her clothes and forget the party after all.

"Okay," he said, grabbing his keys. "Let's go. But there will be one little detour on the way back."

Darcy was intrigued. It really didn't matter where they went or what they did. They fit together. From the moment their eyes had met at a photo shoot, she'd known.

Tyler's mansion was rumored to be one of the most expansive on the island. Darcy had heard all about his afternoon cocktail parties that lasted until dawn the next day. When they drove through the iron entrance gates, she was not disappointed. The long tree-lined drive wove through its own dense woods and flowering gardens and stopped at the valet station next to an exquisite marble waterfall. The house was all and more than she'd imagined: three stories with turrets and fireplaces intermittent with ivy-covered walls and massive windows facing out to sea. These types of functions still intimidated her a bit. "You don't belong here," a familiar voice whispered in her head.

It seemed like all the beautiful people in the Hamptons were there, and their heads turned when she and Luke walked through the front door. Everywhere Darcy went, people recognized her carved cheekbones and emerald eyes. She inhaled a deep breath and squeezed Luke's arm tighter. His smile was reassuring. He always seemed to know what she was feeling.

They walked through the mammoth living room that reminded Darcy of a photo shoot with everyone dressed and posing in designer labels. Small groups gathered around the paintings spectacularly lit by hanging globes from the peaked ceiling. She could see a small orchestra outside and white umbrella-covered tables scattering the kelly-green lawn.

A voice from behind them said, "Welcome, Luke. And who is this charming creature you have been hiding from us all summer?"

Luke turned. "Tyler, I would like to introduce you to the love of my life, Darcy Devereux."

Tyler took Darcy's hand and kissed it with a polished finesse. Debonair was the word that came to her mind to describe this silver-haired man wearing an impeccable summer suit with a salmon-colored tie.

"What a lucky man you are," Tyler said. He turned to Darcy. "A familiar face, I'm sure. ZK chose his model well for his summer spread in Vogue."

Darcy smiled. "Thank you."

"You know the artist, Ian McPherson, of course, but his newest work is the best yet."

"I'm looking forward to seeing it," Darcy said.

Tyler motioned for them to follow him toward the bar. "We must get you some drinks. Tyra from the Tiki Bar is whipping up her luscious libations. Let's get you something wild and daring."

They tried to maneuver through the room, but a crowd of people swarmed Tyler and carried him off to the backyard, where chamber music filled the air.

Tyler waved back at them. "I'll meet you at the bar."

"Let's get a drink," Luke said, taking Darcy by the arm.

The bar featured tropical cocktails and was stocked with imported French champagne and assorted wines from the Pacific Northwest to honor the artist showing his work today. Luke pointed to a Pinot Noir from a well-known winery in

Oregon's Willamette Valley. Glasses in hand, the couple followed the crowd as they admired the massive oil paintings that blended Native American and Asian flavors.

"Hey there, Luke, good to see you, man."

Darcy turned to see a tall, dark, and very attractive man shaking hands with Luke. Even as in love as she was, she could still admire a good-looking man. He turned to her, his hand extended.

"I'm the artist causing all this fuss here today. Ian McPherson."

His handshake was warm, his smile genuine. Humble was not a characteristic she saw much of in New York, and it immediately endeared him to her.

"Darcy Devereux. I can see why Luke admires your work."

"Thank you." Ian waved his hands around the party. "Tyler talked me into all of this. It is definitely not my style, but it does build the career."

Luke put his arm around Darcy. "We'll have to make it out to the end of the world you live in someday."

"Well, it's not exactly the end of the known world. Madrona Island is about an hour north of Seattle and quite civilized."

"You live on an island?" Darcy asked.

"Sure do," Ian said. "Covered in Madrona trees, rocky beaches, and snow-capped mountains in the distance. A few whale sightings and bald eagles circling thrown in, too."

"Sounds like heaven," Darcy said. She looked up at Luke; anywhere would be heaven with him. She wondered if there were any wineries on that Northwestern island. Somewhere the two of them could escape to someday and live happily ever after. At the pace she was going, she was tired all the time. Their dream of escaping somewhere faraway together sounded better and better. She sighed. It was a nice fantasy.

A well-dressed woman dripping in diamonds and gold took Ian's arm and started pulling him away. "You must show me all the new paintings and help me decide which ones to buy for my summer cottage down the road."

Ian spoke back over his shoulder, "Nice to meet you, Darcy. Hope to see you both this week."

"Come on the boat with us tomorrow," Luke yelled after him.

"Text me the time and I'll be there," Ian said, giving in to the patron's persuasions and moving across the room.

"He is in high demand," Darcy said, trying not to laugh.

Luke leaned in and kissed her. "Don't get any ideas. You're taken."

Darcy raised an eyebrow at him.

They wandered around admiring a few more of Ian's exquisite art pieces. When they reached the back of the house, Luke took her wine glass and placed it next to his on a side table.

"And now for the detour," he said. "Are you ready to leave?"

Butterflies flickered in her stomach. He was being very mysterious. "The art is amazing, but I'm not in the market right now for a purchase. We can spend some time with Ian tomorrow on the boat. Let's go."

Hand in hand, Luke led her out the back of the house toward the water.

"What about the car?" she asked.

"We'll come back for that later," he said, guiding her down a footpath to the endless beach below. When they got to the warm sand, they tossed off their shoes and left them behind.

A few stragglers were off in the distance, but they had the beach almost to themselves. The afternoon sun was making its way west as Luke led her in silence to a small, idyllic cove where the ocean water was turquoise and glistened in the sunrays.

"What a beautiful spot," Darcy said.

"I used to run away here as a kid when my parents were fighting, or when Stefan was tormenting me," Luke said. "I'd just float in the cove and wish I was old enough to move away."

Darcy felt for him. She knew the feeling of wanting to leave your family behind and start a new life.

He took her hands in his. "I have never shared this spot with anyone else." He knelt down on one knee. "You are the one, Darcy. The only one." He pulled a small satin box out of his pocket.

Her feet froze in the sand. Her heart raced wildly.

"My love, will you marry me?" he asked.

She looked down at the man who completed her heart and soul. If she said yes, their families would blend and she had no idea how that could ever work. But to say no was impossible. There would never be another love like this one in her life. Tears welled in her eyes.

He opened the box to reveal a large but tastefully designed diamond engagement ring. It was breathtaking, but it was Luke who meant everything to her.

"I do, I will," she managed to get out through happy tears.

A smile spread across his face as he stood and placed the ring on her finger before taking her in his arms and pulling her into a deep embrace. "This is forever," he whispered into her ear.

Forever was the word that echoed in her mind back at home on Monday when the doctor finally called with her test results. Lupus. An autoimmune disease. She had not had the flu last month. There was a reason her hair was coming out in clumps, her joints still ached, and her weight kept dropping. The flare-ups would continue on and off and the disease could progress to her organs. She needed to come in immediately. Steroid treatments were prescribed, and possibly drug therapy.

Darcy had been called one of the most beautiful women in the world, but love was all she ever really wanted and she'd finally found it with Luke. He'd loved her as Darcy Devereux and never known her true identity, Kyla Nolan. Who would she be now?

Chapter One

Present Day
Madrona Island

Kyla stuffed the delicate silk pouch with rose pedals and dried lavender before tying it closed with a gold satin ribbon. These made perfect wedding shower favors, and the soon-to-be-Mrs. DeHaan was picking up the order today. Weddings were in the air on Madrona Island, it seemed.

Lily and Ian's wedding ceremony at the inn last month had been beautiful. Their self-written vows had brought tears to Kyla's eyes. Grandpa John had beamed the whole day, and Ian's young son Jason's smile made the union complete.

Of all the services Kyla offered at Tea & Comfort, wedding preparations were the most painful sometimes. Her road had not always been smooth. Her breath caught remembering Lily's grand opening for Madrona Island Bed & Breakfast last July. Luke had completely shocked Kyla when he'd appeared at the gathering. She had no idea how he'd found her or why. His searching eyes and angry but broken stance still haunted her.

"Kyla?" he'd said.

No one else caught that the name was framed as a question. What he did not say was, "I thought your name was Darcy."

To Luke she was Darcy Devereux, supermodel. Spiky white-tipped hair with flaming red roots. A face painted to perfection. Designer clothes draping her tall, slinky body. That's how Luke knew and loved her when he'd asked her to be his wife. Kyla, the local owner of Tea & Comfort, with long, flowing, red hair down her back and wearing island garb must have been a shock to him.

After seeing Luke for the first time in two years, her joints had ached and the fatigue returned. She'd feared a relapse of lupus and brought out her arsenal of herbal remedies, meditated twice a day, and was feeling much better now. Luke's quick departure had been a relief.

The bells rang over the front door of her shop, bringing Kyla back to the present day. She left her workroom and walked out to the front of the store to greet her customer. Morning sun lit the front window, casting tiny rainbows through the crystal prism along the walls. Audrey, the local librarian, waited at the smooth oak counter where purchases were made.

"Good morning." Audrey straightened her glasses. "Do you have my package ready?"

"It's right here under the counter. I freshly blended it this morning."

Kyla retrieved the monthly herbal tonic she'd prepared. Yellow dock, turmeric, red raspberry, and dandelion with a little molasses taken daily kept the iron up. She placed the bottle in a lavender tissue paper and tied it closed with a piece of silver yarn.

"Thanks so much," Audrey said. "This really helps."

"Don't forget to eat your greens."

Audrey laughed. "I'll try." She held up a jar with a heart charm attached to it. "Love spells?" Audrey asked blinking. "Do they work?"

Kyla hesitated. They certainly hadn't worked for her yet, but then again, her heart was already taken. "They're for focusing your hopes and dreams," Kyla said. "A pink, rose-scented candle helps as well." She pointed to the corner shelf where her handcrafted beeswax candles were displayed.

"Maybe next time." Audrey turned and headed for the door before waving goodbye.

Kyla checked the wooden shelves for stock and placed dried lavender arrangements on the tea tables. She glanced outside and admired the crisp fall day. Hopes and dreams, she thought. She looked down at the empty ring finger on her left hand. Almost.

Her wedding to Alexander Lucas Bradford II—Luke— would have been a huge society affair. Luke's parents would have taken charge and held it at their mansion in the Hamptons. His brother, Stefan, would have made their life hell if Luke had been the first to wed. Kyla caught her breath. The potential for disaster had put her in bed for days with a blazing migraine.

She hadn't told her wealthy-born husband-to-be that her grandmother, Mona, was from a long line of Irish healers and she was proud of her lineage. And her mother was a professional herbalist. Not exactly the type of people Luke was used to associating with at home or school at Harvard. She'd left New York a few days after her diagnosis and never looked back.

Kyla sat back down at her worktable and placed another lovers' sachet in the woven basket. Merlin, her rescue cat jumped up on the counter and rubbed his furry black body against her. The cat's purr was loud and comforting. She scratched behind his ears.

"You always know when I'm feeling stressed, don't you, little guy?"

She looked around for her Siamese cat who had meowed at her door loudly until she had eventually let him in to stay. , Ozzie was curled up asleep on the old velvet chair. Oz was more like a dog than a cat. He fetched rolled-up balls of paper and often greeted people at the door with a full conversation of meows. These two furry angels were great companions during these last couple of years.

She had a lot to be thankful for. Owning and running Tea & Comfort in the charming town of Grandview had brought her more joy than she could ever imagine. Going back to her roots, cultivating herbs and spices, creating products, and helping her customers felt right in a way being a fashion model never had. She was content here on this faraway emerald isle in the Pacific Northwest. She'd finally found a place where she fit in and friends who accepted her for who she was and kept her secrets when she asked. Madrona Island took care of its own, from the lonely seniors to the orphan dogs. Even to runaway women like her, the island and its people opened their arms in a warm embrace.

She stared out the back window of the shop. The maple tree was dropping its amber- and rust-colored leaves, opening up the view to her 1904 cottage behind the shop. Its shake roof and vintage windows beckoned, cozy and welcoming. Tea roses grew profusely up a tall trellis, and flowerpots lined the porch. The first few months, it had been her refuge, a place of healing. Then it had become home.

But seeing Luke again had opened up the lonely places inside her heart. It also brought back the memories of the crazy, narcissistic modeling business and the high-powered players that had run her life until she'd met Luke. The first time Luke smiled at her, a light went on in her heart. Kyla would never forget the day he proposed in the sand. It had been the happiest day of her life. For almost two years she'd tried banishing him from her memory and telling herself they were better off apart. But denial could only last so long.

Chapter Two

*J*ude, perky as ever, walked into Tea & Comfort, pulling Kyla from her memories. Her deep brown hair shone in the overhead light, set off by her red velvet scarf wrapped expertly around her neck.

"Busy day?" Jude asked.

Kyla shrugged. "On and off. How about you?"

"The locals are always hungry, and Chef Ryan's butternut squash soup was a hit today." Jude leaned an elbow down on the counter. "When do you want to go over the plans for the Halloween party?" she asked.

A chill ran through Kyla's body.

"Earth to Kyla, are you there?"

"What?" Kyla asked.

"The Halloween party, remember? Your biggest event of the year."

The sound of the door chimes rang in the air and Kyla glanced up to see Kelly's energetic entrance as she pushed through the door.

"Go ahead and help her," Jude said. "I can wait."

Kyla walked over and greeted the reporter for the local paper.

Kelly handed her a copy of the Island Examiner. "Hot off the presses," she said. "I thought you'd want to take a look."

"Thanks." Kyla stared at the image on the front page.

Jude leaned over her shoulder. "What's so interesting?"

The headline read: "Madrona Island Winery purchased by Alexander Lucas Bradford II." There was a picture of Luke holding up a bottle of Pinot Noir in front of the tasting room.

"Oh," Jude said.

Kyla looked up and the room spun. No wonder she'd been thinking of him today.

"Did you know about this?" Jude asked.

"I do now." Kyla turned back to Kelly, who flashed her a sympathetic smile. "Thanks for always having my back."

Kelly gave her a quick hug. "Let me know if I can do anything. Talk to you later."

"That's the guy from the grand opening, isn't it?" Jude asked. "The one you left behind in New York."

"I don't want to talk about it," Kyla said.

Jude placed a hand on Kyla's shoulder. "Well, maybe we need to."

"You're right," Kyla sighed. "Soon. But not today. Now, what can I help you with in the store?"

Jude stared at her but finally relented. "Hand cream, please. The strong stuff. Running a café is tough on the skin."

Kyla led her to an oak corner bookcase she'd painted a bright periwinkle. Creams and lotions in jars and bottles lined the floor-to-ceiling shelves.

"In this one, I blended shea butter, calendula, and lemon verbena. It should do the trick."

Jude squeezed a little cream from a sample tube on to her hands and sniffed the citrus-scented cream.

"Divine," Jude said. "I'll take the super size."

Kyla's shaking hands reached for the large glass jar. It slipped from her fingers, shattering on the tile floor. The pattern of broken glass spelled out a warning in her head. She backed away and willed her body to stop shaking.

Jude put her arms out. "You look like you could use a hug."

Kyla laid her head on Jude's shoulder. How could Luke still have so much effect on her? She had to pull herself together.

"Can you stay, Jude? I'll make us some tea."

"Happy to. I suggest something calming, but you're the expert."

After brewing a pot of rose petal and chamomile tea, Kyla joined Jude at the round wooden table with the hand-embroidered placemats by the front window. The china cups with a crimson rose pattern were delicate and beautiful. Kyla looked out the lace curtains to the peaceful view, watching puffy white clouds move across the water of the sound. At this moment, she wished she could float away on one. But she'd worked too hard to get healthy and establish her new life here on Madrona Island.

"A penny for your thoughts," Jude said.

"Just a penny?"

Jude's warm laugh filled the shop. "As if you'd share them for even a million."

Kyla frowned. "Perhaps I have nothing interesting to tell. Actually, I hired a part-time assistant named Rebecca, but she prefers to be called Becca."

"About time," Jude said.

"With her short red curls and her nose sprinkled with freckles, she looks just like Shirley Temple in the Rebecca of Sunnybrook Farm movie."

Jude laughed. "How old is she?"

"She just graduated from UC Santa Cruz, so she's only twenty-two. But she has lots of gardening experience and is strong, healthy, and willing to work in the field and shop."

"Glad you found her. When does she start?" Jude asked.

"This week. The sooner the better."

Their conversation was interrupted with the ringing of Jude's cell phone. "I bet it's Ryan wondering where I am." She held up her phone. "It's Lily." Jude answered, "And how is our blissful newlywed today?"

Kyla watched Jude's smile fade.

"What's wrong?" she asked.

"Hold on, Lily. I'm sitting right here with Kyla. I'll put you on speaker phone."

"I'm sorry, Kyla," Lily said. "It's all Ian's fault."

"What's his fault?"

"Without asking me, he told Mary to book Luke at our bed and breakfast until his winery closes escrow. I know how you feel about the man, but he's Ian's friend and he insists it's the right thing to do."

"Traitor," Jude said.

Kyla remained quiet. Her stomach twisted in knots. "For how long?"

The silence rang in the room and echoed in Kyla's head.

"How long, Lily?"

"I don't know yet. Ian said he would fill me in tonight. Mary feels terrible. As the resident innkeeper she still checks with us on any major decisions."

Jude grabbed the phone and switched off the speaker. "Call us as soon as you know. And find out everything." She ended the call and put the phone back in her purse. "I guess he's here to stay."

"And he's bought the Madrona Winery." Kyla could barely get the words out. Her hands were numb and her legs were following. She braced herself against the table for support. "I don't blame Ian for letting Luke stay at the B&B. You know they were buddies in New York. Before…"

Jude pulled her Scottish wool shawl tight around her. "Let's get out of here. Close the shop early. Ryan can prep for dinner service without me at the café. I'll text Lily and tell her we're on our way. We'll go pick her up and take a good, long walk on the bluff."

"Might as well," Kyla said, standing up. "I'm sure not going to be able to concentrate around here now." Kyla zipped up her forest-green fleece jacket. Some fresh air might clear her racing mind. She turned the sign on the door from an open sunflower to a closed rose bud on the other side, locked up, and dimmed the lights.

"I'll drive," Jude said. "Lily is waiting at the B&B. Luke's over at their house and she doesn't want to see him right now."

Kyla tried to slow her breath while Jude's Subaru station wagon headed south on the main highway that divided the island. What could she do? She rubbed the back of her neck, trying to stave off a headache. Out. She wanted out. The island was too small for both of them. Luke would find out everything now. She couldn't bear it.

Mercifully, Lily was waiting on the porch when they pulled up to the B&B. The rolling green lawn that sloped down toward the Puget Sound was turning brown in spots without the summer sun to sustain it. Gone were the lush flower gardens, and only a few herbs remained behind. In the spring, the garden would come to life again. Kyla wondered if she'd still be here to see it.

Lily, her honey-blonde hair catching in the breeze, hurried down the path toward them. "Hi, everyone," she called out.

Through the car window, Kyla saw Grandpa John playing fetch in the field with Gretel, his friendly black dog. She rolled the window down and waved.

He walked over, the dog at his heels.

"You girls playing hooky today?" he asked.

Grandpa John always made Kyla smile. "It was a slow day, so I closed early," she replied. For a minute, she wanted to jump out and cry on his shoulder. It was times like this it would be nice to have a father to turn to.

"Well, you girls have fun," he said with a wink. He looked back at his house. "Looks like Ian's in the dog house. I'm giving him some space."

"I don't blame you," Lily said.

Grandpa John turned and tossed the tennis ball for Gretel, who shot after it at record speed.

Lily slid into the back seat. "Are you all right?" she asked.

Kyla turned to look at her. "What do you think?"

Lily leaned toward her. "I want you to know, Ian and I had our first fight over this. I'm so sorry."

Jude gunned the engine. "And exactly why did Ian offer hospitality to this rake?"

"Ian said we might as well start off as friends and see just what Luke's plans are, instead of being surprised afterwards. He also said Luke is a good guy."

Jude backed out slowly and drove the back road to the state park. "Maybe that is wise. Know your enemy and all."

11

"He's not my enemy," Kyla snapped.

The only sound in the car for the next three miles was the hum of the tires on the asphalt.

Sun reflected off the steep, sandy bluff and washed across the rocky beach below. Kyla and her friends navigated the driftwood-lined path toward the water. Seagulls lined up like little soldiers at the water's edge, as if waiting for a sign to take flight.

The threesome walked along, skirting the incoming tide. A double-decker ferryboat glided across the watery passage to its destination on the peninsula. Kyla unzipped her jacket. Even with the crisp fall breeze, the sun felt warm and soothing. She kicked a wet pebble and watched it glisten in the light.

"How about we take a seat and enjoy the view," Jude said. She pointed to a bleached white tree trunk that had washed ashore some time ago.

"Sounds good to me," Lily said.

Kyla followed and joined them on the driftwood bench. She faced the sound and took a deep breath. Water and sky filled her and calmed her spirit. A whisper in the tides called her to surrender. Let go. It was time to stop running. This was her island now.

Her loyal friends waited for her to talk and tell them why Luke had come back. If he was not her enemy, who was he? She had no idea now. "Thanks for being here, you two."

Jude, always the mama lion, put her arm around Kyla's shoulder. "We're here for you. Just tell me one thing, is he dangerous? Should we call the sheriff?"

"Hardly," Kyla said with a grin. "Only his charm is deadly. It's my heart that may betray me."

Lily nodded. "And sorry again about Ian."

"I about lost it today when you called Jude, but I'm okay now," Kyla said. Her friends stared at her with concerned expressions. "Ian's a good guy, Lily. Don't be angry with him. He was Luke's friend first and sold art to him long before I met him. If it hadn't been for Ian telling me at an art opening in New York about this remote little island in the sound, I wouldn't be here myself."

"Thanks," Lily said. "Ian never turns his back on his friends. I should have trusted his choices."

Kyla sighed. "Back when I left New York—ran away is more accurate—I turned my back on my family and my engagement to Luke. I couldn't face the overwhelming diagnosis of lupus and needed some time alone. Then I remembered Ian and Madrona Island."

"I wondered how you found us," Jude said. "You were never very forthcoming. Part of your mystique and charm."

Kyla watched the low waves crash on the moist sand and inch slowly toward their feet. Soon it would be high tide. Always the same, day after day. A lone seagull screeched as it soared over their heads. Kyla stood and brushed the sand off her jeans. A brown face peeked at her from out in the water. "A seal," she said, walking closer.

Lily and Jude moved alongside her.

"And look, there are grey porpoises out there. See the little dorsal fin popping in and out?" Lily said.

"I suppose Luke will want to know the truth now. Why I left him without a word right after the proposal. I guess I owe him that."

"What will you tell him?" Lily asked.

"The same thing I need to tell you right now. I loved Luke so much but I couldn't face the possibility of him leaving me." Kyla stared at the sand. She'd been a coward and had thought only of herself. Perhaps she was not capable of love.

"Why would he ever leave you?" Jude asked.

"He didn't know the real me or that I was sick. He knew me as the beautiful Darcy Deveraux at the top of my career. His parents disapproved of our engagement, and if they had met my family, that would have been the end."

"Kyla, that's not how love works," Lily said. "He deserves to know the truth."

"I guess I have no choice now," Kyla said.

"Will he understand?" Lily asked.

Kyla met her friend's eyes. "I don't know. Would you?"

Chapter Three

Luke parked on the gravel drive of the inn and unloaded his suitcases from the SUV. The rental car would do for now until he figured out the type of vehicle he would need for island living. The winery came with a truck, so he could use that, too. He surveyed his temporary lodgings: Madrona Island Bed & Breakfast. It was as he remembered it from the summer: a quaint place surrounded by woods on the backside and an expansive view of the water in front. So here he would stay for a little while.

The previous owners of his newly purchased Madrona Island Winery were completing the harvest with their crew before they moved out. Luke looked forward to working alongside them, picking the deep-purple grapes and beginning the process of soaking them. The property would soon be his, including the retail winery, cellars, vineyards, and a two-story log home with floor-to-ceiling windows. Not a neighbor in sight, only miles of cedars, pines, circling bald eagles, and grazing deer. Luke still couldn't believe it was all his. Or would be in about a week.

Ian was his only friend on the island. He hoped that would change soon. Kyla…he was not sure if she was a friend or foe, but he was determined to find out. And now that he'd found the winery of his dreams, he was here to stay. He would get to the bottom of what had happened between them and then move on with his new life here.

Two years ago she had disappeared into thin air. All she'd left behind for him were two short sentences: "Don't look for me. I'm sorry. ~Darcy." She called herself Kyla now.

Those words were embedded into his brain and had ripped apart his heart. He didn't know whom he hated more at that point: Kyla or his parents, who probably had a part in chasing her away.

A screen door slammed and jarred Luke from his reverie. A spry-looking elderly lady in jeans and a flannel shirt hurried down the front steps.

"Young man, are you going to check in or are you going to stand here all day?"

"I'm checking in." He flashed her a smile.

Silver-grey hair contrasted the piercing blue eyes that had him pinned in place. She stood with her hands on her hips looking him up and down. "I remember you. You were at the grand opening in June."

Luke half expected her to pull out a rifle and chase him off the property. Just what had Kyla said about him? Perhaps she had put up wanted pictures around town. Who knew what he was in for now?

"I'm checking in today. Just admiring the scenery first."

"Betty's the name. I live next door. Can I give you a hand with that bag? Mary's making up the rooms."

"I can manage. But thanks for the kind offer." He held out his hand. "Luke. Nice to meet you." Betty's handshake was strong. Luke wasn't sure he'd ever met anyone quite like Betty before.

She squinted and took one last look at him. "I think Ian's in the office. He'll help you out."

"He's expecting me."

Betty nodded. "All right then. I'll be heading off to McPhersons' place across the way. I don't work here, you know. Just a nosy neighbor."

She was gone before he picked up his suitcase. That lady could really move.

Luke walked up the steps of the wraparound porch and knocked on the door.

"Hey, good to see you," Ian said. He picked up Luke's suitcase. "Come on in and I'll show you around."

Luke stepped into the parlor area. "Nice place. Very turn-of-the-century."

"It belonged to Lily's grandmother and has been in the family a long time."

"And where are you living now?" Luke asked.

"Did you see the big ranch house across the field when you pulled in?"

Luke nodded.

It belongs to my Grandpa John and has been in the family forever. He pointed to the kitchen. "Coffee and tea are always available on the counter, and breakfast is at 9:00 in the dining room. Make yourself comfortable down here anytime."

"Thanks again for letting me stay. Was the wife okay with the arrangement?"

Ian shrugged. "She was afraid you coming here would upset Kyla, but I told her you were a good guy and this way she could get to know you."

Luke looked around. "Is Lily here? Should I say hello?"

"Seems an emergency walk on the beach was in order with the ladies after a certain someone's visit was announced."

"I see." Luke frowned. "I can stay at the motel outside of town. I don't want to upset anyone."

"Forget it," Ian said. "You're my friend and it will work out. You'll see."

Ian did not sound that convincing, but Luke hoped he was right. "It sounds like Darcy, I mean Kyla, has made some good friends here."

"That she has," Ian said. "Lily, Jude, and Kyla are inseparable."

"And you, too," Luke said. "You seem a happily married man now and not the reclusive artist I first met. And how's your boy?"

Ian's grin said it all. "He's growing up so fast I can hardly keep up. Lily, Jason, and me live over there in the big house and I added a master suite for some privacy."

"Sounds amazing."

"So, which room is mine? Roses are not really my thing."

Ian laughed. "Actually, I put you in the Honeymoon Suite. It's large, nothing frilly."

Luke narrowed his eyes. "Are you kidding me, Ian?"

"No. It's on the ground floor with a private exit so you can sneak in and out."

"Very funny," Luke said, shaking his head. "Show me to my suite. Please."

The room was a champagne color, very elegant with a large king-sized bed. The gauze canopy was a bit much, but the wood fireplace in the corner was appealing. As promised, French doors led out to a private patio with a path down to the water. A fresh citrus smell permeated the bathroom that had a shower big enough for two.

"I hope you will enjoy your stay," Ian said. "You're welcome here until your place is ready."

"Who would've thought all of us meeting up at that art and wine show in the Hamptons would end up with all three of us here on the island?" Luke said.

"Fate," Ian said. He paused. "Love?"

Luke shrugged.

"When do you plan to see Kyla?" Ian asked.

"You all probably know much more than I do then: why she ran and why here."

"I'm afraid Kyla is going to have to fill you in herself in that area," Ian said.

The talk of Kyla upset him more than he expected. Luke had a moment of doubt about his impulsive purchase of the winery on the island. It was everything he'd ever dreamed of—everything he and Kyla had ever dreamed of—but he'd always thought Sonoma County in California would be his home. He hoped it was not a mistake coming here, seemingly unwelcomed. He shook off the doubt.

"Kyla," Luke said. "She broke my heart. I want some answers."

Ian moved toward the door. "Just go slow," he said as he closed the door behind him.

Luke would go slowly, but he was determined to find out why. He sat down on the edge of the bed, sinking into a down comforter. He'd never gone slowly with anything in his life, and he didn't know how to do it now. He thought for a moment about the rushed affair and quick engagement he'd had with Kyla. They were so in love; they were racing to their new life together. And then she was gone. None of it happened. Not a wedding. Not a honeymoon in a perfect room like this. Not a life together.

Maybe he could go slowly now if it meant finding out the truth. Luke walked over to the French doors and stepped outside on the porch. He had to give it to Kyla. She'd found one of the most beautiful places he'd ever seen. He breathed in the sea air and listened to the gulls calling. With a pang he thought of the many things they'd dreamed of together and the many things they'd lost.

The late afternoon sun dipped behind the snow-peaked mountains and a small shadow cast across the water. A car door slammed in the driveway of the inn. A voice called out, "You take care, Kyla. I'll call you tomorrow."

"Thanks for the walk, Lily."

Luke recognized Kyla's voice and quickly stepped back into the doorway of his suite. He listened as the car pulled away and thought of the woman inside and wondered who she really was.

Chapter Four

"Luke just left," Lily whispered. "He had breakfast with us first."

"You don't have to whisper if he's gone," Kyla said back into her cell phone.

"Right," Lily said. "I don't want Ian to hear I'm reporting back to you either. Luke asked all about the town and…"

"What else? Did he ask about me?"

"He mentioned Tea & Comfort and wondered how long it had been open."

A million thoughts ran through Kyla's mind. He was checking up on her. Wondering how long she'd been here. Was he also checking her financial stability?

"And what did you tell him?"

"I told him the truth, of course. That it was one of the most wonderful and successful shops in town."

There was a satisfaction in that and Kyla smiled. But hearing about Luke's every move was not bringing her peace of mind. "Thanks, Lily. For now, I think I'll just imagine he isn't here."

Kyla hung up the phone. She could imagine all she wanted. Luke was not going away. She had too much to do today to sit around and wonder what he was doing anyway.

"Morning," Becca said as she entered through the front door of the shop. "I stopped by the lavender field and did a little pruning this morning. The plants are looking hearty." She slipped a purple apron over her jeans and T-shirt and tied it in the back. "Shall I brew some tea?"

"There's plenty of hot water and I just brought the tangy orange scones out of the oven," Kyla answered. "I do have to run out this morning to do some errands and pick up some fresh cream. Think you can handle the place alone for a few hours?"

"No problem. You just go do your business and I'll take care of everything. The afternoon tea items will be ready when you return."

Becca was a real find. Kyla used to have to close the shop to do errands and rush back to open it again. She walked into the back room and scooped the envelope with the deposit off the desk and picked up her to-do list. The bank was first, then the fabric store for ribbon, the post office box to retrieve mail, and last was the small grocery store in town. Cascade Market was a bit of a drive and she only needed two items. She looked at the teapot-shaped clock on the wall. It was a little after eleven in the morning. If she hurried, she could be back for afternoon tea, when her customers often came in for little moon-shaped sandwiches and moist scones with clotted cream.

Kyla walked down Front Street, peeking in the windows as she went. A delivery truck blocked Island Thyme Café as it unloaded supplies. She waved at Ryan, who was out front directing the workers. As the new chef, Ryan had made a positive difference in the food and Jude's workload. Something else was clear: He'd touched Jude's heart as well.

She noticed a sign in the window of Books, Nooks & Crannies. She remembered when it had been called Frank's Books. Now it was for sale. No, Kyla thought. She loved hanging out in the various little nooks spread throughout the store and reading books and magazines. What if a new owner changed the quaint store or, worse yet, closed it or turned it into yet another gift shop for tourists? Kyla pushed opened the door and went inside.

"Morning, Miss Kyla," Frank said. "I got some new gardening books in if you're interested. They're in the back by the window."

"I'm more interested in knowing why you have the shop up for sale. Is everything all right?" He was pushing seventy, she knew, but he always seemed happy to see a customer. And he lived upstairs, so this was his home as well.

"I've had this shop close to twenty years," Frank said. "I think it's time I pass it on to someone else and do a bit of travel. I want to see my grandkids in Arizona and spend winters toasty warm in the blazing sun. The book business is not what it used to be."

"Can't argue with that," Kyla said. "But we'll miss you so much."

"I'll still be around some. You can't get rid of me that easily."

Kyla looked around at the nooks and crannies filled with new and used books. "Are you selling the whole building, including your upstairs home?"

Frank straightened a few books on the counter. "If I can. The stairs are getting harder to navigate. I thought I might get one of those modular places and spend half my time here. You know, be a snow bird or goose or whatever it is."

Kyla laughed. "You might just enjoy that. I hope the new owner doesn't change a thing."

"They may have to change a bit to make this rent. My grandson, Marco, in Seattle has his eye on the place. He thinks adding a fancy coffee bar inside would up the profits."

"Not a bad idea," Kyla said. "How old is Marco now? I haven't seen him in years."

Frank pulled a picture out of his wallet and showed it to Kyla. "Twenty-three years old, and a handsome young man. He's been away to university and just moved back home."

"He has grown up," Kyla said, looking at the picture. If this young man moved to town, the young girls' heads would be spinning.

"Marco's coming over to the island next week to discuss things. It might work out to keep it in the family."

Cherise from the art gallery peeked her head in the front door of the shop. "Is my book in?" she asked Frank.

He shook his head. "Not yet. Sorry."

"No problem," Cherise said. She hesitated at the store and stared at Kyla. "Are you at Tea & Comfort this week?"

"Every day," Kyla said. Cherise had never been in Tea & Comfort before, so Kyla was curious what her interest might be.

Cherise was gone as fast as she appeared.

"Okay then," Kyla said turning back to Frank. "I'll come by later to look at those new gardening books."

She reluctantly left the shop and headed toward the bank. Just as she turned the corner, she saw Luke walking in the front door of Island Bank. He looked very Pacific Northwest in his jeans and sweatshirt, and she almost didn't recognize him. But his sunlit hair framing his striking profile was unmistakable. She ducked back around the corner. "This is ridiculous," she said aloud to herself. "Why am I hiding in my own town?" Fine, she would go to the fabric store first and then the bank. She walked up the street. Was this how it was going to be now? Wondering if he was around every corner?

Purchase complete at the fabric store, Kyla headed back to the bank. The teller greeted her with a bright smile. At the post office she met with the same. She never retrieved her mail without seeing a familiar face. Just stepping out of the shop and taking a run through town brought up her spirits. She would not let Luke's invasion spoil that. Besides, he'd probably be at the winery most of the time after he moved in. Lily said the escrow was closing next week.

Kyla looked at her watch. If she hurried, she could get to the store around the corner, buy a few things, and make it back to the shop within an hour. Once inside the market, she grabbed a wire basket and headed to the produce section. The fresh brown eggs from 3 Brothers Farm looked delicious and would make some good breakfasts. She reached up for a couple of glass bottles of cream from the local dairy and heard a familiar voice behind her.

"Need some help?"

Luke's deep, warm voice was unmistakable. Kyla turned to face him. His nearness set her on edge as sparks moved between them.

"No thanks," she said.

Kyla tried to step around him, but Luke blocked her path. "Nice little market," he said. "And they carry my new wine label."

She met his eyes with what she hoped was a fierce look. "The brand is popular on the island. So were the old owners."

"And hopefully the new owner will be popular, too," Luke said.

His smug grin made her want to punch him. She knew that look of his, daring her to respond. "Nice seeing you," she said, trying again to push around him.

"Is it?" he asked.

"Are you going to let me buy or not?"

He grinned. "And if I don't?"

She glared at him. "What do you want, Luke?"

"Answers, plain and simple."

Kyla looked around and was relieved no one seemed to be watching them. The basket was getting heavy and Becca was waiting for her.

"Right here and now?" she said, raising her voice.

Luke shrugged. "Of course not. How ungentlemanly of me. May I take you for lunch this week? We could catch up."

"Why, of course," Kyla said with the same pretense of civility. She might as well get it over with before she had too much time to think. "Tomorrow. Island Thyme Café. Noon."

He tilted his head to her and stepped out of the way.

"Tomorrow," he said.

Luke watched her walk away, head high, back straight, holding the basket almost as a prop in a runway show. Despite her apparent paleness, she looked even more beautiful now than she had in New York. Her cascading, auburn hair trailed down her shapely back. Her hastened strides toward the checkout stand drew his gaze to her long legs. Even in faded jeans and fleece, she moved with inherent grace.

For a minute he forgot why he was even in the store. He'd had appointments all morning with the various local merchants to introduce himself as the new owner of Madrona Winery. But when out of the corner of his eye he'd caught Kyla hiding from him near the bank, he'd decided to shadow her and see what she what up to. He was not proud of himself stooping to being a spy, but it did have its planned effect. Tomorrow he would finally come face to face with the only woman who'd both won his heart and broken it.

Chapter Five

Kyla arrived early to Island Thyme Café. Somehow she'd managed to stay calm when she called Jude and reserved a private table by the window. The last thing she wanted was for the whole town to hear this conversation.

Jude hugged her when she walked in and escorted Kyla to the table. She laid a menu before her. "Can I get you a mocha for now?" she asked. "Lily swears by them as a cure-all."

"I'll have one of those Mexican mochas Ryan makes, with the cayenne in them. Double tall, please."

Kyla looked around the large dining room. Only a few locals hung out at the bar, drinking beer and eating hamburgers. A couple she didn't recognize sat in the corner by the woodstove completely absorbed with each other. Alone for a moment, she stared out the large window overlooking the cove. Sky and water blended into one grey image. Not even a peek of sun. These days made her tired, and she had so much to do to finish the Halloween party plans. But she would have no peace until she faced Luke and put her past behind her.

"Double tall, extra chocolate," Jude said placing the coffee drink before her. "I hope it helps. I'll be at the bar. Just yell if you need me."

Kyla sipped the sweet and spicy mixture through the thick straw and let it warm her insides and spark her brain. But when the door opened and Luke entered, there was no drink on earth that would settle her heart.

He tossed off his parka and put it behind the chair. He just stood there looking at her for several seconds. Why did he have to be so devastatingly handsome? His gold-streaked hair brushed across his forehead, setting off his silver-streaked eyes. His full bottom lip still appeared to be in a perpetual pout. Kyla caught her breath and tore her eyes away.

"Good afternoon." Luke sat down and perused the menu.

She kept her eyes glued to her menu, but choosing something to eat was not appealing.

"What's good here?" he asked as if they were out for a casual lunch.

"Their homemade soups are excellent and about everything else, too. Ryan is a top chef. Jude is lucky to have him."

Jude walked over to take their order. "Hello, Luke. I don't think we officially met at the grand opening. Jude Simon, owner and proprietor."

He shook her hand. "Luke Bradford, owner and proprietor of Madrona Island Winery."

Kyla watched the exchange. Jude's smile was forced, and her eyes never left him. Luke was cautious and polite.

"What's your soup today?" Kyla asked.

"On demand, Ryan has cooked up his famous butternut squash and apple soup, and the other option is chicken chili. Comes with homemade honey bread."

"I'll have a bowl of the soup," Kyla said.

"Which is your favorite?" Luke asked Jude.

Jude met his gaze. "You don't look like a chili sort of guy to me, and the squash is probably too sweet for your palate. How about an order of our fresh-from-the-cove garlic mussels over linguini?"

"Perfect," Luke said. "You got me."

Jude smiled and walked back toward the kitchen.

Kyla sipped her mocha while Luke fidgeted with his napkin and avoided eye contact. This was ridiculous.

"When do you move into your new home?" she asked.

"As soon as they finish with the harvest, which is in about a week. It's a beautiful piece of property."

"That it is." She really wanted to say, Just like we always dreamed of. She looked away before he could see the tears forming. "I hope you'll be very happy there," she managed to get out.

His eyes bore into her. "Do you?"

She could feel her resolve weakening. "Of course."

"It's pretty hard to be happy when the love of your life walks out on you without even a goodbye."

She met his eyes. "I'm sorry."

"A bit late for that, wouldn't you say?"

Kyla released her pent-up breath. He was right in every way.

Luke placed his hand on hers. "Why, Kyla? You owe me that much. Was it my parents?"

She couldn't bear to see the pain in his eyes. "No, they had nothing to do with it."

His race reddened. "Tell me the truth. Did they buy you off?"

"Absolutely not," she said. "How dare you even think…?"

Luke glared at her, but behind the mask of anger was true devastation. Kyla's heart broke. He sagged in the chair and looked like a lost little boy.

"Then what? What possibly would make you run like that?" he asked.

Images of the sterile doctor's office where she received two treatments that first week ran through her mind. Blonde clumps with red roots of hair filling her sink, fatigue and morning-like sickness that had her fearing pregnancy. She had thought she was sparing him a life saddled with a sick wife and spared herself the pain of rejection when he would surely have cancelled their engagement.

"I had my reasons, Luke. Believe me, I thought it was for the best."

"The best? I loved you. Asked you to marry me. You left me wondering what the hell happened to you. I didn't know if you were dead or alive. Or if I'd done something terrible or perhaps Stefan or my parents had bought your passage to a distant planet."

At the sound of Stefan's name, Kyla froze. Luke's brother had called her when he'd heard about their engagement and let her know they'd never accept her into their family. In his snide, superior way, he'd told her to have fun while she could still enchant Luke and until Luke's girlfriend, Lizbeth, came home. She'd hung up the phone—mind finally made up—and packed her bags.

Jude brought over their lunch and placed it before them. Neither one of them lifted a fork.

"Anything else?" Jude asked.

Kyla shook her head. "We're fine."

"Okay then," Jude said. She hesitated before turning to go.

Luke picked up his fork and then threw it back down on the plate.

"Kyla," he said, his voice gaining volume. "You owe me an explanation."

"And what about Lizbeth?" Kyla asked. "What explanation were you going to give her when you proposed to me? And conveniently forgot to tell me you had a girlfriend?"

His shoulders dropped. "Kyla, I was going to tell you. I only dated her a few times to make my parents happy, but I never loved her. We really were just friends. As soon as she returned from Europe, I was going to break it completely off."

"And when were you going to tell me about her? Or was that why you had Stefan do it?"

"You never gave me a chance to tell hardly anyone about us, Kyla. You just disappeared." Luke paused. "Stefan told you? When?"

Kyla fought back the humiliating tears that stuck in her throat. "Imagine how I felt, Luke, when Stefan called and was only too happy to tell me you were engaged to Lizbeth."

His face paled. "To be honest, from the moment I saw you, I never gave Lizbeth another thought."

Kyla narrowed her eyes. "So you didn't go back to her after I left?"

His eyes flashed with anger. "If you believe that, you don't know me at all."

"You don't know me either," she said. "A few whirlwind weeks and you were ready to marry a stranger." How dare he follow her across the country and pressure her like this?

"I was under the impression you felt the same way about me as I did for you. Perhaps I was wrong," Luke said. Deflated, he sank back in the chair.

"Perhaps you were wrong," Kyla said impulsively. She wanted to bite her tongue after the words poured out. She couldn't stand to see him like this. But was it fair to get his hopes up again?

Luke pushed out his chair. "Lunch is on me. It's the least I can do after taking your time." He turned, paid the bill at the counter, and was out the door before Kyla could catch her breath.

Chapter Six

Hell may have no fury like a woman scorned, but watching Luke's face made Kyla wonder at what depth of hell she had put him through when she'd left him behind. So much had changed in the last two years. She'd like to think she'd matured and would not have acted so rashly now. He at least deserved an explanation, a chance to know the truth. But she had not wanted the Cinderella story to end. For once in her life, she was the princess being swept off her feet and going to live happily ever after. But like Cinderella, she had a family who did not fit in the castle and a past that certainly did not make her deserving.

Jude rushed over to the table. "Are you all right?"

Kyla was not sure how to answer. "He hates me."

"Just the other side of love," Jude said. She patted Kyla on the shoulder. "Give him some time. Have you considered telling him what's really going on with you?"

"I can't. Not yet."

Jude nodded. "I guess you didn't mention that you grow your lavender on the winery property either?"

"Nope," Kyla said.

"Well then, perhaps a bit of a distraction would help. How about we go over the final details for the Halloween party?"

Kyla looked up at her good friend. "How do you always manage to stay so upbeat and happy?"

For a moment Jude's mask slipped and a wave a grief crossed her face. Kyla was surprised she'd not seen it before. Jude was like the sun, always shining.

"That's how I get through," Jude said. "Focus on what's in front of me and find the joy in it."

"Halloween, right?" Kyla said. "I've been letting things slip and it's coming up fast."

"Next week to be exact," Jude said, putting on a goofy smile. "Let me go get my fancy new iPad to take notes. Be right back."

Outside the window, the beauty of nature mixed with the grey melancholy of the misty day. The tide was out in the cove, and Kyla saw a blue heron perched on one leg near the water's edge. In the distance, where the clouds thinned, she saw the snowy peak of Mt. Baker.

The pain in Luke's eyes…she could hardly bear the fact that she'd been the cause. But, like Jude said, that was her past. She'd let her fear swallow her up, but she had not meant to hurt him. And now they both needed to move on.

Jude slid into a chair opposite her. "So, just like last year, some of the merchants will stay open late and we'll all dress up." Jude looked up from the tablet. "Have you decided on a costume yet?"

"Don't laugh," Kyla said. "I was thinking of going as Mother Nature."

Jude did laugh. "Well, if anyone can pull that off, it would be you. I'm sticking to a new version of my tavern wench costume."

"It suits you well," Kyla said. "What's Lily wearing?"

Just as Lily's name was mentioned, Chef Ryan leaned out of the kitchen door and yelled, "Lily's on the phone for you, Jude."

"Mind reading again?" Kyla asked.

"That's your talent, not mine," Jude said with a smile. "I'll be right back."

A warm wave rushed up Kyla's spine. Something was up with Lily. She rose from her chair and walked toward the counter.

"We'll wait for you," she heard Jude say.

Jude turned. "Lily would like us to wait until she gets here. She has some news. Meanwhile, we can finish."

Kyla half-listened as Jude confirmed which treats every-one planned to serve.

"What are you making?" Jude asked.

"I'm making mulled cider, hot chocolate with cayenne and lavender, and I'm trying out a pumpkin-filled chocolate truffle."

"No fair," Jude said. "Everyone always likes your treats best."

"But you have Ryan working here now. I bet he'll come up with something amazing."

Jude grimaced. It was obvious there was more going on here, at least on Jude's part. Kyla would take a close look at the two of them together next time. She hoped it was mutual.

Lily blew in the door, propelled by a hearty gust of wind. She tossed her blonde hair out of her eyes, scanned the room, and waved before hurrying over to them.

"So glad you were both here so I can tell you together." Lily pulled off her flannel scarf and unbuttoned her coat.

"Give," Jude said.

Crimson colored Lily's cheeks as she held back a smile. "Don't tell anyone else yet, okay?"

"Of course," Kyla said.

"We just found out I'm pregnant!"

Jude jumped out of her seat and hugged Lily. "What wonderful news."

A single tear rolled down Lily's cheek. "I never thought it would happen."

Kyla held her breath, willing herself to be calm. A child. Pain surged through her heart. It would probably never happen for her. She could still hear the doctor talking. May be too high risk. Kyla's medications could cause problems for a baby, etc., etc. But Lily looked blissful and she was happy for her.

"What a blessing," Kyla said. "Ian must be over the moon."

"He is," Lily said. "You should see him pacing the floor, making plans, and asking me if I need to lie down."

Jude laughed. "Men."

The three women joined hands. "Friends for life," Lily said.

"Friends for life," Jude and Kyla echoed back.

They squeezed each other's hands, letting their love for each other fill the air.

"Hey, can I pay my bill up here, ladies?" a guy barked from the cash register.

Jude rolled her eyes. "Be right back."

"Enough about me," Lily said. "What are you doing here on a work day? Who's minding the shop?"

"I met Luke here for lunch." Kyla stared down at the table.

"And you didn't tell me? How did it go?"

Kyla glanced up. She was sure misery filled her eyes.

"I see," Lily said. "How can I help?"

Chapter Seven

Luke parked his car in his driveway in front of the log house that now belonged solely to him. The wood deck wrapped around the house and two Adirondack chairs faced out over the vineyards. He was glad a few of the workers stayed on to help with the winemaking. The first part of the fermentation process would start soon and when everything was ready, they would start pressing the grapes.

Ian parked right behind Luke and jumped out to help carry in some boxes.

"Nice place," Ian said. "The view must be amazing from that top floor." He lifted a box out of the back of Luke's SUV. "Where do you want this stuff?"

Luke held the keys up in his hand. "Follow me." As he walked in across the smooth wood floors, his eyes took in the wall of windows and towering stone fireplace. He could hardly believe this was real. He dropped his suitcases in the front hall and then directed Ian to put the few boxes he'd brought with him in the front room behind the leather couch. A large basket filled with wine waited for him on the formal dining table. A note was propped against it, and he walked over to take a look. "A housewarming present from the previous owners," he said to Ian. "Nice people."

"They sure were," Ian said. He looked out the window that faced the vineyards. "This is a magnificent piece of land. You have your own forest, too."

"I do," Luke said, stepping beside him. "I don't think I'll ever get tired of looking out this window and knowing I live here. Thanks for the heads up on this island paradise."

"You're welcome," Ian said. "I wish you luck with this venture." He turned and scanned the room. "A few good pieces of art would brighten up this room."

Luke laughed. "I have some of your work being shipped here from my storage, and I was planning a trip to the art studio in town soon to see some of your new work. I was also hoping you'd help design my new label for the winery."

"That could be interesting," Ian said. "I think I'd like to do that."

"Great. How about a toast then, to my new home?"

Luke pulled a bottle of Pinot Noir from the basket, found a corkscrew on the counter in the kitchen, and a set of wine glasses on a shelf. He'd bought the house furnished and they'd left quite a bit behind. The sellers had been downsizing in preparation for their retirement and had asked him if they could leave some kitchen appliances and other supplies. Luke had readily agreed. This was his first real home.

Luke and Ian held up their glasses for a toast. "To neighbors and friends," Ian said.

From the doorway, Luke waved goodbye as Ian got in his car and headed up the long tree-lined driveway to the road. A wave of melancholy engulfed him. Neither the big house nor the dream property changed the fact that he was alone here. He needed to meet with Hank, the assistant manager, soon. There was an extraordinary amount of work to get the winery up and running with his new ideas, so he would be busy. Too busy, he hoped, to notice the emptiness that crept up sometimes and shook him to the core.

To ward off the chill, he put some of the stacked wood in the stone fireplace and lit it up. He warmed his hands and watched the flames take hold. His thoughts drifted back to his meeting with Kyla. He still felt bad that he'd walked out on her, but she still held the key to his emotions. No amount of promises to himself to stay calm would help when she snapped back an answer to him. Her words of not loving him were false. As much as they hurt, he saw the fire in her emerald eyes and the pain. If love was still there—and certainly he felt it for her—that made Kyla leaving even more confusing. He'd never forgive Stefan for taunting her. All that pent-up resentment imagining his parents had paid her off had done nothing but tear him apart. Anger was a good motivator, it turned out. It sent Luke packing up out of New York and that lifestyle that had never fit him anyway.

He'd spun out of control the first few months after she'd disappeared. His dear father had said good riddance and tried to tell him it was for the best. Trying to drown his sorrows and wallow in self-pity didn't last long. He still had his dream of owning a winery, and the money in his grandmother's trust was waiting for him to find the right one. He'd moved to Napa County in California and worked his way up in his

uncle's winery, from picking in the fields to managing pro-
duction. And now it had all paid off. Chasing a dream was one
thing, but finding it was another.

Kyla would love this place; it was everything they'd ever
imagined. Why? What a horrible word. What wasn't she telling him? He probably hadn't made it easy for her after being
a jerk the other day. He had to figure out a way to build
trust between them. Nothing was the same without her. Luke
stretched out on the couch. He looked up to the wooden loft
where his empty bedroom awaited him, then closed his eyes
and fell asleep.

Chapter Eight

Kyla considered sending Becca over to check on the lavender that grew in the field next to Luke's vineyards. Rain was threatening and she wanted to get over there while everything was dry. She needed to pick some mint for her teas, too. But it was better if she went herself. Nothing had been decided on whether Luke would continue to lease her the field the way the previous owners had and she didn't want Becca ending up in the middle of what might be an issue. If she drove in the back way and kept quiet and low, there was a good chance Luke wouldn't see her there over the white picket fence she'd put up.

On the drive over, she replayed their lunch meeting the other day. It had ended in a disaster and she wasn't ready for another interrogation. He owed her an apology, she thought. And truly, she owed him one. And more…an explanation. Kyla had let fear drive her away from the man she loved and guilt keep her there. One secret led to another until all she had were her secrets and her fears. It was not the way she wanted to live anymore. She didn't know where to begin with Luke, which lie to untangle first. Kyla had never thought of herself as a liar. She'd lived in a make-believe world where a poor girl from a broken family could become a famous model and live happily ever after. Darcy Deveraux had no past, only a glamorous future. So who did Luke love if Darcy Devereux was but a cardboard cutout?—a paper doll that others hung clothes on and accessorized with pretty things? She'd smiled and posed and pretended.

Kyla turned down the narrow dirt road to the west of the lavender field and parked behind an old barn. She scanned the area. Relief flooded her when she realized no one was around. She tossed her bag over her shoulder and quietly shut the car door. The gate that led to the rows of plants was open. Becca had probably forgotten to close it last time or some critters had gotten in.

The damp, sweet smell of fall soil filled her senses and calmed her. Kneeling on a patch of grass, Kyla pulled a few weeds loose from around the plants. Tending this peaceful garden brought her back to her roots, reminded her of working in the yard as a little girl with her mother and grandma Mona. She drew a clipper out of her bag, hunched over the peppermint, snipped off some stalks, and placed them in the canvas bag. "Thanks for a bountiful harvest this year," she whispered to the plants.

"You talk to plants, too?"

Kyla's head jolted up. Quietly standing on the other side of the fence, head tilted, watching her every move, was Luke. His new look suited him. Faded jeans and a button down shirt with rolled-up sleeves over a T-shirt only made him more alluring.

"How long have you been there?" Kyla asked.

"Just a moment or two. I wondered who was poking around in my field."

His field. He'd said that very clearly. "I had to do a little pruning and picking and I didn't want to bother you. I'm sure you're very busy with the winery."

"Very busy," he said. "But I still don't miss much." Luke leaned over the fence, checking everything out. When he looked up, his grin was maddening. "When did you learn how to grow herbs?"

"A long time ago," she said.

"I didn't know that."

"There's lots you don't know about me," Kyla said.

His look was gentle. "I'm sure there is. But I'd like to know more."

Kyla stood. She didn't miss how Luke's eyes followed her hands as she brushed off her bottom. She walked along the fence toward the gate, and he trailed her on the other side. A light breeze brushed through the plants, and a faint scent of lavender caught in the air.

She knew the subject of her garden had to be addressed. "This land is very important to me," Kyla said.

Luke nodded. "At least we have that in common."

Kyla stopped walking and faced him. "I hope you'll continue to lease me this land so I can grow my herbs on it."

"I'll think about it," he said. His eyes wandered to her canvas bag. "What are you picking today?"

Kyla pulled out a sprig of mint, its sweet scent mixing with the sharpness out of the air. She held it up to him for a smell. "It's mint and can be very calming in tea."

Luke touched her hand with his long, graceful fingers as he pulled the mint closer to smell. "Perhaps we should have had mint tea instead of coffee the other day?"

Very clever, she thought pulling her hand back. "I'm not sure that would have helped anything."

"Well, you're the expert," Luke said. "But I'd be willing to try."

She looked up at him. A glimmer of hope crossed her heart.

"Kyla," he said, holding her gaze, "I'm sorry for the way I acted at the café."

She paused, staring deep into his soul. "I understand." Kyla pulled a few more sprigs of mint from her bag and handed them to Luke.

"For you. A peace offering."

Chapter Nine

Kyla held her breath tight and cinched the laces on the muslin bodice of her costume. The emerald-colored satin gown with the flaring sleeves complimented the green shoes she had decorated with fall leaves held in place with tiny sequins. She tilted her head, admiring her sparkly headpiece adorned with dried flowers, herbs, and berries. In her family's culture, she was celebrating Samhain, or All Hallows' Eve, the Celtic New Year's Eve. Kyla remembered as a child, her grandmother made mulled wine and delicious Colcannon with a buttery center. And Barmbrack cake with a ring baked into it. Whoever found the ring was sure to be married before the year was out. Kyla used to hope it was not her.

Kyla entered the shop and smiled. It was the most magical night of the year and she and Becca had worked all day to get ready. Lights twinkled where they'd strung them around the shelves, and the scent of cinnamon and cloves floated in the air.

"You look amazing," Becca said.

"And you make the perfect sprite in your gauzy little dress and tiny wings," Kyla said.

"Trick or treat," someone yelled from the front of her shop.

Kyla slipped a copper bracelet on. Her mother had given it as a gift. She hurried out to greet her early guests.

Jude and Lily waved hello. "What do you think?" Jude asked. She twirled around in her old-fashioned bar maid costume with a scooped neckline and short, full skirt.

"Seductive," Kyla said.

"Ryan will certainly take notice," Lily chimed in.

"Kyla, you are a knockout," Jude said. "You look more like a nature goddess than Mother Nature."

"It is all in the eye of the beholder," Kyla said. She looked over at newly pregnant Lily. "And you, Lily, look radiant as a member of the faerie folk," Kyla said.

"Ian made my gossamer wings. I love the way they glow in the light."

Kyla walked over and gave them both a hug.

"Look at the three of us," Jude said. "Great friends and all so different. Kyla here could rule the world, Lily dwells with forest folk, and I hang out in a bar!"

"Earth, air, and fire," Kyla said. "We are missing the water element."

As if on cue, Ian walked in looking handsome as Neptune, King of the Sea. He held up his pitchfork. "Trick or treat, ladies, or I will bring the ocean waves upon you."

Lily giggled. "You better get him some of your famous truffles before the floods begin."

Kyla offered each of them a treat. Guests were pouring into the store, so she waved her goodbyes as Jude hurried out back to the café. The town folk loved when the shops stayed open late and offered treats or, in some cases, tricks. People gathered around tasting her fragrant, hot apple cider mulled with spices from her own garden. Some purchases were made, but the night was about celebrating with your neighbors and friends.

"Trick or treat," a deep voice said behind Kyla. She turned to see Frank from the bookstore dressed as a deep sea fisherman. "And look who's hooked on my line," he said. "Mr. Darcy himself."

Kyla smiled at the handsome young man. His dark hair curled over his forehead, setting off his black eyes. Long sideburns, a black waistcoat, and vest accented with an old-fashioned cravat fit his character perfectly.

"Marco?" she asked. "It's been a few years."

"You recognized me," he said with a grin.

Kyla noticed Becca at the counter, her eyes transfixed on the young man. Kyla swore she saw sparks fly off her.

"Some good news," Frank said. "Marco is going to take over the bookstore next month and I can head south for the winter."

"Congratulations," Kyla said. "Let me know if we can be of any help getting you settled."

"Thanks so much," Marco answered.

"Please help yourself to some treats." Kyla pointed to the tables of goodies. She watched as Marco turned and Becca came into his line of sight. The jolt through his body was visible. This new neighbor might prove quite interesting.

Would Luke make an entrance tonight? Her heart fluttered. She was sure he would.

Luke couldn't take his eyes off her. Kyla's red hair glowed from beneath her flowered crown. Beauty surrounded her as she flitted around the customers. Luke was impressed by the quality of Kyla's shop. Its offerings were much more than tea. Handmade candles, lotions, and culinary herbs, most in Kyla's own brand, lined the shelves. The round, wooden tables by the window were covered in baked goods, and the smell of cinnamon filled the air. Tea & Comfort was an apt name for the cozy place with its nooks, shelves, and displays filled with decorative tea sets.

Suddenly he was face-to-face with a goddess. "Nice shop you have here," Luke said. He watched her face register his presence. Her eyes scanned his carefully constructed costume.

Kyla raised an eyebrow. "A pirate. And just who do you plan to rob and pillage?"

He gave her his best smile. "No one, ma'am. I am more the pirate of the Caribbean type."

"You certainly look like one in your black, laced-up shirt and bandana. The dreadlocks are particularly effective."

She started to turn away. "And where is my treat?" he asked.

Her eyes narrowed. "If you are looking for a bottle of rum, you best go to Jude's place."

"A piece of bread or a cup of tea would do, my lady."

Kyla's eyes twinkled. For a moment he almost reached out to kiss her.

She pointed to the tables filled with spiced brownies and cookies. "Help yourself," she said, turning again to go.

"I am settled in at the winery now. When would you like to discuss continuing to grow lavender in my newly acquired fields?"

His words stopped her in place.

"If looks could kill" crossed his mind as her eyes bore into his.

"Not now. If you haven't noticed, we are in celebration mode. Perhaps you want to trick or treat some other place in town while you have time." He watched her back straighten as she crossed her arms in front of her.

He stood his ground. "I will give you a call then."

"I'm sure you will," she said.

She turned her back and left him standing there. Satisfaction raced through his veins. A part of him wanted to see her working in the lavender field next to the winery, force her to see him almost every day. But who would it be torture for? Her or him? Something was very wrong. Her eyes betrayed her and showed the same love and connection with him they used to. Luke was sure of that, just as he knew his own heart. Of course he would let her grow her lavender at his place. But why wouldn't she tell him the truth?

He watched her smile at neighbors and friends mingling in the shop. Her laugh rang through the air as a masked man flirted with her. Perhaps he was fooling himself and it was disdain he saw in her eyes, not love, or her laughing at his pathetic attempt to chase her across the country. On second thought, maybe he would evict her rights to the field until she confessed. Blackmail? Maybe.

Luke stomped out of her shop and headed down the street. Witches and princesses paraded by in all shapes and sizes. A strong brew sounded pretty good about now. He walked into the Island Thyme Café and almost turned around and left. The noise level was off the chart. The place was packed with people celebrating the holiday in high spirits. He noticed Ian dressed as Neptune, pitchfork and all, sitting at the bar. Lily, in gossamer wings, was squeezed in next to him.

"Hey, buddy," Ian said. "Come join us for a drink."

"I could use one," Luke said.

"Nice costume," Lily said. She held up a cup of coffee. She must have been the only one in here without an alcoholic beverage.

Luke ordered a glass of the award-winning blend Jude bought from his winery. He loved the mix of Merlot, Cabernet Franc, and Malbec.

Jude placed a full glass before him. "A booth just opened up over by the window if you guys want to run over and grab it. It would give you more room."

Ian jumped up wine in hand. "I'll get it."

Lily laughed. "So sweet." She turned to Luke. "I'm pregnant, and he wants me to be comfortable."

"Congratulations to you both." Luke put his hand out to help Lily off the barstool. He grabbed his wine glass and Lily's coffee and followed her over to the booth.

Chef Ryan waved over to them. He made his way across the room carrying a platter of appetizers. "Some eyeballs," he said with a grin as he held the tray before them.

"Are we supposed to eat those?" Lily asked.

"Of course." He pointed to the deviled eggs. "This one is mixed with avocado with the desired green appearance and drizzled with a red pepper aioli to create the bloodshot effect and topped with a black olive."

Luke lifted one off the tray and took a tentative bite. "Surprisingly delicious," he said.

"And the other one?" Lily asked.

"Ah, the green eyes appeal to you," Ryan said. "Freshly made mozzarella cheese with a green picholine olive."

Lily nibbled a piece. "Why don't you leave them here for us," she said with a smile.

Ryan put the whole tray in the middle of the table. "Mind if I join you?" He scooted in next to Ian. "Good to see you in here, Luke. So, how's the winery business coming?"

Luke was glad to get his mind back to business. "Actually, I was hoping to talk to you and Ian about a few plans I have."

"What do you have in mind?" Ian asked.

"Starting in the spring, I would like to start having a concert series at the winery with tastings and small bites included. I was hoping to feature some of your artwork as well, Ian."

"Done," Ian said.

"Spanish tapas are my specialty," Ryan said. "Happy to be included."

Luke shook both men's hands. "Let's plan a meeting for next week." He turned to Lily. "I was hoping you might have some ideas for local musicians. The ones at your grand opening were top notch."

There was hesitation in Lily's eyes. It was important to Luke to have them all as friends. To show them he was not "the bad guy" after all.

"I'll see what I can come up," Lily finally said.

Chef Ryan rose and took the now-empty platter with him. "I better get back in the kitchen before the boss fires me."

That was never going to happen if Luke was right about the way Jude looked at Ryan. He knew that look and it was definitely not about firing anyone. Ian's hand covered Lily's on the table. Luke knew their look, too, and was happy for them both. The familiar ache in his heart surfaced. He would be patient. Kyla was worth it.

"Cheers," a group at the bar yelled, holding their glasses in the air.

Luke glanced over to see what the commotion was for. "Looks like someone has some good news," he said.

Lily stood up and waved toward the bar. "It's Grandpa John, my neighbors, Betty and Shirley, and someone else," she said.

The group was dressed like they'd all just come from a country square dance: the ladies in full skirts and the men in suspenders. A waiter followed behind them with a tray of wine glasses.

Luke stood to shake John's hand.

"Nice to see you again, young man," Grandpa John said. "I hope you're settled in to your new place."

Luke nodded. "I am. The next sunny day, why don't you come over and I'll give you a tour of the vineyards."

Grandpa John laughed. "That might not be 'til spring, but I'll take you up on that."

"Or summer," Betty said with a grin.

Shirley edged her way in front of the group, pulling an older gentleman with her.

She waved the waiter to put the drinks on the table. "I'd like to introduce you all to Ron."

Luke noticed Betty roll her eyes. That one was a character all right.

"Drinks are on us tonight," Shirley said, her cheeks flushing red as she stared into Ron's eyes. "We've found each other again after almost fifty years."

Everyone lifted a glass and held it up to make a toast. "I hope you don't mind my using water," Lily said, "with the pregnancy and all."

Shirley beamed. "Of course not. The next toast is for you."

Grandpa John held up his glass. "To two lovers reuniting," he said.

The glasses clicked as they repeated the toast.

"Are we the last to know?" Lily asked.

"No, dear. I haven't told a soul until today. Ron has been courting me for a few weeks. We've decided not to waste any more time, so he's moving to Madrona. We wanted to wait to surprise everyone until all the plans were made."

Betty coughed. "And that you have."

Luke wondered if love was in the water on this island. He'd certainly come to the right place. Shirley must be at least eighty, and Ron looked the same.

"We're just going to take a seat in the booth here next to you," Ron said, leading his group to the table.

"I want to hear the whole story tomorrow," Lily yelled after them.

Shirley turned and winked at her. "Tomorrow."

Chapter Ten

Kyla slipped on her jeans, pulled on a soft black sweat-shirt, tied her tennis shoes, and slung her purse over her shoulder. She ran out her front door. Jude was waiting in her car to pick Kyla up and whisk them over to Madrona Island B&B for a 10:00 a.m. girls' powwow. Important news required full attendance of the trinity—Kyla, Lily and Jude—so Tea & Comfort would have to open late today. There was a promised special guest as well.

"Morning," Kyla said as she snapped in her seatbelt.

Jude held up a chai-latte-to-go from the café. "For you."

"You're a life saver," Kyla said, taking a long sip. There would be great coffee at Lily's, but Kyla's favorite was spicy chai.

Jude backed out of the drive and headed for the main highway that split the island east and west.

"So, what's the 'can't wait to tell you' news?" Kyla asked. She hated to be the last to know.

Jude looked over and winked. "There's another romance a-brewin' on the island."

Kyla thought she might throw up right there in the front seat. If it was Luke...

"Hey, it's good news," Jude said. "Cheer up."

"Give," Kyla said, staring down her friend.

Jude slowly sipped her latte, drawing out the suspense until Kyla wanted to hit her.

"It seems our friend Shirley has been very busy surfing the Internet."

"Doing what?" Kyla asked. "Looking for garden supplies? Baking pans?"

"Not exactly. Something, or should I say someone, much more interesting. Shirley's been holding out on us. She tracked down an old flame from her college days. His name's Ron. He has been coming over here from Seattle and dating her for a few weeks."

"That's great." Kyla considered the eighty-two-year-old Shirley. She was an attractive woman, well-coiffed, and, except for her arthritis and bad hip, her health was good and her will strong as steel. She was happy for Shirley, but something did not sit right in her heart. Seeing Shirley's once-lost-love rekindled caused Kyla's own hope for her and Luke to flicker. She forced the thought out of her mind when they pulled up to the inn.

"One other thing," Jude said. "Your, ah, friend, Luke, spent some time in the bar last night."

"Did he? Doing what."

Jude coughed. "Mostly making friends and a few plans."

"Like what?" Kyla asked.

Jude pulled into the driveway of the inn. "He asked Ryan to do some cooking for him for events at the winery. And Ian some artwork."

"Next thing you know, he'll ask to join the writing group at the library."

"Writer's group?" Jude asked.

"Why not? He's ingratiating himself everywhere else." Kyla opened the car door and headed up the porch steps. She turned to Jude behind her. "I don't want to hear any more about him."

Jude put up her hands. "Fine with me."

Inside, the momentary sunlight streamed through the window, lighting up the parlor. The room was toasty warm, and Lily had the formal dining room table set with rose china, a silver coffee pot, and a glass serving dish piled hot with sweet-smelling blackberry scones. "Ode to Joy" played softly in the background. It was one of Kyla's favorite pieces of music.

Shirley was already seated in the place of honor at the head of the table. She waved. "Hello, ladies. Did you come for the "tell all"?"

For a moment, Kyla felt underdressed. Shirley was in a purple pant suit, full makeup, coiffed hair, and sporting pink saltwater pearls around her neck. Kyla gave Shirley a hug and then sat down next to her. "I hear you have some exciting news to share with us."

Shirley beamed. "I do."

Jude scooted in next to them. "We want *all* the details."

"Wait for me," Lily said, pouring coffee and laying cream and sugar on the table. She pulled a chair up next to Kyla. "Now tell us, just how did you find Ron?"

Shirley poured cream into her coffee and added a teaspoon of sugar before stirring. She was obviously enjoying being the center of attention, Kyla thought. How cute.

"Search and find," Shirley said, as if it were so simple. "Google can find anyone. And if they can't, you can pay someone to find them." She smiled. "Even long-lost loves like Ron."

Kyla had to chuckle. Shirley looked so pleased with herself. Kyla hoped Ron was all Shirley found on that search and not some of the weird people out there in cyberspace.

A log snapped in the fireplace with a loud pop, releasing a fragrant smell of pine.

"How come we've never heard about Ron before?" Lily asked.

"I hadn't thought of him in years," Shirley said. "We dated in college at UW. I met him at a fraternity party, and it was love at first sight for both of us."

Kyla felt her stomach clench. She remembered what love at first sight felt like. One look into Luke's eyes and she'd known she'd met her soulmate.

"And then?"

Shirley looked off dreamily into space. "I couldn't eat or sleep, thinking about him all the time. Ron wanted to be a veterinarian, and in those days there weren't many schools. We were thrilled when he got accepted to Iowa State Vet College." Shirley sighed. "Our plan was for both of us to work and save money to get married when he finished school. In those days, girls didn't live with their boyfriends unless they were married."

"What happened?" Jude asked.

"Iowa is a long way from Seattle and a lot can happen in between. My mother got ill. I had to drop out of college to stay home, take care of her, and put my dreams on hold. Phone calls were expensive. Vet school demanded every second of his time. His letters grew further and further apart."

Kyla saw a tear trickle down Shirley's cheek. Love found. Love lost. But in Shirley's case, it was love found again. No longer hungry, Kyla laid her fork down on the antique tablecloth.

"It was the 1950s," Shirley continued. "My mother was dying and my father never home. They pressured me to marry. Ron told me it would be years before he could even think of marriage. He understood and suggested we date other people and stop writing for a while. I was twenty-three years old. Lonely and afraid. When Fred asked me to marry him, I said yes. A telegram congratulating me from Ron, and that was the last I'd heard of him until now."

"How sad," Jude said.

"Don't get me wrong, ladies. I had a good marriage. After Fred died, I moved over here to live with my sister, Betty, and life has been good. And now it's very good."

Lily rubbed her stomach softly. "So what's the story with Ron? Did he ever marry?"

"He did eventually. I saw a clip in the local paper one day and cried my eyes out. By then I was pregnant with my son. Ron had opened his very own veterinary clinic in Iowa. I was so proud of him."

"Does he still live in Iowa?" Lily asked.

"Oh no. He's eighty-four years young and has been retired close to twenty years now. He moved back to Seattle last year after his wife died. Boy, was he surprised when I emailed him on Facebook. He said he'd never stopped thinking about me."

"How romantic," Lily said. "And how does Betty feel about the new development?"

"How do you think?" Shirley said, scrunching up her nose. "She's pouting, banging around with her damn hammer when Ron is visiting, and barely saying hello."

"It seems long-lost loves are springing up all over. Like Luke coming back for Kyla." Jude popped a big bite of scone into her mouth.

There was a collective gasp in the room at the mention of Luke's name and then silence.

Jude put her hand over her mouth. "I'm sorry, Kyla. I was just…"

"It's okay. But don't count on us having the same happy ending." If she were honest with herself, Kyla had never stopped thinking of Luke either. She pushed his memory further back in her mind every day, but her heart never forgot.

"Stupid me," Jude said. "I was just hoping one might ride up on a white horse looking for me. too."

Shirley winked at Jude. "What about the hot chef you hired for your café? I see the way he looks at you."

Kyla caught Jude blushing. It didn't take a tealeaf reading to see love was brewing there.

"We'll see," Jude said with a shrug. "We're here to talk about you, Shirley. Any wedding plans?"

Shirley almost spit out her coffee. "Not so fast. If it were up to Ron, we'd be married already. He thinks we should spend all the time we have left together."

"Ron's completely smitten with you," Lily said.

"And I with him. But I want a little courtship to make up for lost time. Ron said he has a big surprise for me today."

"Sounds mysterious," Kyla said. "Perhaps it's the big question."

"Perhaps," Shirley said with a mischievous grin.

Kyla remembered her fast and spellbinding courtship with Luke in New York. Was there a chance for them to rekindle what they'd once had? Slowly this time, with their feet on the ground?

The sound of a car door closing echoed inside the house.

"Knock, knock," Ron said as he stepped through the front door, flowers in hand. "I hear you girls are having coffee. I hope I'm not interrupting."

"Of course not," said Lily, heading toward the door to greet him. "Come in and join us."

Ron looked over to Shirley. "You look beautiful this morning. Are you ready to go on our little adventure?"

Shirley set her cup down on the table and stood up gracefully. "Sorry, ladies, Ron and I have plans for the day. Thank you for the lovely scones, Lily."

Ron offered Shirley his arm and the two turned to go.

"Have fun," Jude called after them.

Kyla watched them walk out the door hand in hand. A longing pulled at her heartstrings.

"Betty doesn't sound too happy about those two," Jude said.

Kyla nodded. "I have a feeling Betty could use a little support about now."

"You're right," Lily said. "Let's bring over some scones and say hi."

Betty answered the door wearing overalls and holding a wrench in her left hand. "What are you all doing over here? Everything okay?"

"We're just being neighborly," Lily said.

Betty eyed them suspiciously. "All three of you?"

Kyla stepped forward. "We wanted to know how you're doing with Shirley's new development."

"Oh, that." Betty rolled her eyes in her classic fashion. "Fine, just fine. You're all here, so why don't you come in for coffee? It's been in the pot a while, but it's still warm."

They walked through the entry into the living room. Oak floors covered in rugs supported couches and recliners and various antique pieces of furniture. Milk-glass vases filled with fall flowers added color. At the end of the long room was a dining alcove with table and chairs facing the water.

"What a lovely room," Jude said.

Kyla thought the room was exactly what she'd imagined with these two sisters. Shirley was just over eighty and Betty was the younger one in her late seventies.

Betty motioned toward the table. "Go ahead and have a seat. Cream and sugar for any of you?"

"Black," they all said at once.

Kyla set the scones on the table and took a seat by the window. She never tired of the incredible view on this side of the island.

When the tea was set, Betty joined them at the table. Kyla looked from Jude to Lily, but neither spoke up. "So, Betty," she finally said, "what's it like having a man around the house?"

"Don't need one," Betty said.

Lily laughed. "They can be nice sometimes."

"You're young and got a good one." Betty sipped her coffee and bit off a corner of a scone.

The room was silent. Kyla nudged Lily to say something. She was her closest neighbor and knew Betty the best.

"It is pretty amazing how Ron and Shirley got together after all these years," Lily said.

"Not really, if you saw how much time Shirley spent on Facebook searching for him. That girl got it in her mind to find him and that's what she did. Thank goodness they stay most of the time in Shirley's wing of the house."

"She seems happy," Kyla said. "So does he."

Betty sighed. "All I wanted the last year was to get a dog. But, oh no. Too messy, Shirley would say. Can you tell me what's more messy than a man?"

Jude laughed out loud. "Amen to that."

In her mind's eye, Kyla could see Betty with a perky little dog to keep her company when she worked. "That sounds fair to me. How about we all take a ride over to Madrona Island Animal Shelter and find a dog that needs a new home?"

Betty's eyes lit up. She popped up from her seat. "Let's go. Won't Shirley be surprised."

Kyla could swear that for a fraction of a second Betty had sported an evil grin.

They piled in Jude's car and drove a few miles down the main highway to the makeshift MIA shelter. It was one small building and a grouping of kennels, but it served—with a few small outreach sites—all of the island's stray animals.

Sean, the front desk attendant, guided them into the back and pointed out where they could find the dog kennels. "Just let me know if you want me to take one of them out for you," he called to them as he shut the door to the office behind them.

Betty leaned up close to a few kennels, cocked her head, and then moved on. "I'll know him when I see him," she said.

Kyla knew that feeling.

"Well at least we know it will be a boy," Lily whispered to Jude and Kyla. They walked behind Betty, watching her inspect each dog. A gigantic chow threw himself against the cage door, and Kyla prayed he was not the one of Betty's choosing. As strong as Betty was, the dog was way too big and strong for her. The echo of dogs barking reverberated through the shelter.

Up ahead, Betty squatted down in front of a kennel and put her fingers through the bars. Kyla watched her talk sweetly to the dog and try to pet him.

"Any guess what kind it is?" Jude asked as they approached.

Kyla was surprised to see a small, about-ten-pound, brandy-colored poodle. That was the last dog she expected Betty to pick out. She did have a soft center after all. The dog jumped in the air, hoping to make a good impression.

"He sure has a lot of zing," Betty said. "Those poodles are smart, you know. And they don't shed. Shirley will like that."

Lily leaned down and tried to pet the little guy. "You could call him Zinger."

Betty stood hands on her hips, a smile slipping across her face. "Zinger it is. Now let's get this guy out of his cage and take him home."

"Don't you even want to hold him first?" Kyla asked.

"Nope. I told you I'd know him when I saw him."

When the attendant removed Zinger from the cage, he leapt straight up in the air into Betty's arms.

While they filled out the paperwork to adopt the dog, Lily spotted a flyer on their bulletin board. "Hey, Betty, look at this. They need volunteers to help build the new animal shelter."

Betty read over the flyer. "I can bring my tools and help out for sure."

A lady behind the counter gave Betty a skeptical look.

"Don't underestimate this lady," Kyla said. "She was up fixing her own roof last week."

"And she fixed my kitchen plumbing," Lily piped in.

The woman smiled. "We can always use new volunteers. Welcome aboard, Betty."

The happy crew headed home, dog and all. Kyla wondered how Shirley would like this development.

If only it were that easy to ease her own ills, Kyla thought. A headache played behind her eyes. A long nap, that was all she needed.

Chapter Eleven

Kyla stepped out of the shower and towel dried. She ran a comb through her hair. A handful of red strands slipped between her swollen fingers and spilled into the sink. With a long sigh, she examined the small butterfly rash starting on her cheek.

"No, not now," she said. "Not after over a year in complete remission."

Every time she tried to focus on all the things she had to do, overwhelm sent her back into a spin.

Luke had only been on the Island a few weeks and her past was creeping back up to her present. The dreams of love she'd long since put to bed were waking up and haunting her racing mind. She didn't know what to expect next from him. One minute he was sweet, the next angry or unreadable.

And now Lily was pregnant. Even with all the joy of the announcement, fear tinged Kyla's thoughts. Her gut would not stop churning. She wasn't sure if it was a warning about the pregnancy or her own fears of never being able to have a child coming to the surface.

Luke was here to stay. That left only two options for Kyla…stay or go. The thought of packing and running brought immediate relief. She could disappear again, reinvent herself. But why would she run from everything she'd always wanted?

It was Luke's fault she was even thinking that way. If only he hadn't come to the Island. In the whole country, he had to pick Mardrona Winery to follow his dreams. Well, she had settled here first.

Kyla tossed her hair into a ponytail and put on a warm robe. Back to her routine. No one was going to interrupt it. Breakfast first. She cut up spinach and mixed it with almond milk and frozen blueberries in the blender, then added some Greek yogurt and flax seed. The water was boiling for tea. She poured it into a cup over the fresh tealeaves and joined Merlin in the rocking chair by her small fireplace in the den.

Merlin curled up in her lap and purred. "Sweet little guy," she said. "Don't worry, I won't let anyone take away the peace we've found here." He purred louder as if in answer to her words. Oz was bundled up under his blanket in his fuzzy bed with his tail hanging out.

Kyla was glad the Halloween party was over and there were no events she had to prepare for until the Christmas season. But now there was Shirley's wedding to deal with. Ron had popped the question all right. All she really had to do was make it a gift for the couple. But Kyla was not pleased it was being held at Luke's winery.

"Isn't it sweet of him to offer?" Shirley had said. Real sweet. It was like Luke was throwing all the dreams they'd had of marrying in their own winery right in her face. But it was not about her and Luke. It was about Shirley and Ron's sweet story of finding each other again after all these years. Luke had found Kyla again too. The image of him in his dashing pirate costume sent heat through her body. His devastatingly good looks, black plunging neckline with golden hair running over his shoulders had taken her breath away. Every cell in her body longed for his. The pain in her limbs, the aching of her heart, how was she going to heal that? Rescue remedy helped with trauma, but she and Luke were linked beyond this time and place, and it had to be played out.

She wandered into the kitchen and placed her teacup on the sink. The leaves had formed distinct patterns at the bottom and she was transfixed with the images. Right in the center was clearly the symbol of purest love—a heart. A bird took flight in the upper right corner…a message was coming. But cloud images prevailed throughout. Trouble. Was Luke out for revenge? Kyla tossed the leaves into the sink and rinsed out the cup. Her way of dealing with conflict had always been to run. All the way to Madrona Island. She'd told her family where she was but with strict instructions not to contact her.

Kyla dropped back into the rocker. She was tired all the way to her bones. She thought of the courage her grandmother had shown coming to a new country and facing possible ridicule with her Irish ways. When she sought customers for her herb and healing business, she told Kyla, "They will come to me, and I can help them. All will be well. You will see."

Her mother had cried when Kyla told her about the lupus. But her grandmother had immediately mailed Kyla a list of remedies and told her she would be praying for her. But Kyla had turned her back on them. Now, more than anything, she wanted to call her family. She picked up her cell phone from the side table and waited for the familiar voice to answer.

"My Kyla, how are you?"

"Not that great, Grandma. I miss you." Kyla burst into tears. "I am so sorry I didn't call sooner."

"Don't worry yourself. Your mother and I knew you would find your back to us," Grandma Mona said in her soft, steady way.

Kyla wiped her tears. "I did everything you both told me and was in full remission. Everything I used to make fun of was exactly what healed me."

She could hear her grandma sigh. "Was in remission?" she asked.

Kyla heard the click of another line picking up. "Is that you, Kyla?" her mother asked.

"It is, Mom. I miss you both so much."

Kyla poured out the story of Luke finding her and everything that she had been running from finally catching up to her.

There was silence on the other end of the line. Finally her mother said, "Why don't you come home? Your grandmother and I can take care of you and you can just rest."

For a split second, Kyla imagined closing the shop and packing her bags. But it would just be another form of running. "Thank you for your kind offer and for being there for me after the way I have treated you both."

"We love you," the both said at the same time.

"I know you do, and I love you both too. But this time I need to stay and face my demons."

"Challenge them to a duel," her mother said. "Imagine holding the sword Excalibur and cut right through them."

Kyla laughed at the image. Her mother was always so dramatic.

"Just know we're here," her grandmother said. Worry laced her tone.

"I do, Grandma. And I promise, I'll see you soon."

Kyla hung up the phone and felt amazingly better. The heavy weight on her chest had lifted some. She even felt hungry. All she needed was a plan, and what better way to make one than over at Captain's Cove real country breakfast to make up for the cold smoothie she hadn't finished? Now all she needed was her best ally. She dialed Jude's cell number. It was Monday and the café was closed today. Her friend readily agreed and offered to pick Kyla up in fifteen minutes.

Dressed in jeans and a warm sweater, Kyla pulled on her fleece coat and locked the door behind her. Jude was waiting for her in the front driveway with a warm car and a bright smile.

They drove along a Madrona-tree-lined road to the old log inn that had been first opened at the turn of the century. A low-hanging fog drifted across the water, misting up the car windows. Jude parked and they walked into the quaint dining room with its log walls lined in antique mirrors. A raging fire burned in the ancient stone fireplace.

"Hello, ladies, are you here for breakfast?" the waiter asked.

"Definitely," Kyla said.

He escorted them to a small table by the window that overlooked Eagle's Bluff and handed them the menus. Jude slipped off her purple down jacket and put it behind her chair.

"Our special today is crab cake eggs Benedict with home-style potatoes."

"I'll have that," Jude said, handing him back the leather-bound menu.

"Me too," Kyla said. "And some of your island roasted coffee."

The waiter nodded in approval and headed for the kitchen.

"I'm glad you called," Jude said. "It's nice to eat somewhere else besides my café once in a while."

"I'll bet." Kyla sipped her water and looked over at her friend. "You look different."

"You and your x-ray vision!" Jude said. "There is a new development in my love life department. Perhaps you could shed some of your perceptive light on it."

Kyla groaned on the inside. Love was not what she wanted to talk about today. Or maybe it was.

"You do have a certain glow about you," Kyla said.

Jude giggled. "I haven't been kissed like that since…I can't remember."

"I assume you mean by Ryan?"

"Yes, I do," Jude said with a grin. "He finally figured out I don't bite. Although I can't make any promises after last night." Jude looked at Kyla with hope in her eyes. "Do you get any feelings about this relationship?"

A light whisper echoed in Kyla's mind. "He has secrets," the voice said. "Secrets."

Kyla did not want to lie to Jude. Nor did she want to withhold the truth. "It shows good taste that he knows who to trust with his affections."

The waiter placed two heaping plates of food before them and a mug of coffee on the table beside Kyla. "Enjoy your meal."

The lemony smell of the Benedict sauce mixed with the garlic roasted potatoes made her stomach growl. Kyla dug her fork in and broke the gooey yoke over the fresh crab cakes before taking a bite.

"Amazing. Just what I needed," she said.

"Speaking of what you need, how is it going with you and that dashing pirate that has taken residence in the winery?"

Kyla's stomach made a flip and her appetite waned. She laid her fork down and sipped her coffee.

"Better now than it was this morning when I was thinking of closing Tea & Comfort and leaving the island."

Jude almost spit out her mouthful of breakfast. "What? Why?"

"Luke. I don't want to face him. I'm not completely sure why he's here."

Jude's sympathetic expression steadied Kyla's nerves. She remembered her grandma and her mother's loving support on the phone. She was not alone anymore.

"No one is worth having to run away from the place you love. And the people who love you," Jude said.

Kyla let the words settle in her mind. She picked up her fork and stabbed a big bite of crispy potatoes. She was allowed some comfort food once in a while. Love. Wasn't that really what she was running from?

"You're right," Kyla said. "I think I've been running in one way or another for the last ten years."

"That's probably long enough then," Jude said. "It did get you here to Madrona Island. Perhaps this is where you were meant to be all along."

A warm flush filled Kyla. Every step and every turn she had made brought her here. There was no reason to run anymore. This was where she wanted to be.

"When I'm ready, I'll tell Luke the truth," she said.

"My best advice is don't wait too long," Jude replied. "You know that saying about the best of intentions and all that."

Outside the window, a lone fishing boat moved slowly across the misty cove. How long was too long? Kyla wondered.

Kyla unlocked the door to Tea & Comfort and turned on the lights. Merlin and Oz jumped out of the window seat and greeted her with a loud meow. Oz purred against her leg and then made a mad dash for the kitchen.

Merlin preened as she petted him. "I know you have a tough life," she said to the cat. "Lie in the window all day, eat treats, and play with your catnip mouse."

Time for work, she told herself. Shirley was due in today to pick up her arthritis-soothing tea blend. Kyla went into the back room and mixed up the alfalfa-based tea and bagged up some fresh peppermint as well. She placed her silver label on each and laid them on the shelf just in time as Shirley sprung open the front door and made her entrance. She looked dazzling in a rose-colored pantsuit, full makeup, and blonde hair sprayed to perfection.

"You're looking all aglow today," Kyla said. "How's it going with that special someone?"

Shirley blushed. "I have my secrets, you know. I might be old, but I'm not dead yet!" Shirley plopped her bright pink leather purse on the counter. "Are my magic potions ready to pick up?"

Kyla pulled the bags off the shelf and laid them on the counter. "They're not exactly magic," she said.

"Oh yes they are," Shirley insisted. She held out her hands. "Look at these fingers." She flexed them with ease, waving her age-spotted hands in the air.

"Not bad," Kyla said. Shirley looked darn good for eighty-plus years old. Some of Kyla's customers responded quite well to her complementary natural treatments in addition to those prescribed by their medical doctors. They certainly had made all the difference in Kyla's own well-being.

Shirley did a twirl. "I almost feel like a schoolgirl again."

"I can't take all the credit for that," Kyla said. "Love can do wonders for the spirit."

Shirley beamed. "Don't underestimate yourself. Having someone who actually listens to me about my aches and pains and really cares makes a big difference too! Those doctors just keep telling me it's old age. Can you imagine that?"

"Glad to be of service," Kyla said. Shirley sure gave old age a new face. "How are the wedding plans coming along?"

"That Luke is a dear, letting us use the winery for our ceremony and reception. He's so handsome too. He's offered free wine, Jude is providing appetizers, and Lily is baking the cake."

"And what can I do?" Kyla asked.

Shirley thought for a moment. "How about some of those little love potion wedding favors?"

"I'm happy to make them special just for you and Ron."

Shirley paid with cash, counting out each dollar and change. "We're so lucky to have you here on the Island with us. My whole knitting group would be packing up their needles if it wasn't for you."

"I'm pretty lucky to be here too," Kyla said. If they wanted to think her herbal potions were magical, that was fine with her. The mind was a powerful tool for healing.

Shirley clutched her bag to her chest and headed for the door. "See you soon," she said with a wave.

Kyla watched her hurry out the door. It felt good to be wanted and to make a difference in someone's life. Her grandmother and mother had helped so many people with their healing and caring skills. Kyla had that same gift, one she had previously discarded. But here on Madrona Island she could share it with people she loved. It would work out with leasing the land from Luke. She visualized her field of lavender stretching across to the horizon. Bright yellow sunflowers shot up here and there against the deep purples and framed by a clear blue sky. And she would be here to harvest it.

Chapter Twelve

*L*uke stared out the window. The vines had turned a golden orange and the fruit trees were losing their leaves. He watched Kyla drive down the shadowy lane toward his tasting room. She was coming to him. That was a good first step. Even though it was only to ask to use his land.

He walked out to greet her and watched her hesitate before she opened the car door and stepped out. The sun glinted in her hair and his heart skipped a beat.

"Good morning. Welcome to my vineyards."

"And lovely ones at that," she said.

Luke gestured with his hand toward the tasting room. "Would you like the grand tour?"

Kyla held her head high and stared at him as if weighing his invitation. Luke knew it was important for her business expansion to be able to use his field. If nothing else, he knew he had her attention. For now.

"Why not," she said, apparently trying not to seem too interested.

He started with the tasting room, pointing out its low ceilings and wood-paneled walls. He showed her the various labels and gift items. Kyla's eyes didn't miss a thing.

"The reds sit in the oak barrels after fermenting in bins," he said. "The whites won't be ready until next year."

"I've never been inside the tasting room before. It's very cozy and welcoming."

He led her outside for a walk through the fall-colored vineyards. "The crush pad and bladder press are out back," Luke said as she followed him down the path. "We grow only the Pinot Noir grapes here; the rest come from central Washington."

Kyla nodded and glanced out over the fields.

In his discomfort, he found himself blabbering on and on. "You know, it was a dairy farm before grapes were grown here. In March, the buds will burst, and then a new cycle will begin. I have plans for a wine club, catered events, and, of course, weddings."

"It was nice of you to offer Shirley this venue for her wedding," Kyla said.

"My pleasure. They make a sweet couple." Luke took her alongside the old, red barn with the new tractor outside. Maybe he was showing off a little, he thought. Chickens and roosters pecked around inside their pen as they passed on their way toward the land he leased to her.

Kyla trudged ahead of him. She had not smiled once, but he noticed her eyes did not miss a thing. Luke hoped she loved the place as much as he did. Why did he care? he asked himself. Did he want her to see what she was missing? Did he hope she'd want him and all these trappings? What he really wanted was to see pleasure in those deep green eyes.

"Would you like to see the newly remodeled barn where we're holding Shirley's wedding?" he said. "It's right over here."

Luke took her along the west side of the pond and slid open the freshly varnished cedar door to the event barn.

He heard Kyla sigh before stepping in.

"It's beautiful," she said.

Guilt played at the edge of Luke's conscience. He knew this must be painful for Kyla. It was just how they had planned it back in New York. It required everything in him not to take her in his arms, kiss her passionately, and say, "Let's forget the past and just start where we left off." But he was hesitant to do so until he knew more.

"About the lavender fields," Kyla said in a businesslike tone. "Have you considered my offer for leasing the land?"

"I have," Luke said. He purposely said nothing more.

"And?" Kyla stamped her foot.

Luke smiled at her cute gesture.

"Excuse me," she said. "What are you smiling at?"

Luke stepped over and whisked her into his arms and kissed her. Lost in the moment, it felt like they'd never been apart.

"I've missed you," he whispered.

She laid her head on his shoulder and melted in his arms. "Everything's such a mess." Kyla looked up at him, her emerald eyes misty with tears.

"It doesn't have to be," he said.

She turned and walked over to the window overlooking the vines. After a moment, she looked back. "It's all we've ever dreamed of. Why, Luke?"

"I never stopped dreaming," he said. "You're the one who left."

Her face clouded over. Abruptly, she turned back.

Luke took a few steps toward her. "I acted like an idiot the other day at lunch. I'm sorry. After you left New York I fell apart. I had blamed my parents and vowed never to speak to them again."

"I told you, they had nothing to do with it," Kyla said.

"I made sure Lizbeth knew there was no chance of marriage and never would be. She was as relieved as I was. My dad cut me off financially. I left town to live with my Uncle Joe in the Napa Valley on his thriving vineyard. I wanted to get as far away from New York and everyone in it as I could find. And I've never felt freer since."

"Have you spoken to your parents all this time?"

"My mother contacted me when my grandmother was ill. She knew we'd been close. I flew home to see Grandma and had a few last days with her."

"I'm sorry," Kyla said. "I know she was special to you."

"After the funeral, my parents and I were cordial to each other. Stefan was almost polite. After the reading of the will, I realized my grandmother had left me a small inheritance. That's when I decided to buy a winery of my own. There was nothing my parents could do about that." Luke felt his throat tighten. "I don't know how I would have survived my childhood without her."

"My Grandma Mona is very special, too," Kyla said.

"Perhaps someday I'll meet her," Luke said.

"Perhaps," Kyla said.

Luke touched Kyla's shoulder. "And you? When did you come here? Open Tea & Comfort?"

Kyla stared at him. If he could only read her mind. But it seemed she was the one who did that.

"There's so much you don't know," she said.

"Then tell me."

Her gaze locked on his. "I just can't. Not yet." With that, she turned her back to him and headed for the door.

"You can lease the field. Same terms as the previous owner," he called after her.

Kyla stopped for a second before walking out the door. "Thank you."

Luke followed her outside and watched her get in her car and drive away. It was a start. He looked at his watch. It was only 11:00. He had two hours to get some work done before Shirley and her wedding gang showed up for a meeting.

Promptly at 1:00, two cars drove up to the winery and parked in front of the tasting room. Luke strolled over to greet them. He shook Ron's and Ryan's hand, and gave Shirley a quick hug.

"What, no hug for me?" Jude said.

Luke was surprised Jude was letting her guard down with him. "Brides-to-be first," he said then leaned down and hugged Jude. "Shall we walk over to the barn where the event will be held?"

The stone-lined path meandered down to a quaint red barn. The previous owners had installed shiny oak floors, completely insulated and painted the walls, and added a low stage area with track lighting. Skylights lit the room during the day and large picture windows looked out to the vineyards and turquoise pond.

"A perfect place for a wedding," Ron said, wrapping his arm around Shirley's shoulders.

Luke hoped, when he was that age, he would still be holding the love of his life in his arms.

Jude and Ryan discussed the number of tables, chairs, and
basic logistics while Ron and Shirley explored the stage.

"We can have two buffet tables along the wall," Ryan said,
"and put the round tables at the front of the room. That way
the guests can watch the ceremony from the seats." He paced
the area by the stage. "I'll make sure the stage has flowers and
candles for the ceremony. And we can have dancing in the
back area after dinner."

"Dancing," Shirley said. She stepped down from the stage
as Ron gave her his hand. "I'll have to practice my steps. I'm
a bit rusty."

"I'll help you practice," Ron said, moving into partner
position. "May I?"

Shirley giggled and placed her right hand on his shoulder
and her left hand in his.

As they watched the couple glide around the floor, Luke
noticed Ryan slip his arm around Jude's shoulder. Watching a
couple fall in love was very contagious.

"How adorable they are," Jude said.

Ryan and Luke made eye contact and smiled.

After the dance practice, Luke invited everyone into the
tasting room for a glass of wine to celebrate.

He put five glasses on the counter and filled them with
a wine created by the previous owner combining apples and
pears grown on the property. They had called it "A Perfect
Pearing."

"To Sherry and Ron," he said, clinking glasses with everyone there.

Luke was sourly aware as each couple faced each other that he was the only one standing alone. Without Kyla, everything had a half-empty feel. But at least he'd found her now. Hope brightened the edges of his loneliness. His kiss had been returned that morning and, ever so briefly, he'd seen inside her heart.

Chapter Thirteen

Kyla sketched out a label to expand her Internet business for Tea & Comfort. There had been a big demand for her T&C tea blends, candles, and soap. More than she could keep up with. Her energy level had really dropped lately, and she was glad she had Becca to help. Next she would need a bigger space to make and store her products. Now that she knew she could continue to lease the field from Luke, the T&C health and beauty cream formulating could begin. She imagined the label clean and white with a small bundle of lavender and golden chamomile flowers tied in a pine-green bow. The beauty line would offer a magical youth blend for the face and a silky hand cream. She would box them as a set with a bar of creamy goat milk soap.

Ian had promised to create the final label, and now that the field was secured she could decide which other herbs to plant with the lavender. She had enough stock to do a test run on the product, but if she started advertising it on the Internet, she would need a much bigger supply by next summer. Kyla was grateful Luke hadn't tried to stand in her way. Had she really expected him to? Her gut still felt uneasy. She'd left him almost standing at the altar. He wanted answers. He was being patient. But for how long? And then what?

She rubbed her sore neck and tried to push the thought of him from her mind.

Lily was just walking in the door and Kyla remembered this was the day Lily had volunteered to help her blend the herbs for Shirley's wedding favors.

"Morning," Lily said before dropping into the nearest chair. "I'm sorry, but I've been a little woozy in the mornings lately."

Kyla took a close look at her friend's eyes and skin. She was a bit pale, but that was to be expected the first trimester. But there was something else, just below the surface, and it left Kyla uneasy.

"Can I fix you some tea?"

"Nothing feels right going down right now, so I'll pass."

"Are you up to helping with these today?"

Lily sat down at the table covered in herbs, ribbons, and small pink nylon bags. "Looking forward to it. Can you share some of your trade secrets with me?"

"I've mixed in a touch of soothing lavender with jasmine, known for its sweet smell. It creates a feeling of euphoria and is rumored to ignite passion for centuries."

"Ah," Lily said.

Kyla pulled a basket of rose pedals toward them. "The sensual smell of rose relaxes you, and I added some chopped vanilla bean for happiness." Kyla handed Lily a box of the pink bags embroidered with tiny flowers. "Now all we have to do is add the mixture and wrap them up and tie the heart charm on the ribbon."

Lily leaned forward. "The smell…" She closed her eyes and grabbed the table. "Excuse me." She jumped up and ran for the bathroom.

Kyla heard the sounds of morning sickness, groans and all, radiating from behind the door. Would Kyla ever feel that way herself? What were the chances she ever become pregnant?

"Are you okay, Lily?" she asked by the door.

She heard the toilet flush and the water run in the sink. Lily opened the door looking a bit peaked. "I think so. But I don't think I can stay. The roses are turning my stomach."

"I understand," Kyla said, leading Lily to the door. She walked her to the car. "Are you all right to drive? I can take you."

"I'm fine now in the fresh air. Sorry," Lily said. "I was hoping to spend some time together."

Kyla hugged her friend. "Go home and get some rest. I can handle this just fine."

"We haven't gotten to talk much," Lily said. "How are you doing with Luke and all?"

"He leased me the land, so all is well."

"And?" Lily asked.

"And that's all," Kyla answered.

Lily scrunched her face. "I detect something you're not telling me."

"I'll tell you another time," Kyla said.

Lily leaned against her car. "Not fair. You know everything about me. I'm feeling fine now, so I'm not going home until we talk a little."

Kyla leaned on the car next to her friend. "Luke gave me a tour of the winery today. I have to admit, it hurt my heart to see our dream come true before my eyes and not have it be ours to share."

Lily patted Kyla's back. "It must be really hard. I've seen the way he looks at you and he's wearing his heart on his sleeve. How do you feel?"

"One minute I want to push him away and the next I'm returning his kiss with equal desire."

"Kiss?" Lily said.

Kyla felt her face heat up. "Only one kiss," she said.

Lily chuckled. "And maybe more to follow?"

"Or not," Kyla said, trying to sound firm. Her lips tingled with longing betraying her words.

Lily's knowing smile was maddening.

"You better get home now and get off your feet and rest," Kyla said. She helped her friend into the car and watched her leave. It was nice to have friends she could trust.

Reluctantly, she returned to her workroom and put together all fifty love spell charms. A novelty item or real? she asked herself. The one person she hadn't made one for was herself. Maybe it was time to do so.

The day went by quickly serving tea, selling products, and baking another batch of lavender chocolate chip cookies. They were her favorite and the locals and tourists loved them. I bet Luke would love a batch, she thought to herself. She imagined taking them over to his house and curling up with him on a sofa while they had tea and cookies.

What was she thinking? They were barely speaking and she had some big decisions to make. Was it time to tell him about her diagnosis and why she'd run away? Plain and simple, back in New York she hadn't trusted that with her so sick, his love was strong enough to handle what lay ahead for them. If he'd done that to her, she would have been devastated. And angry.

She collapsed in her overstuffed velvet chair. Oz rubbed his head against her leg and purred. Merlin jumped into her lap. Kyla stroked his sleek fur.

"My little friend," she said, kissing him on his pink nose. "What should I do?"

In response, Merlin gave a loud meow.

"Really?" Kyla said. "And just what does that mean?"

The cat jumped off her lap and ran to the door. He looked back at her as if he wanted her to follow. Kyla opened the door and followed him back toward her cottage.

"You're a pretty wise kitty," she said. "It's dinner time. For us both."

She hadn't eaten all day. She hadn't slept for two nights. When she passed the big mirror in her living room, a gaunt image stared back at her. Fear crept up her spine. Lily had a good excuse for feeling poorly. Kyla knew only too well what was probably causing her fatigue.

"Come here, kitty," she said. She fed Merlin and Oz and headed for her bedroom. There was no way she could eat a bite. What she needed was to sleep, and for a long time.

Chapter Fourteen

It was a perfect fall evening, rain-free, wind-free, and mild. The small caravan of cars was led by Ian, with Lily and their son Jason beside him. The bridal couple cuddled in the backseat until they pulled in and parked next to the winery barn. Kyla pulled her car in behind them. She'd brought Betty and Grandpa John with her. With its twinkling lights and lanterns, the setting looked magical. The golden light pouring out the windows and the sweet smell of applewood smoke from the chimney was inviting.

Luke stood in the doorway dressed in a charcoal suit that showed off his broad shoulders and slim waist. Ron, wearing a dark pinstripe suit, stepped out of the car and offered Shirley his hand. Shirley looked radiant in a satin and lace dress in the perfect shade of plum to match her bouquet of purple calla lilies, red and white roses, ferns, and huckleberry branches.

Luke stepped forward and shook Ron's hand. "A perfect night for a wedding," he said.

"I'll say," Shirley piped in.

Luke continued to greet everyone and offered Kyla a warm smile. His timberwood grey tie matched his eyes that focused for the moment only on her.

"Let's go in," Kyla said.

Luke guided them through the double doors and guided the guests into the elegant barn. The wood floors gleamed under the mock candlelight of the three antique chandeliers hanging from the beams above. The buttercream-painted walls set off the tables which were perfectly draped in white tablecloths. As a centerpiece, plum-colored candles in brass holders splashed light over the lush flower arrangements.

Kyla watched Luke take the couple up on the little stage area to their regal seats of honor. He put a small microphone on each of their collars. He'd thought of everything. He usually did.

Cate Pearl, the local minister, sat in a chair on the other side of the stage. Luke had constructed a small trellis along the back wall lined with rustic wrought iron candleholders and fresh flowers.

Grandpa John walked up beside Kyla. "Let's sit together," he said. He pulled out a wood chair for Betty and another for Kyla before sitting between them and putting his arms around both of their shoulders. "I have the two most lovely dates in the room. Beside the bride, of course."

"Oh c'mon," Betty said.

But Kyla could see she enjoyed the compliment. Cherise, attending alone, asked if she could join them at their table and they all welcomed her.

This was the first time Kyla had seen Betty in a dress. Well, a denim skirt and glittery cowgirl shirt was close enough. The guests took their seats and Kyla recognized most of the other guests except for a few relatives of Betty and Shirley that had driven over from Seattle. Mary Gibson, who helped out Lily at the B&B, and her husband, Will, sat at the next table with

Dan—the grocer—and his family. She recognized Audrey from the library and a few of the book club members.

Kyla watched all the pieces come together. Jude and Ryan were arranging a buffet on a couple of tables to one side of the stage. Next to it was another table piled with brightly wrapped presents they had brought over ahead of time in the café van. A piano player sang soft love songs in the corner. Perfect.

Luke made his way around the tables, checking on the guests. Kyla could feel his presence behind her when he approached them.

She felt a warm hand on her shoulder.

"Good evening," he said.

Kyla looked up at him. His eyes twinkled. "A very good one," she said.

"You did a wonderful job decorating this barn," Grandpa John said. "I remember when there were cows in here before the remodel."

Luke laughed. "Thanks. I'm hoping to have many more weddings here."

His eyes bore into Kyla's with his last statement. She could barely catch her breath.

"I'm sure there will be plenty more weddings here. And soon," Grandpa John said.

Thankfully, the piano player broke into the song "As Time Goes By" to signal it was approaching time for the ceremony. The words to the old love song drifted in the air, and Grandpa John joined in, not quite getting the words right.

"You must remember this kiss," he sang, "as our love goes by."

Kyla smiled. She'd heard he'd been in love with Lily's grandmother, Maggie, a few years ago. He was quite the romantic, it seemed.

"Here's looking at you," Luke said, not taking his eyes off her.

Kyla blushed.

Luke flashed a dazzling smile. "I'll go take my seat now. Please save the first dance for me, Kyla."

She stumbled on her words as the music got louder. "I will," she said, watching the dashing figure walk to the front table and take his seat.

Betty squeezed her arm gently. "What a nice young man. Not bad-looking either."

Kyla frowned, wishing everyone would stop trying to push them together. The chandeliers dimmed and a golden spotlight hit the stage. The minister, in a purple gown, walked in front of the altar and into her position. There would be no bride and groom walking down the aisle, probably because of Shirley's hip, Kyla thought.

The music ended, and Shirley and Ron stood in front facing the altar.

"Welcome," Cate said in her booming voice. She did not need a mic. "We are here today to join together Shirley Rose Prescott and Ronald Alan Bueller. The couple have written their own vows. So, Ron, will you begin?"

Ron turned to face Shirley and took her hand. "Here I am at eighty-four, more in love with you than I was before."

The whole audience sighed. Kyla could already feel tears working their way up from her heart as Ron continued.

"For as long as we both shall live and beyond that as well, I am forever yours," Ron said.

Kyla had to reach into her purse for tissue. After all these years, still their love grew stronger. She looked up at Luke's table, and he was staring right at her. He held her gaze, and the meaning was clear.

"And now we'll hear from Shirley," the minister said.

All eyes faced the stage. Shirley cleared her throat. "You are and have always been the man of my dreams. I will treasure every moment we have together, and my heart will forever be yours."

Kyla heard Betty sigh beside her. "Are you okay?" Kyla asked her.

Betty wiped away a tear with the back of her hand. "I have to admit they do look happy together."

Kyla squeezed Betty's hand.

Shirley walked to the altar on the stage and picked up an unlit candle. The pianist played "Moonlight Sonata" as Ron did the same. Then they walked back in front of the minister and she lit each candle with the blazing flame of a large white pillar candle.

"As we light these candles, they symbolize unifying two into one," Cate said.

The crowd held their breath as the beautiful melodic chords of the sonata filled the air with their passion and beauty.

The ceremony was much the way Kyla would want her wedding to be. Her wedding. She looked around the barn. The stars out the side windows sparkled. It was the perfect spot. Beyond her imagining.

The pianist finished the tune and Kyla could hear people blowing their noses.

The minister spoke again. "With the power vested in me by the state of Washington, I now pronounce you husband and wife!"

Everyone stood and cheered as the couple, assisted by Luke, walked down the few stairs and stood in front of the tables to receive their guests.

"I give you Mr. and Mrs. Bueller," Luke announced. At the same time, Jude and Ryan came around with a tray of champagne glasses. "Please lift your glasses for a toast," Luke continued. "To the bride and groom and many years of happiness."

After the clapping died down, Kyla followed Grandpa John and Betty to join the reception line. When they reached the front, she hugged Shirley. "You look radiant. Beautiful." Kyla moved on to Ron and shook his hand. "Thank you for making Shirley so happy."

Ron smiled. "It's her that has made me the happiest man in world."

Ron's words were still ringing in her ears as Kyla began to walk away and ran right into Luke standing directly in her exit path.

"It was a lovely ceremony," Kyla said, keeping her voice even.

"Almost perfect," Luke answered, still not letting her pass.

"Almost?" Kyla said without thinking.

Luke took a step closer. "It wasn't you and I."

She froze in place. No words would come. His searching eyes were relentless.

"Here you two are," Grandpa John said. "Luke, you put on a darn good wedding."

Luke broke his gaze with her and turned to Jim. "Thank you, sir. Now, if you both will excuse me, I have to make sure the buffet is ready and then prepare the dance floor."

"If he keeps up like this," Grandpa John said, "Luke will certainly be successful here on the island."

"Probably," Kyla said. Luke was here to stay, but so was she.

"Who's hungry?" Betty asked coming up beside them. "Let's go get in the buffet line before it gets too long."

The buffet tables were covered with tablecloths and huckleberry branches, and pine boughs mixed with candles were the centerpieces. Chef Ryan handed them a plate at the head of the line. "Step right up, folks. We have platters of poached salmon with blackberry salsa, baked cod with lemon caper butter, roasted garlic red potatoes, and much more."

"Look at these flaky biscuits," Betty said, heaping two onto her plate and a generous helping of honey butter.

Kyla scooped some sautéed chard, glistening herb butter, and goat cheese and pear salad on her plate then headed back to their table.

Mary and her husband were already eating. She looked up at Kyla and said with a full mouth, "Delicious."

During the meal, the wood floor was cleared toward the back and chairs were placed at the side where people could sit and watch or rest if they wanted. A local disc jockey arrived with his laptop computer and a PA speaker.

After the plates were cleared, Luke stood front and center.

"Time for the bride and groom's first dance," he said.

Luke offered his hand to the bride, bowing slightly. She stood up, holding his hand and smiling.

"Who could resist him?" Kyla thought.

Luke walked Shirley to the center of the dance floor, and the candlelit barn encased them in a warm glow. The disc jockey played a slow waltz. Luke slipped his broad, capable hand around Shirley's back and danced for a few seconds before Ron moved into place and pulled Shirley into his arms.

Luke stepped back to the edge of the dance floor but did not sit down.

Kyla watched the couple dance gracefully across the floor. She'd never seen Shirley look happier. Together they danced in graceful motion.

When she looked up, Luke was watching her. Kyla knew he was going to ask her to dance next. Her eyes flew to the nearest exit. She couldn't just drive off. Betty and John needed a ride home and were counting on her. The sound of clapping brought her focus back into the room. A new song started playing, and John asked Betty to dance.

Luke walked slowly in her direction. Kyla's whole body flushed with heat as the room spun around her. He did a mock bow. "May I have this dance?"

Kyla wanted to say no, but her hand reached out to his.

He led her to the floor, and from the moment he put his hand around her waist, she was lost in the warmth of his arms. Their bodies melded together as one as they danced; she was unaware of anyone around them. His familiar scent and the feel of his strong body next to hers felt so right. To have and to hold as long as we both shall live, echoed in her mind. It was as if they'd never been apart and everything that kept her from him was just a dream.

When the music stopped, so did the illusion. Were her limbs trembling from weakness? From his closeness? She was not sure, but she had to sit down.

Kyla walked to her table. She leaned on the back of her chair and slid down into it. She noticed that Luke stood still on the dance floor, watching her. His eyes held so many questions but none she was ready to answer. She was not sure she would ever be.

The Bee Gees' old song, "More than a Woman," sent several older couples scurrying back to their seats. Luke moved out of sight and Kyla sighed with relief. She watched Becca dancing some flashy moves with Marco, Frank's grandson from the bookstore. Ever since she and Becca had walked over to the bookstore with a welcome gift for Marco, he'd been a regular at her shop. He came for tea and Becca crossed the street for coffee. Marco was quite attractive with his olive skin and ebony hair brushing against the collar of his button down shirt. The women in the room were probably swooning, but Kyla could tell Marco only had eyes for Becca.

"Betty, do you remember disco?" Grandpa John asked. "My wife and I even took lessons. She loved to dance."

Kyla would like to have seen that.

Betty shook her head. "I'm not the dancing type."

The music stopped and the DJ announced it was time for the bride to throw the bouquet. "All the single women in the audience, please come forward," he said.

Kyla was glued to her seat. Jude flew onto the floor and Audrey reluctantly sauntered out with a few other women. John and Betty looked at Kyla.

"Go," Betty said.

"I'm tired, and I don't really want it," Kyla replied.

John put his arm around her shoulder. "Kyla, dear. Don't be afraid. You're too young to live without love."

Kyla shivered and found herself standing up. Betty gave her a little push and she walked out onto the floor but hung to the side.

"Are you ready, ladies?" Shirley asked.

Shirley turned her back to the single women and the crowd slowly chanted, "One, two, three!" As if in slow motion,

Kyla saw the bouquet fly up into the air and head her way. In front of Kyla, Jude jumped up to catch it, but the beautiful plum-red, and white bouquet ricocheted off Jude's hands and landed perfectly in Kyla's.

All eyes turned to Luke.

The room spun, and it was all Kyla could do to not pass out. Heat flashed through her body and the noise from the crowd became painfully loud. She could barely catch her breath. All she knew was that she had to get out of here now. Her eyes scanned for the nearest exit and her body followed.

Chapter Fifteen

The next day, Kyla closed the shop early and gratefully returned to her house behind the shop. She fell on her bed and curled up into a ball. Her fingers dug into her palms as she willed back the tears. "It's too much," she said into her pillow. "Make Luke go away."

At the sound of his name, she burst into tears. Her body shuddered from impact. She was so tired. Bone-deep exhausted and it was getting worse. Every joint and muscle in her body ached. Depression wasn't even the word for her mood today, and throwing up this morning hadn't helped. Unlike Lily, she was definitely not pregnant. There had been no one since Luke. "Luke," she whispered. Her head pounded. The room spun in reply, then everything went black.

From a far distance, she could hear a woman's calling her name, "Kyla, Kyla, are you okay?"

The woman shook Kyla's body, but Kyla did not want to come back. Not to him. Not to a hopeless situation and an ugly disease taking over her body again. She floated somewhere far away, pain-free finally. A bright light pulled her into the distance and a warm voice filled her head.

"It's not your time," the benevolent voice said. "Go back…go back."

Kyla felt herself whirl through space and wake with a jolt, lying in a speeding vehicle. Jude was by her side, her face lined with worry. A paramedic adjusted the IV line.

"You're awake," Jude said. "Thank God."

Kyla stared into the face of her beloved friend. She reached out and clasped Jude's hand. "How did I get here?"

"I came into the shop and no one was there. I called after you and wandered back to your house. The door was open and I found you in the bed unconscious."

Kyla wondered how long she would have lain there if Jude had not come. It was Becca's day off, and no one checked on her on a regular basis. She could feel the self-pity creeping up as the ambulance pulled into the Island Hospital emergency area. No more, she told herself. She would call on the same inner strength and guidance that had led her to Madrona Island and helped her achieve full remission. She did it once, she could do it again.

Luke pounded on the door of Grandpa John's house. Ian would know what was happening. When in town, he'd seen an ambulance at Tea & Comfort and a woman being wheeled out by paramedics. There was a "closed" sign on the door. Panicked, he wondered if it might be Kyla. They may not be on the best of terms yet, but he cared. More than he wanted to admit to himself.

Grandpa John opened the door and his dog, Gretel, ran up to greet him. "Luke, come in."

"Where's Ian? I want to know what happened at Tea & Comfort today."

John pointed to the old couch. "Sit down, Luke. I'm headed over there myself. Let's talk a minute first."

The dog followed Luke and sat at his feet. "Was it Kyla?" Luke asked.

"Yes, it was," John said, patting Luke's hand. "There's no hurry, son. She's fine."

Luke stared into the old man's compassionate eyes. He'd heard that John had been through a lot of loss in his lifetime. Everyone loved and trusted this man, and Luke could see why.

Luke leaned back on the couch. Gretel pushed his hand with her nose to get him to pet her. He ran his hand over the silky dog's head. "What is it? What's wrong with her?"

"That's not for me tell you," John said. "But I can tell you want to help her. She needs kindness right now, support, friendship. That is what will heal her."

"I don't understand."

"Trust her, Luke. I've seen the way you look at her and she looks at you. There's not a mean bone in the sweet lady's body, I will tell you that. You're hurting, she's hurting, but right now you need to be the calm one."

The tension drained from Luke's body. He knew in the depths of his soul John was right. He'd let anger cloud his vision and his words. It was time to tell Kyla how he really felt and how much he wanted her back. No matter what. If he was honest with himself, he had to admit the truth…he'd bought a winery on the island just to be near her.

"I understand," Luke said. "Why don't I drive us over there? I'm ready."

John's smile lit up the room and Luke's dark heart. "I see you are, and it makes me proud. I knew if Kyla loved you, you had to be a pretty good sort."

Loved him. John just said Kyla loved him. Why had he ever doubted it? Luke had blamed his parents, then Kyla, and then hated himself. It was time to find out the truth.

Luke stood back at the doorway of Kyla's hospital room and let Grandpa John enter. Lily, Ian, and Jude were huddled around the bed. Kyla was conscious but looked pallid and drawn.

"And here we all are," Grandpa John said with a smile. "Everyone who loves you, sweetheart."

Kyla's eyes flew to the door and Luke froze. In that moment, the fire of his anger completely faded and all he saw was the question in Kyla's eyes. He stepped in and stood at the foot of the bed.

"Hello, Luke. Thank you for coming," she said.

Luke could almost hear the room sigh in relief.

"Wouldn't be anywhere else," he said, reaching his hand out to her.

She wrapped her fingers in his. The room was silent as Luke and Kyla communicated with their eyes.

Jude stood and stretched. "I think it's time I got back to the café. But I'll see you tomorrow."

"Thank you, Jude. For everything," Kyla said.

"Anytime." Jude walked toward the door then turned. "Lily, perhaps you should go home and get some rest."

"Right," Lily said. She leaned over and kissed Kyla's cheek. "Take care, my friend." Lily grabbed Ian's hand. "Come on, husband."

Ian looked from Kyla to Luke and back again. "Go on home," Kyla said. "I'm fine."

"Wait," Grandpa John said. "Can you two drive me home? I rode over with Luke."

"Come on, Gramps," Ian said. He looked back one more time and Kyla waved him to go.

It was just Luke and Kyla now, and he had no idea what to say. A monitor beeped softly as his thoughts drifted. If he lost her now…no, that was not an option.

He leaned forward. "What happened?"

"Luke," she said, her voice strained. "I've been ill."

Ice filled his veins as fear surged through his body. "Are you…are you?"

"Probably not dying yet," she said. "Not if I take good care of myself. I have lupus. SLE to be exact. It is a chronic autoimmune disease, but the symptoms can be controlled most of the time and I can live a normal life."

"Why are you in the hospital?"

"The disease can flare if I get too tired or stressed and then the symptoms get worse. I remember having some chest pain and must have passed out. Jude found me and called 911."

Kyla had always seemed so strong. He remembered his parents talking about one of their friends suffering with this disease. But Kyla?

"How long have you known?" he asked.

"I found out in New York."

New York. He sat back in his chair. That long. "Why didn't you tell me?"

Tears filled Kyla's eyes.

Luke handed her a Kleenex. "Please don't cry. You don't have to tell me anything now if you don't want to. I just want you to feel better."

She wiped her eyes. "I want to tell you. No more lies. No more running. It's only hurting both of us."

Her green eyes looked up at him and all he saw was love. For a moment Luke did not want to hear the truth. He just wanted to sit in the small, sterile room with Kyla forever and pretend everything was perfect.

"I'm sorry," she said. "I was so afraid of ruining everything we had. And of course that is exactly what I did."

Luke shook his head. "I don't understand."

"You loved Darcy Deveraux…supermodel. My hair was falling out and I could barely get out of bed in the morning. My career was over and, with it, the life I'd known with you. And you hadn't even met my family. I couldn't bear seeing your face when all of the truth came out. So I ran." She blew her nose. "And not just from you, Luke: from my career, from the public, from myself."

"I see." And he finally did.

"I now realize that coming to Madrona Island helped me to heal. I had been in remission for over a year."

Kyla looked so weak and fragile. When Luke had shown up on the island and given her a hard time, it must have set off her relapse. He didn't want to make it worse; he only cared about the woman in front of him, the woman he loved. "Kyla, nothing you tell me will change the way I feel about you."

To his dismay, she broke out in tears. "It's okay, Luke, they're happy tears." Her tears turned to laughter. "All this wasted time…"

He brought her hand to his lips and kissed it softly. "That is behind us. We'll work it all out."

Her beautiful, emerald eyes stared up at him, and he had no doubt she loved him the same way he loved her.

"Lie back and rest, Kyla. I'll be back tomorrow and every day until you're better and back home."

He stood to go, but hesitated. He hated leaving her alone.

"Go," she said. "I'll be here waiting for you in the morning."

Luke laid back on his leather recliner in his living room and stared out the window at the dormant vineyards. Exhaustion had set in the minute he got home from the hospital. Seeing Kyla so sick filled him with guilt and remorse. He'd been so damned self-righteous about her leaving him, he'd never stopped to think there might be a good reason why she'd disappeared.

He thought back to the day he realized that she wasn't just ignoring his calls, texts, or emails; she was gone. Just the memory made his heart race. Shock, anger, denial, blame, and finally the choice to bury himself in a life he hated. He'd drunk anything that came his way at every jet set party he could find. Women came and went in a blur from his Manhattan apartment. No one and nothing had any meaning for him. He'd cut off his parents, assuming they'd either scared her away or paid her off, and hated them even more. Most of all, he hated himself. Maybe she didn't love him. He'd tortured himself with every scenario. Surely if she were dead the media would have picked that up. At times he wished she were. At least it would have been over.

He sipped a glass of Madrona red, a popular product in his tasting room. The oak-beam ceiling with the track lighting sent a golden glow over the rustic furniture and massive living room. A small fire burned in the river rock fireplace that reached through both stories of the house. Luke longed for a dog like Gretel to curl at his feet. One like he'd had as a little boy. A big dog, maybe, to take hiking. But most of all, the emptiness would never be filled without Kyla.

There was no doubt in his mind he could handle her illness. The man he was now could forgive her and let the past go. But would that really have been his attitude if she'd told him the truth a few years ago when they were engaged? She was a dynamic creature then: a top model and ardent partner in bed. How would he have reacted to her diagnosis? The pedestal he'd put her on was so high, would she have fallen off when he knew the truth? Were her doubts about him justified? After two years of hell and soul searching, he was not the same man anymore. Thank God.

Chapter Sixteen

"I'm fine," Kyla insisted as Jude and Lily rushed around her, trying to make her room comfortable. "Ladies, they released me from the hospital, I'm home now, and I can go back to work. And besides, I have Becca to help me in the store."

Lily fluffed up Kyla's bed. "How about a little nap first?"

"Good idea," Jude echoed.

Kyla stood her ground. "I appreciate you both being here for me, but I don't need fussing over. I promise I will take good care of myself."

"And call us if you need anything?" Lily asked.

"Yes, I will. Now why don't you both head home? You've got businesses to run."

Kyla watched her friends walk down the driveway. How could she have ever considered leaving here? She knew who she had to call next. He'd come every day while she was in the hospital. Her heart fluttered as she called his number.

"Madrona Island Winery," Luke answered.

"I'd like to order a thousand cases of your best wine," she said.

"Kyla? I'm sorry. I forgot I was answering my cell phone. Are you home?"

She hesitated for a moment. Why hadn't she waited until the business day was over? "I'm fine. You're obviously busy. Give me a call later when you can."

"Hold on," he said. "You are not escaping that easily."

Her laugh rang in the air. Relax, she told herself. It's okay. "I wasn't planning on going anywhere," she said.

"Is that a promise?" he asked.

Without hesitation she answered, "Yes. Yes it is."

"All right then. How about I pick you up at 6:00 and whisk you off for a nice dinner?"

"I'll be ready and waiting," Kyla said. It felt like the last years apart melted away and they were back where they started…in love. Only this time the secrets—well, most of them—were out on the table.

After a long afternoon nap, Kyla put on her favorite lime-green cashmere sweater. It was a few years old but still soft and flattering. She wondered where Luke would take her for dinner. It really didn't matter. All she wanted to do was be with him.

She heard him knock and steeled herself for the confrontation. This time she would be honest with him no matter what happened. He stood at the door, his sandy brown hair curled slightly against his cheek, setting off his sculpted jaw and beguiling smile. His black pullover sweater hugged his body and made her want to do the same. In his hand was a bouquet of stunning deep pink-and-white lilies. They'd always been one of her favorites.

"Come in," she said. "I'll put these in some water. Have a seat."

She watched Luke sink into her sofa and take in the quaint living room with her overstuffed couch, oak rocker, and slow-burning flames in the brick fireplace. She felt his eyes follow her into her cozy kitchen. She loved the faint scent of lavender from the dried bundles hung from her ceiling.

"The cottage is charming," he said. "And so are these two," he said pointing.

Oz and Merlin had leapt in his lap, and he was stroking both of their furry little heads. "Yin and Yang," he said. "One black and one white."

"They keep me good company," she said. Kyla placed the flowers in a vase and laid them on the dining room table. "They add enchantment to the room," she said.

He patted the section of the deep purple couch next to him. He looked up at her with his translucent grey eyes, rimmed with long dark lashes, a devastatingly handsome combination that left her lightheaded. She felt like a schoolgirl with her first crush as she sat a few feet away from him.

Luke frowned. "So far away?" He reached out his arm and she scooted to snuggle against his body. "I've arranged a special surprise for dinner," he said. "I hope you like it."

"Are you going to tell me first?"

Luke stroked her hair. "I didn't want to tax you your first night home, so I had Chef Ryan cater a dinner for two to go. I thought we'd go to my house, sit by the fire, and have a quiet dinner at home."

He looked like a little boy hoping for approval. "That sounds perfect," Kyla said. And she meant it. She'd not been looking forward to crowds, noise, or having to socialize.

Luke helped her into her coat. "It's getting chilly, so bundle up."

They drove the five miles on wooded roads to his winery. He turned down a small drive and pulled in front of a log house. Against the evening sky, the house was lit up by tiny white lights that were nestled in the trees and bordered the stone path to the front door. A warm glow radiated out of the large peaked windows.

"It looks like something out of a fairytale," she said.

"I'm so glad you like it," he said.

He walked around and opened her car door for her, then offered his hand. Together they walked up the path and into the house. The living room had a two-story, open ceiling with skylights on both sides. A wooden staircase spiraled upstairs to a loft bedroom and beyond.

"Did this home come with the winery?" she asked.

"It was included, but I did a little redecorating before I moved in."

Kyla walked through the main room into an open country kitchen, complete with an old wood butcher block. Assorted pans hung from a stainless steel rack above a tiled island right in the center of the space. They walked through the kitchen to a dining table set with wine glasses that glimmered in candlelight.

"Shall we?" Luke pulled a chair out for her.

"Will the food magically appear?"

Just at that moment, there was a knock at the front door. "Delivery," Jude yelled.

Kyla looked at Luke. "I texted them when we arrived," he said with a grin.

Jude walked in with one of her waiters carrying a box of food and laid it on the kitchen counter. The waiter pulled ceramic plates out of the box, removed their aluminum coverings, and placed one before Kyla and then Luke.

"Bon appétit," Jude said, winking at them before leaving as fast as she came in.

The plates smelled of fresh salmon laced with dill and lemon. Crispy red potatoes drizzled with olive oil and sprinkled with rosemary complemented the broccoli rabe lightly covered with butter and garlic.

"A feast," Kyla said.

Luke held up a chilled bottle of white wine. "Our exceptional pinot gris," he said.

Kyla enjoyed the flex of his muscles as he uncorked the wine and poured her a glass.

"How about a toast?" he asked.

Kyla held up her glass to his.

"To us," he said.

"To us," she returned and clinked her glass with his. "I hope you don't mind if I just have a few sips," Kyla put the glass down. "I'm still pretty tired."

"Of course. Can I get you something else? Some sparkling cider or...?"

She placed her hand on his arm. "I'm fine, Luke. Let's just enjoy the wonderful meal."

Each bite was more delicious than the next. A roaring fire that opened into the living room and dining area kept things toasty as they finished their meal. "I don't think I've eaten this much in a long time," Kyla said.

Luke's smile lit the room. "I couldn't be happier," he said, standing. "Let's move to the living room and sit by the fire for a while."

She followed him over to his brown leather couch and settled in beside him.

"The place has a true rustic feel to it," Kyla said.

He pulled a wool throw over them. "It could use a woman's touch here and there."

"Perhaps it could. No dog?" she asked. She remembered Luke loved dogs and always talked about getting one when he settled down.

"Not yet. But one or two are in my plans."

"You should see the cute poodle we helped Betty adopt from the shelter the other day. It was the color of burgundy."

He pulled her closer and together they sat in silence watching the yellow, orange, and blue flames crackle over the sweet-smelling wood. Kyla felt…what was it? Content. It was not a feeling she was used to. She laid her head on Luke's shoulder.

"I could sit like this forever," she said.

He hugged her closer. "That's the idea."

Kyla sat back up and turned to face him. "Is it?"

"I have to admit, when I got here, I was determined to make you feel as bad as I had the last few years," Luke said. "But the minute I saw you, I knew I could never do anything to intentionally hurt you."

"You mean like I did," Kyla said.

Luke tried to look brave, but Kyla could see the deep pain behind his eyes.

"I never wanted to hurt you, Luke. That's why I left. I know that doesn't make any sense, but there are still things I haven't told you."

He tried to lighten things up. "You mean like you read tea leaves?"

"And so does my grandmother," Kyla said. She watched his face, waiting for it to sink in.

"So you come from a long line of gypsies?" Luke said with a chuckle.

"Actually, I do." This time Kyla saw surprise in his eyes. "We've been called that before and probably had a few Irish relatives in the old country who truly were. But when my grandmother came to the United States, she was known for her herbal healing remedies. And a few love spells," Kyla said with a smile.

"What about your parents?" he asked.

Kyla felt the old shame creep up into the pit of her stomach. What did Luke know of a single parent struggling to make a living? Or a little girl named Kyla too embarrassed to bring friends home?

"This may be hard for you to imagine with your upbringing," Kyla said, "but my world consisted of being raised by only my mother and grandmother in a small brownstone in Brooklyn. We were lucky to pay the mortgage each month when I was a kid." She sat up straight and reminded herself that her past was not something to be embarrassed of. "Stefan would not have given me the time of day. And can you imagine how your parents would have taken that news?"

"Not well," he answered honestly. "And I would have been surprised myself, but it wouldn't have made a difference in my love for you."

His eyes were sincere, but Kyla sensed a place deep inside him still trying to make sense of who the Darcy Devereaux he knew actually was.

"Wouldn't it?" she asked. "My hair was falling out. I had bruises up my legs and not enough energy to get out of bed some days. What kind of bride would I have made?"

"Mine," he said simply.

Kyla thought about all that wasted time they could have spent together. And how much time would they have had left if her lupus worsened "I couldn't do it to you, Luke. A sick bride from a family that never even heard of the social register."

"You couldn't do it to me or you thought I would run?"

"Both."

She felt him pull away. They sat in silence and listened to the crackling of the fire. Her secrets were mostly out in the open now. It was up to him to accept them or move on.

Chapter Seventeen

uke had spent the cold, windy November morning in the vineyards cleaning up the vines before they went completely dormant. He was proud to be known as the only winery on the island producing hand-crafted Pinot Noir. The fields, barns, woods, and orchards—all twenty-two acres of them—were his. And the rich soil and moist climate were perfect for a small estate winery. His plans for expansion spun in his head. The previous owners had let the place go a little after the husband's heart attack, and Luke had his work cut out for him.

He went into his office and warmed his hands at the woodstove before sitting down at his desk. A glance at his calendar reminded him that Ian was showing up at 2:00 with sketches for his new wine label and for a painting of the vineyards he could use for promotion. First on his agenda was to start a wine club. His uncle in Napa had done very well with that addition. And next summer Luke visualized wine pairing dinners with Chef Ryan in the orchard under the trees.

No matter how hard he tried to block it, anger raced through him. A week had gone by since he'd had Kyla over for dinner. When he dropped her off that night and they kissed goodnight, Luke had wondered just who was he kissing, Kyla Nolan or Darcy Devereaux. Who was this woman he loved? She had a family that she'd never trusted Luke enough to tell him about. He'd told her everything—how he hated his father, had run from their wealth and the strings that went with it. They talked about their dreams of escaping the city and settling together on their own idyllic winery. Had that even been true? Had she just been telling him what he wanted to hear? He didn't want to ruin what they had now, but the doubts would not leave him alone.

He'd called Kyla every day to check on her just like he said he would. But each time he'd had to fight back the urge to ask her if there was anything else she was hiding. But she was still recovering after the hospital incident and he did not want to upset her. Neither one of them had suggested getting together again. But as the days clicked by, Luke longed for her. No matter how busy he stayed or how much he loved running the winery, there was an emptiness that followed him.

Luke heard Ian's car skid onto the gravel drive and went to the door to greet him. The rain was falling in earnest now and the fields were already muddy.

Ian hurried inside and shook the rain off his hair. "It's a wet one," he said laying his art case down on the floor. He put his coat on the hook by the door. "Nice and warm in here."

"The woodstove is airtight and keeps this place pretty toasty," Luke said.

Ian picked up his sketches, carried them over to the oak tasting bar, and spread them out for Luke to see. "Have a look."

Luke surveyed the two watercolors side by side. "This one. It's perfect."

He held the painting to the light. Golden letters read "Madrona Island Winery" across the top of a burgundy label. Underneath was a panorama of the vineyards bathed in morning sun with the barn in the distance. Two dogs slept in the foreground.

"My choice, too," Ian said. "The image will look great on a T-shirt as well."

"Ah yes, merchandise." Luke reached behind the bar for a bottle. "Here's a thank you bottle of the holiday blend I just released. I can't take credit for this year's release, but next year our reds will have come directly from my fields and my hands."

"That must feel great."

"It does." Luke put the wine in a gift bag and handed it to Ian. "How's the wife doing? Feeling any better?"

"She's tired a lot. I'm trying not to worry. Speaking of that, have you seen Kyla lately?" Ian asked.

"Not in a few days. You?"

"She and Lily talk every day, but you know Kyla. She's busy working hard at the shop and doesn't say much."

Luke jolted. "Actually," he said, "I don't know Kyla all that well as you seem to."

The two men stood silent, facing each other. Ian rubbed the back of his neck. "I hope you understand. I was in a tough position."

"How so?" Luke knew he was pushing Ian, but he'd been part of this whole cover-up as well. Only Ian had known the truth about Kyla these last few years.

Ian walked over to the leather chairs facing the wood stove. "Why don't we sit down?"

Luke took a seat. He stared at the scorching flame through the glass door of the stove and waited for Ian to begin.

"Just know, Luke, that your friendship was always first in my mind. I considered helping Kyla carefully before I did it."

"Helping her…" Luke trailed off.

"She called me a few weeks after I returned from the Hamptons that summer after we all went sailing together. I thought she wanted to buy a painting. She wanted to know if she could trust Maggie, the owner of Madrona Island B&B, to keep her stay there a secret."

"And you didn't think that was strange?" Luke asked.

"Her request seemed strange at the time, but then, I didn't know her well. She said she needed to get away and have complete privacy. She sounded terrible and I hoped you two hadn't broken up."

"What'd you tell her?"

"That Maggie could be trusted completely."

Luke stood up and paced in front of the fire. "So Maggie knew, you knew, who else knew?"

"Actually, only I knew. Darcy used the name Kyla when she registered. Maggie took good care of her and eventually Kyla decided to settle here. I was the only one she told about her illness. She begged me to keep her identity a secret and not press her for details."

Luke stopped pacing and glared at Ian. "Why you?"

"Perhaps because I was your friend, Luke, and she knew you trusted me."

Luke sank back into the chair and put his head in his hands. "Why didn't she tell me?" He looked up at Ian. "What am I supposed to do now? Act like none of this happened?"

"She loves you, I know that," Ian said. "And you two have a second chance at a future together."

"I love her, too. At least, I know I loved Darcy Devereuax. But who is Kyla Nolan?"

Ian smiled. "She's an amazing woman. You ought to get to know her."

"Will she let me?" Luke asked. "What other secrets is she hiding?"

"The only way to find out is to give her a chance. Go on a date. Have some fun." Ian stood up and walked toward the door to get his coat. "I better get back before I have to float home. Why don't you both join me and Lily this weekend for the Holiday Crafts Fair at the Loganberry Farm Café & Bakery? Their pie is amazing."

"A double date." Luke grinned. "I'll ask Kyla."

Luke walked Ian to the door and watched him run toward his car. "Hey, thanks, Ian," Luke yelled after him.

Ian waved back. "Any time."

Chapter Eighteen

Luke was right on time to pick Kyla up for their double date with Ian and Lily. Kyla knew his invitation was for more than a day together. It meant he had considered everything she told him and still wanted to see her. His disarming smile put her right at ease.

He helped her into her down jacket. "You might want mittens," he said. "It's pretty crisp out there. But clear blue skies."

She slipped on her fuzzy mittens and took his arm. Luke's SUV and Jude's Honda, with Ryan in the passenger seat, were parked in her driveway.

Luke opened the front car door and Kyla jumped in. "Morning," she said to Ian and Lily in the back seat. "I see our double date has turned into a triple."

"Jude heard where we were going and wanted to come, too," Lily said.

Kyla turned to Lily. "I'm not a bit surprised."

They followed Jude down the road to the Loganberry Farm event. A big banner was strewn across the front of the barn with the words "Island Country Christmas." The place looked so different in the winter. The pond's surface was icy and the ducks were skittering around it, finding holes in the water. Gone were the blooming flowers and vines. The browns and dulled shades of orange and yellow remained.

They parked side by side in the lot. Jude jumped out of her car first and opened the door for Kyla.

"Great to see you," she said, leaning in for a hug.

"I see you let Ryan out for the day," Kyla said.

"Hey, I heard that," Ryan said, coming over and shaking Ian and Luke's hand.

The inside of the barn was warm and festive. The smell of hot apple cider filled the air. The walls were lined with booths of homemade crafts, from hand weavings to carved wooden bowls, jams, jellies, honeys, and tempting baked goods. The couples strolled along while the local musicians Holly and Ken played guitar and sang Christmas carols in the background.

Kyla watched Ian and Lily stroll hand in hand ahead of them. She glanced up at Luke, and he turned and smiled. It still dazzled her and sent chills down her spine to look up into his eyes. Luke slipped his arm around her shoulder and guided her over to a table with handmade jewelry that Lily was admiring.

"Look at this necklace," Lily said. She held up a silver chain with a blue heron spreading its wings on the inlaid pendant. She looked at the price tag and sighed before moving on to the next booth.

Ian lingered behind and slipped some money to Luke. "Grab it when she's not looking," he whispered.

Luke winked. Kyla lingered back with him and held up a necklace in the shape of a bald eagle. "They are beautiful."

"You never know what Santa will bring," Luke said.

Kyla shook her head. "I guess not. Now hurry up and get that necklace for Lily before she turns around."

Necklace carefully stowed in her purse, Kyla hurried down to join Lily at the apple cider booth. Jude and Ryan were already sipping theirs out of paper cups.

"Try some," Jude suggested. "Warms you to your toes."

Ryan tossed his empty cup into the trash. "On to the fudge," he said with a grin. Jude trailed along and so did Ian and Lily, leaving Kyla alone with Luke.

"Speaking of chocolates," Luke said. "I've been thinking about having someone craft some fine truffles using some of our wines for flavoring."

"I know a pastry chef in town who would be great for that. You might consider adding a little lavender to one as well."

Luke considered the idea. "Lavender chocolate Merlot could be a killer combination. Let's talk business one day next week."

"Sure," she said. To be close to him again was what she wanted. There could be no more lies between them. It was time to confront the past they'd both been bruised by.

Heat blew fiercely into the barn from the overhead vents and the crowd grew larger.

Jude and Ryan waved from the corner by the door and motioned for them to follow. "Let's go," Kyla said, her hand on Luke's back.

They made their way through the crowd and happily out the door into the cool, fresh air.

"Yes. Oxygen," Jude said exhaling, her breath rising like mist in the air.

Ian and Lily were already outside huddling close to keep each other warm. "Let's go get pie," Lily said.

Kyla was glad to see Lily was hungry again. But she still hadn't put much weight on.

"I've heard about this famous pie place since I moved here," Ryan said. "My boss finally gave me a day off to try it."

Jude punched Ryan in the arm. "Can't help it if we've been extra busy since you started cooking."

They followed Lily to the old silo-shaped building that housed Island Pie Café. Ian held open the door and the group seated themselves at a table by the window facing the dormant gardens and duck pond. A waitress dropped menus at the table and took coffee orders.

"So, what's good?" Luke asked.

"Everything," Kyla said. She couldn't decide between the seasonal pumpkin pie made from scratch or her favorite loganberry pie hot with ice cream.

"I'm having the salted caramel apple pie," Lily announced.

Jude put her menu down on the table. "Me, too."

"Me three," Luke said.

Kyla decided on the loganberry à la mode, and Ian ordered the rhubarb pie.

"This is one of my favorite places on the island," Kyla said. "Fresh peach pie in the summer and every berry imaginable. And in winter, perfect lattes and soups made from scratch."

"Good thing it's a bit of a drive from Island Thyme Café or we'd have lunch competition," Jude said.

Ryan coughed.

"Of course they don't have a five-star chef like we do," Jude said.

The pie came and the conversation stopped as everyone dug into the buttery crust and perfectly filled slices. Kyla glanced out the window and watched the ducks huddling up together to keep warm. In the spring there would be baby ducks and geese everywhere. She'd have to bring Luke back here.

Lily pushed back her chair. "Excuse me all. Off to the ladies' room."

Kyla followed close behind as Lily hurried off. Once inside Kyla asked, "How are you doing with the morning sickness? Did the herbs I gave you help?"

Lily leaned over the sink. "They did some, but I'm still dizzy several times a day and I'm up half the night."

Kyla scrutinized Lily. She did not like what she saw. There was a green tinge to her skin and dark circles under her eyes. Eyes that displayed fear.

"What if…?" Lily started.

"It will be fine," Kyla said. "Come into my shop tomorrow and let me make you a tea blend to help."

"Will you do a tea leaf reading for me at the same time?" Lily whispered.

Kyla hesitated. She didn't want to scare Lily or use the tea leaves to predict anything like this. "I don't need to," she said. "I can see a pretty little tow-head girl running around your porch. All will be well."

"Is it a vision?" Lily asked.

Kyla tuned deep inside herself. The child's image glowed in the sun, but a dark cloud was blowing by. "It is," Kyla said. "There may be a rough patch, but it will pass."

Lily looked visibly relieved. "Thank you," she said. "Let's get back. I don't want to worry Ian."

Back at the table, everyone was talking about the upcoming holiday parade.

"You all have to come," Jude said. "Even the fire department shows up with the firemen and women in Santa Costumes and drive down Front Street."

"That is something I'd like to see," Luke said.

Kyla nodded.

"It's a date then," Jude said. "We can all meet up at the café and stand out on the sidewalk and watch together."

It was something to look forward to for Kyla. This would be her third parade since she'd moved to the island. But if all went well, it would be her first one standing beside the man she loved.

Luke turned on the car lights before he pulled out of the parking lot from the pie café. It was 4:00 in the afternoon, and already the moon was lighting up the darkening sky. He waited for the car to warm up a bit and then turned up the heat.

"Look at the clouds," Kyla said. "They have a pink hue. Perhaps we will get a little snow."

"A little snow?" Luke asked.

"It's not New York, Luke. We don't even get snow every winter. Mostly dustings and a foot here or there. But when it does snow, the whole island closes down."

Luke upped the heat. "It's cold enough outside, that's for sure."

"When we get to my house," Kyla said, "why don't you come in for my special hot chocolate."

"Count me in," he said. It would also give them some time to talk. Alone.

Luke was glad Kyla had left her propane heat on so the house was warm. The cats were cuddled together on the rocker in the corner. He sat on a stool by the eating bar and watched Kyla make hot chocolate from scratch. She poured in the milk and whisked in the chocolate. Her hair looked like fine brandy as it curled down over her shoulders. Her sweater and jeans showed off her soft curves. She was as beautiful as he remembered, and it had nothing to do with fancy clothes and stylists.

She smiled back at him. "My specialty for all that ails you."

"And what makes it special?" he asked.

Kyla added some herbs into the warm milk. "A pinch of cayenne to warm you and a sprinkle of lavender for relaxation."

He thought about what was ailing him. Tonight he was going to have to clear up a few things with her if he was ever going to free his mind and move forward.

Kyla poured the warm mixture into some tall mugs, placed them on the counter, and pulled a stool up next to Luke.

He sipped the spicy hot cocoa and felt warmth race through his body.

"It has a bit of a kick," she said.

"That it does," he said with a laugh. "And just in time." Luke pointed out her dining room window where a light snow had started to fall. The back porch light illuminated the large flakes drifting slowly down from the sky, coating the ground in a thin white carpet.

"I wonder if it will stick," Kyla said.

Luke watched her childlike expression as she watched the snow and longed to pull her outside and dance in the icy shower.

She moved over to the window. "I'd love to go outside and feel it fall on my face. But I guess it's best if I wait until I feel a little stronger first," she said with a sigh.

He stood behind her and put his arms around her shoulders. "Soon. I'm sure it will be soon."

Kyla turned her eyes, glimmering like dark emeralds, staring into his. He pulled her into his arms and kissed her. She tasted of sweet chocolate with a bit of spice. Her arms clung to him as she pressed her body to his. Luke ran his fingers under her sweater and caressed her warm back. He wanted her, all of her. Now. He forced himself to step back and see her reaction. She swooned. Her lips parted and her eyes pooled with longing.

"Darcy," he said before he realized the wrong name he had used.

She snapped back to attention, fear lacing her eyes. "Darcy is gone, Luke."

"I'm so sorry," Luke said, but the mood was broken. Outside, the snow had really picked up and it was sticking. He considered driving home while he still could. But he had to know more. That winter in New York after Kyla had disappeared had been the coldest of his life. At one point he'd walked through the freezing wind and ice and considered lying down in a snowdrift and never waking up. The melodrama of the moment had sent him into laughter before breaking him into tears. He'd left New York for sunny California and not looked back. Until now.

Kyla turned, walked over to the loveseat, and curled up in a corner. She pulled her knees up and hugged them, looking like an innocent young girl. Perhaps she was. She was only twenty-seven, Luke reminded himself. And she'd been alone, it sounded like, for most of her life. He wanted to hold her, protect her, and tell her everything was going to be all right.

He sat down in the opposite corner of the small sofa and kept his distance for the moment.

"For the record," Kyla said, "I was going to tell you everything right after you proposed to me in New York."

The words broke Luke into a million pieces. "Why didn't you?"

"We'd only known each other a month. I was so shocked by the proposal and so blissfully happy. I knew it was time to throw my fear to the wind." Kyla sat up straight and looked him directly in the eye. "Then three things happened."

"And what were they?" he asked.

Her voice was raspy. "First, it was your brother's call. Imagine my shock when Stefan notified me that you were all but engaged to Lisbeth."

"We were never engaged or even really dating," Luke said. "I'd forgotten she existed."

Kyla held up her hand. "Let me finish."

Luke leaned back into the couch. He should have told her, but when he did remember about Lisbeth, he hadn't wanted to mention anything that might break the incredible rightness of their love.

"Second, I was going to call you and find out why you'd lied to me. The phone rang and I picked it up thinking it was you. It was the doctor, and everything I knew and everything I was came abruptly to an end with that call."

Luke nodded. "I can understand that."

She looked right through him. "Could you really have?" she asked. "You knew me as a wealthy supermodel, glamorous and free. When all that came crashing down, would you have stayed?"

Kyla stopped to calm herself.

"And three, I loved you. For the first time in my life, I loved someone enough to care about them first. How could I saddle you with a sickly wife? How would I ever know whether you stayed out of guilt or love? You deserved more. And so I left."

The weight of her confession crushed him. All the anger, regret, soul searching, and longing had brought him here back to Kyla. And she deserved more than a man who'd spent the last few years feeling sorry for himself.

He reached his hand out to her. "How can you ever forgive me?"

She burst into tears and he scooped her into arms and cradled her. Luke kissed her silky hair and wiped her warm tears with his fingers. "No more crying, Kyla. I love you. I always have and always will."

She gazed up at him. "And I love you."

Kyla jolted awake. Someone was in her kitchen. The smell of coffee brewing alerted her. She lifted the blanket, and memories returned. Luke had stayed over last night. On the couch. The snow had been too heavy for him to drive home and he'd volunteered to sleep in the living room. She'd been torn, but they still needed time before they jumped back into their relationship. She slipped on her turquoise silk robe and slippers and wandered out to the kitchen.

"Good morning, sleepyhead," Luke said, grinning at her. "How do you like your eggs?"

"Any way you like them," she said.

Having a shirtless man with sculpted abs in her kitchen was a first. Nor could she remember the last time someone had made her breakfast. And never in this house.

"Got any fresh herbs?" Luke asked.

"Is that a joke? In the middle of winter?" she said.

Luke winked at her. "Fresh dried will do."

Kyla went to her spice cabinet and brought down two bottles. "I have rosemary and a special Herbs de Provence I mixed up this summer."

She watched him scramble the eggs with a whisk and pinch the herbs before dropping them in.

"Hope you don't mind," he said. "I took out the goat cheese and spinach as well."

"Don't mind at all." Kyla cut up some slices of the local sourdough bread she'd bought in town and popped them into the toaster. The fresh garlic-and-herb butter she'd made would go perfect with the meal. She poured the coffee and brought cream to the table, then handed Luke two royal blue ceramic plates.

She watched as he slid the eggs off the pan onto each plate next to the buttered toast and carried them to the table. Outside the window there was a coating of snow on the pine boughs, but the rain had started and the snow was melting fast in her yard. He would go home soon, she realized. But he was here now and that is what counted.

"You are quite the cook," she said.

"I had a little practice when I was living with my uncle and training with him at his winery. Breakfast is my specialty. Perhaps dinner at my place this week?"

"I'll think about it," she said grinning. She savored the delicious blend of herbs masterfully mixed with egg and creamy cheese.

"Okay. I get the hint. You want to take it slow. How about lunch?"

Kyla pretended to ponder the idea. Slow was good. "I want it to last this time," she said, blushing at her boldness.

He put his fork down and met her eyes. "Whatever it takes. Just tell me."

She nodded, sipped her coffee, and decided to change the subject. "So how's business coming along?"

Luke put his fork down on the plate. "I've been meaning to tell you. Kelly, the reporter from Island Times, is doing a big write-up on my new ownership. Do you know the magazine, Island Vineyards?"

"I've seen it around town," she said.

"They're widely read and they contacted me for an interview. It will be great publicity."

Kyla was happy for him but still uneasy. "My little island escape won't be staying private much longer, I fear."

Luke paled. "I hadn't thought of that."

"Let's just hope the tabloids don't get wind of the long-lost model found at last."

"I guess if I found you, others will, too," Luke said. "Sorry for being so thoughtless."

Kyla stroked his smooth cheek, letting her fingers linger. "It's not your fault or your problem."

He attempted a smile. "I don't want it to be yours either."

Kyla pushed her fork around her plate. The tabloids could make her life hell. She enjoyed her anonymity here, her privacy, and wanted her fans to remember her as she'd been. In the past, she'd done everything she could to avoid exposure, but it no longer seemed that important.

Kyla forced a smile. "Perhaps it is time to show my face to the world again."

"And a very beautiful face it is," Luke said. "If you're ready, I'll do all I can to help."

Over the last couple of years, Kyla had thought often of calling her booking agent, Arlene. She felt terrible that she hadn't at least told her the truth. Arlene still deposited her commissions in the account they agreed on and asked no questions. But they'd been very close and Kyla knew she'd hurt Arlene's feelings.

"I think I'll call Arlene. It's time."

Luke leaned across the table and kissed her on the cheek. "Brave girl."

It was about time courage took the lead in her life and cowardice fell to the wayside.

Chapter Nineteen

Luke looked out the misty window of the tasting room at the dormant vineyard stretching across the hill. Grey clouds hung low over the vines and barren pasture. Yet he was happier than he'd ever been. Orders kept pouring in for the holiday blend all month. The Saturday afternoon wine tastings and small plates with Chef Ryan had also been successful. The biggest hit of all was the new chocolate loganberry truffles he had commissioned Michaelene, the local pastry chef, to create. She used the liqueur from the island distillery down the road, and a pinch of lavender from Kyla's harvest added magic.

The loganberry liqueur was made in small batches by distilling brandy into local wines, including Luke's blends. The juice was aged with skins of locally grown loganberries, Luke's favorite. The liqueur had won medals for its garnet color and exotic aromas, and when mixed with the finest dark chocolate, it was pure bliss in the truffles.

Kyla never left his thoughts. He'd fallen more in love with her every day. Luke had thought long and hard about the type of engagement ring he wanted to buy for her. He had returned the last one, with its seven-carat brilliance, a few years ago. That was not what he wanted this time around. This ring would not be about impressing her, but something meaningful instead. Luke had called his jeweler friend in Sonoma County and told him a bit about Kyla's heritage and taste. He had suggested a Celtic claddagh ring in exquisite rose gold with a marquis center diamond and two small emeralds embedded on the sides. It sounded perfect, and the custom-made ring would be delivered tomorrow. A day before the parade and two days before Christmas. Just in time. Luke thought of his mother and how she'd always wanted to see him happily married. Instead of an obligatory holiday call, he decided to call her and share all his good news.

The phone rang at the family home and Luke silently hoped his father would not answer. The housekeeper answered on the fourth ring. "Bradford residence."

"Merry Christmas, Rose. It's Lucas. Is my mother there?"

"Merry Christmas, Lucas. Will you be coming home for the holidays?" she asked. Luke could hear the hope in her voice. She'd been with the family since Luke was a little boy.

"You never know," he said.

"I'll go get your mother. She'll be so happy to hear from you."

It felt good to do something to make his mother happy. Luke had walked out on the family and hardly called during the last year. It wasn't fair to his mother, but Luke could not take one more minute of his father's controlling and dismissive attitude. He'd almost laughed when Luke had told him he was going to marry the model Darcy Devereux back then. Wait until he heard Kyla was a shop owner now. Luke couldn't care less. He'd probably never please his father and still please himself too. And the last two years had taught him the importance of living your own life and following your own passion.

"Luke, is that really you?" His mother sounded almost giddy.

"It is, Mom. Merry Christmas."

"It is now," she said.

Luke imagined his mother hurrying around, directing the staff and decorating their massive house for the holidays. He didn't miss the endless parties and empty conversations. But he was glad to hear her voice.

"Tell me how you're doing," she said. "How's the winery?"

Guilt tugged at his heart, and Luke made a quick note to overnight them a case of his wine for a gift. "The winery is everything I hoped for and more."

"What good news. I'm so happy for you, Luke. I saw an article in Wine Review about you taking over the vineyard, about the changes you're planning, and how you are turning it into a real destination."

"Well, I haven't won any awards yet," he said with a laugh. "My new chocolate truffles with loganberry liqueur might, though. I'll send you a box."

"Sounds divine. And what can I send you? Do you need anything?"

Luke knew his mother was asking if he needed money. She was sweet to worry, but his inheritance from his grandmother and the profits from the winery kept him very comfortable.

"I'm absolutely fine, Mom. Thank you."

"I'd love to send a housewarming gift at least," she said.

"How about you come visit in the spring when the buds break in the vineyards? Seeing you would be wonderful."

He heard the catch in his mother's voice and knew she was pleased.

"I'll be there. Just let me know when."

"Well," Luke said, drawing it out, "I do have some other news." He hesitated. His mother tried to be supportive, but she, too, had worried about Luke marrying a model. Her main concern had been how fast it had all happened and she didn't want to see him hurt.

"I'm in love," he said.

His mother was quiet. "Is it someone on the island?"

"As a matter a fact, it's someone I knew in New York who lives on the island now. Someone I have never stopped loving."

"I can't think who…Darcy? Did you find her?"

"Yes, Mom. I did. She's been here all along. It's a long story. She's not been well. Before I tell you everything, I want you to know we are more in love than ever and I am going to ask her to marry me. If she says yes, the wedding will probably be here at the winery in June."

"I'll put it on my calendar," she said. "As long as you're happy, I wouldn't miss it. And if you need help with anything, I'm here and pretty good with event planning, as you know."

"I'm sure it will be small," Luke said. Her support meant everything to him.

Luke told her the whole story, and to his mother's credit, she stayed quiet and listened.

"A happy ending," she said simply. "I'm so glad."

Luke took a deep breath. "How is Dad? Stefan?" It was hard to ask about his half-brother, but he knew it would make his mother happy. Stefan was from his father's first marriage. They'd never been close as kids, even though Luke had tried. And from what Luke could tell, his brother had turned into an arrogant and ambitious man. His mother had always hoped they'd get along. Luke had given up.

"You know your dad. He's always busy and working too hard. But he's fine. There is some news about Stefan. I was going to email you." His mother hesitated. "Stefan has been dating. I didn't mention it because Stefan never sticks with one woman for long. But it looks like there may be two weddings in the family next year. Stefan is engaged to Lizbeth."

The room spun. It was just like Stefan, going after the richest, prettiest girl in New York. The fact that their dad had really wanted Luke to marry Lizbeth and bring her into the family made it worse. Luke had disappointed his dad's wishes and proposed to Kyla instead. Stefan finally had their father's approval and must feel triumphant. Luke reigned in his temper and tried to sound civil. He hoped his brother at least loved Lizbeth. She deserved that.

"Why don't you send me his address? I'll send them a case of wine to congratulate them." The thought of sending sour wine raced through Luke's mind, but he did not need to fuel the sibling rivalry by being a jerk himself.

"That would be nice," she said. "I'll email it to you. Let me know when to book my airline reservations."

The door opened and three customers raced into the tasting room, shaking rain out of their hair and laughing.

"I've got to go, Mom. I'll call you soon," Luke said.

He put his cell phone under the bar and gave the guests his full attention.

"Would you like to try today's tastings?" Luke asked the couples. He went through his speech about the wines, the special cheese, and the chocolate, but all the while his mind lingered on the conversation with his mother. It was good to talk to her. But how would he tell Kyla about Stefan and

Lizbeth? His stomach dropped at the thought of upsetting her. He sighed and poured more wine.

He'd tried to live without his family, but at his core, he loved them. It was just so hard to be around them. He wanted to create a new family with Kyla and hoped there was a way to put both of their past issues behind them. His mother had reached out and Luke would reach back. He did not have to react in the old ways, and he no longer had to run or justify who he was and what he wanted.

"Dad, let's buy a case of this one for our family holiday," a pretty young woman said, smiling at her father.

"A great idea," the man answered. "And what would your mom like?" he asked, putting his arm around the beautiful, obviously happy woman next to him.

"The truffles, boxes of them," she said.

The man laughed, turned to Luke, and winked. "You heard the lady. How many boxes do you have?"

"I have a dozen in stock," Luke said. "They're custom made. If you want to order more, I could ship them to you."

"We'll take all you have and a case of the Pinot Noir as well." The man pulled out his credit card. "Gotta keep the ladies happy."

Luke rang up the purchases and watched the family teasing and laughing with each other. That was what a happy family looked like. That was the kind of husband and father Luke was determined to be.

Chapter Twenty

Kyla pulled her pine-green cashmere sweater over her head and smoothed down her plaid wool skirt over her warm tights. The round neckline would set off her silver necklace with the large garnet and moonstone perfectly. She brushed her hair out and applied a berry-colored lip-gloss.

"Good enough" she said. She did not have time to waste this morning. She had spicy scones to make, gifts to wrap, and so much to get done before Luke arrived for the Christmas parade in town. Jude had called at dawn and asked if she could come over for a quick chat before the shop opened at ten. Kyla wished her request had come on another day when crowds wouldn't be flooding the streets and swarming her shop, but Jude was a friend, and friends came first.

She was glad she'd started up the wood burner in her living room the minute she'd slipped out of bed this morning. Merlin curled up right in front of it, as close as he could get without singeing his whiskers, and stretched his long, black body in contentment. Oz was still burrowed in her bed. It was a nippy day and would probably not even get up to 40 degrees. Her heavy skirt and wool tights would help keep her warm. And a sip of Jude's holiday cider would assure it. Luke would arrive at 3:00 sharp to watch the parade with her.

Kyla poured hot water into a mug and steeped some green tea. A smile spread across her face. She'd finally figured out a holiday gift for Luke. She had commissioned Ian to paint a picture of Luke's vineyard and barn, radiant with sunlight from a photo taken in the summer. It would fit next to the tasting menu on the wall behind the counter. Ian had delivered it yesterday, discreetly wrapped, as promised. She would give it to him Christmas Day.

Everything was going so well, it was almost scary. Her call to her agent, Arlene, had gone perfectly. Not a word of complaint about the sparse communication for the last two years. When Kyla told her the whole story, Arlene assured her that she was there for Kyla for the long haul. In sickness and in health. But, she'd said, don't tell my husband that. Arlene always made her laugh. She'd even come up with the idea of Kyla possibly being a spokesperson for the Lupus Association. The idea of helping others through her own experience excited Kyla.

She reached down and scratched under Merlin's chin. "We'll see what happens." The cat's purr radiated throughout the room.

"Knock, knock." Jude stepped in the front door of Kyla's cottage. "Hope I'm not too early."

Kyla held up her mug. "Want some tea?"

"Well, actually," Jude said, "I would, but not that kind."

Kyla frowned. "I have black tea and peppermint and…"

"To be honest, I was hoping for tea and comfort today. You know, a tea reading."

Kyla laughed. "Why didn't you just say so? Let's go into the shop and I'll brew some China tea that I just got in."

Jude followed Kyla through the back door of the shop into the parlor area, sat down at the small round table, and watched Kyla brew the tea. "Thanks for doing this."

"I'm happy to. Just make yourself comfortable while I get ready."

Kyla brought the side-rimmed teacups to the table then lit the bayberry-scented candle in the middle. "Sorry the room is so cold. I turned up the heat."

"It's fine," Jude said as she ran her fingers through the fringe of the tablecloth.

Kyla handed Jude a cup of steaming water with loose tea leaves floating on the surface. "Just wait until they float to the bottom," she said, "then take a few sips and think about your questions."

Jude's hand shook slightly as she lifted the pure-white bone china cup to her lips for a sip.

"Now," Kyla said, "put the cup in your left hand and swirl the tea leaves around three times in a clockwise direction." Kyla watched closely, noticing Jude's movements and expression. "Please hand it to me."

"I love the ritual of this," Jude said. "So mysterious."

Kyla tipped the cup sideways and drained any remaining tea into the saucer. She placed the cup on the table in front of Jude and leaned over it to see the patterns.

The cup showed many issues, but the most prominent one was a love relationship. Not a smooth path and many obstacles were clear, but she was not sure Jude was ready to hear that. "Small worries are scattered around like little pebbles," she said, "but the main issue is the large heart right in the center of the cup."

"You got it. My heart flutters every time Ryan comes near, but sometimes he is so distant."

Kyla closed her eyes and let the images in the cup sink deep into her mind. Danger danced at the edge of her feelings. She looked back at Jude. "Love is the central question, but many images surround it." She pointed to the first quarter of the cup. "Roses dance along the edges here, symbolizing love returned."

"Really?" Jude asked hopefully.

After a moment, Kyla continued. "But here, directly across from the handle, is a clear image of a dragon."

Jude looked closely at the cup. "I think I see it. Here's the head and the tail trails along the bottom. What does it mean?"

"Halfway through a year, so six months from now, it signifies a sudden change."

Jude frowned. "A bad one? I'm due for some good luck in love for once."

Kyla's eyes circled the cup as she listened to her inner knowing for guidance. "The need for caution is there, but in a few months' time, there is a broken sword pointing toward the handle. Triumph over an enemy. The sign of Venus sits at the end of the journey. Love."

Jude sat in silence, staring at the cup. She looked up at Kyla. "How long?"

"The full transit through the cup from handle to handle signifies about a year, but I think it will be sooner."

Jude shook her head. "He's worth the wait, whatever it takes." She cast off her troubles and gave Kyla a bright smile. "Dinner is on me anytime at the café."

Kyla rose and started cleaning off the table. "I better go open the shop and get ready for the parade. See you around three in front of the café to watch?"

Jude hurried toward the door. "See you then."

Kyla wished she could spare her friend the trouble she'd seen coming ahead. She recognized a fellow runner in Ryan. But from what she could not see.

Kyla mixed up a batch of mull spiced apple cider and began warming it on the stove. She stirred the mixture and inhaled its invigorating scent then placed thermoses of hot water in the back room of the shop. Love. She wondered what the tea leaves would show for her and Luke. But she'd made a promise to herself long ago not do to readings on herself. It was too hard to stay objective.

On the way out front, she flipped on her acoustic music track of harp and piano. The holly berry reefs on the tables supported thick, white candles that needed to be lit. They looked perfect with the white tablecloths and ruby-red napkins rolled up in crystal holders. She flipped on the twinkling lights she'd placed in the window and turned the sign to "open" in the window.

Becca arrived in a flurry. "Sorry to be late," she said. "Traffic and parking were impossible."

Kyla shrugged. "Christmas is always busy here. Glad you made it. And I love the outfit."

"Thanks," Becca said. She twirled around in her red and white velvet Mrs. Santa dress and adjusted her wire glasses.

"And what would you like for Christmas, Kyla?" she said with a smile.

Kyla laughed. "It's been a long time since anyone asked me that."

"Well, I have a feeling this year you'll get everything you want. But only if you've been a good girl," Becca said.

Kyla thought about her year. She'd certainly done more this year to turn her life around in a positive way. Did that count? Was there really anyone keeping score?

The sleigh bells over the front door announced their first customer. Becca hurried to the counter.

Shirley and Ron walked in wearing bundled-up wool coats, matching knit hats courtesy of Shirley, and fuzzy mittens.

"Merry Christmas," Shirley belted out.

Kyla hugged them both. "Are you here for morning tea or shopping?"

"Both," Ron said. "Shirley's been counting the minutes until you open."

Kyla seated them by the window and wrote down their order. "Where's Betty today?"

"She's getting ready to be in the parade. Can you believe she's going to ride on the float for MIA Animal Shelter holding Zinger? She even got Zinger a special holiday coat to wear."

"Can't wait to see that," Kyla said.

The sleigh bells over the door rang out as customers poured into the shop. Kyla and Becca ran around taking orders and ringing up purchases.

"Can we get this gift-wrapped?" a customer asked at the front counter. She held up a delicate teapot with glittering gold stars across a midnight-blue background.

Kyla centered herself. The holidays were great for business but the stress could get overwhelming if she let it.

"Of course. Do you have a color preference for the paper?" Kyla pointed to the back wall where three gift-wrap samples hung. One had burgundy satin paper with a green velvet bow, another had shiny silver paper with a blue ribbon, and the final option was gold tissue paper with a dried lavender ornament.

The customer stared at the wrapping samples. "They're all so beautiful," she gushed. "It's for my mother. She's always loved stars. She's so sick, I think this will be our last Christmas together."

The holidays brought out the best and worst in people, Kyla thought. Most people were more generous and caring, but some were sad and lonely. "How about I make up a special wrapping just for your mother?"

The woman teared up. "Thank you. That means a lot."

Kyla chose the gold paper for its uplifting color. She wrapped the pine-green ribbon around it and decorated it with a sprig of holly.

"Thank you, she'll love this." The woman held the gift to her chest.

The line at the cash register was so long it almost reached the front door. Kyla looked at the black cat clock on the wall. It was already 2:00 and she was closing in an hour. She hoped. All these last-minute holiday shoppers were cleaning out her shelves. It would help get her through the lean winter months.

Becca rushed by with a tray of teacups in her hand. She rolled her eyes at Kyla.

"Almost done," Kyla said. What would she do without Becca? Perhaps she would take a few days off after Christmas and close the shop. Give Becca a few paid days off. She imagined sitting by a fire with Luke. As if on cue, he walked through the door. His slate-colored jacket with its high collar set off his carved face and pale eyes. His smile made her stomach flip.

He walked up to the counter and pulled off his gloves. "How can I help?" he said.

She still had so much to do. "Do you mind bussing tables?"

"No problem," he said. "I even have experience from when I bussed at the country club at sixteen years old. My first real job."

"A man of many talents," she said. "There's hot apple cider if you want some."

She watched as he hung his coat on the rack, picked up a tray, and headed over to the now, thankfully, almost all empty tables. Finally, after ringing up a few more items, the last customer walked out the door. Becca hurried over to lock it and turn the closed sign. She leaned against the door, her red hair falling in her face. "No more customers today."

Even after a busy day, Kyla was amazed how high her energy still was. "Let's turn off the lights and get out of here so we can see the parade." She put on her warmest down jacket and knit hat then pulled on her mittens.

Luke reached his hand out to her and together they slipped out the back door to meet up with Jude and the gang.

Chapter Twenty-One

Luke glanced at his watch. Three o'clock on the dot, just in time to get a spot to watch the parade. When he'd first walked in and seen Kyla's red hair catching the twinkling lights, her frazzled smile and flushed cheeks, his heart had leapt into his throat.

The town looked like a turn-of-the-century movie set. Wreaths hung from the old-fashioned streetlights, and every store window basked in colored lights. "This is the first Christmas I've been excited about in a long time," Luke said to Kyla as they navigated through the crowds in town.

She stopped, her soft eyes meeting his. "Same for me."

He leaned down and kissed her lightly on the lips. "And we have so many more to look forward to."

A brisk wind raced across Main Street. Luke pulled Kyla close to keep her warm. This winter was nothing like he'd grown up with in New York, where the snow and cold cut through his bones. Still, he was concerned for Kyla. "Are you sure you want to stand out here and watch? We could go inside and watch through a window."

"Luke, it's fine. I'm fine. Jude will have plenty of her secret holiday brew ready for us. That always keeps me warm."

"Secret?" Luke joked.

Kyla winked at him. "It is rumored to have a touch of whiskey in it."

Bundled-up children danced around the curb and into the closed-off street. After only a few months living here, Luke recognized many of the families. Madrona Island was starting to feel like home.

Kyla squeezed his hand. "Who would have thought just a year ago we'd be standing here together watching your first island Christmas?"

"There's nowhere else I'd rather be," he said.

"Over here," Jude yelled. She waved her hands wildly at them.

They slid behind the crowds lining the sidewalk and joined Jude on the curb in front of Island Thyme Café. Shirley and Ron were huddled together next to Chef Ryan.

"Merry Christmas, you two," Jude said.

Luke shook hands with everyone and gave Shirley a kiss on the cheek. She winked back at him.

"I hear Betty is going to be in the parade," Kyla said.

"Can't wait to see that," Jude said. "Why don't you two run inside the café and grab a cup of holiday cheer? We'll hold you a place."

After popping inside the café, now with cups in hand, Luke escorted Kyla back out to their place on the sidewalk. Ian, Lily, and their son, Jason, rushed over to join them and wished everyone a Merry Christmas. Jason could barely contain his excitement as he strained his head, looking for Santa Claus. A son like that would warm up any family.

"I'm happy to see that Lily bundled up in a down jacket and wool hat," Kyla whispered to Luke. "I'm a bit worried about her."

Luke frowned. "I'm sure everything will be all right." That family deserved only the best and Luke hoped he was right.

A police car turned the corner with its light blinking and siren looping. A large wreath decorated the grill. Over the car's loud speaker, "Frosty the Snowman" started to play. A couple of officers followed on foot asking people to clear the street for the parade. Luke watched as kids, cheeks flushed and with big smiles across their faces, hurried over to the curb. Ian's son made sure he was right up front.

Luke snuggled in close to Kyla and put his arm around her. He could hardly believe the scene before him. His new best friends were at his side. The only woman he would ever love stood beside him, and the whole town lined the streets and rode in the country Christmas parade.

Following a police car, a classic convertible Cadillac turned into the street in front of them. In the back seat, Janet Collins, the mayor, was dressed as Mrs. Santa Claus and waving to the crowd on both sides of the street.

"A lady mayor," Luke said.

"Lots of powerful ladies on this island," Jude quipped.

A young girl about four years old tugged on her mother next to them. "Look, Mommy, it's the bus we take to Grandma's house and an elf is driving it."

Luke watched the expression on Jason's face as a shiny red fire truck with several firemen and women hanging on the sides with Santa hats turned the corner. Ian was lucky to have such a great son. The firemen tossed wrapped candy canes to the kids as they passed. Jason caught a few midair and gathered several from the sidewalk. Speakers on the top of the truck played "Jingle Bells" as they passed. Kids ran everywhere trying to scoop up the candy lining the curbs. Luke would have loved this when he was young. It was quite a contrast to the Macy's Christmas Parade.

Ian reached down and retrieved a candy cane and handed it to Lily. "I know you love them," he said.

Lily protested for a second. "But they're for the kids."

"They won't miss one." Ian pulled the wrapper off for her. He patted her tummy and winked. "It's for the baby."

Those two were so in love. Luke hoped for the same kind of relationship with Kyla. He watched Kyla and the obvious pure delight she took from watching the event. He thought about the ring waiting at home. Perhaps tonight.

Kelly from the local paper darted in and out of the crowd, taking pictures. When she pointed the camera toward them, Kyla turned her head into Luke's shoulder. The woman he'd known in New York had certainly not been camera shy. Then it hit him. She was still hiding her face. Avoiding exposure.

He hugged her close. "Are you all right?"

Kyla peeked back toward the street.

"Kelly's gone," Luke said.

"That's not…"

Luke put a finger to his lips. "Shhh, we're going to have to face this one day." She looked like a panicked animal caught in headlights. "But not today," he said.

The noise of the crowd blurred out further conversation as the next float turned the corner on Main Street.

"There's Betty!" Shirley yelled. She pointed to a float being hauled by a pickup truck. The float was decorated with oversized dog bones wrapped in big red bows and rolls of yarn and catnip. Sitting in one of the throne-like chairs was Betty holding Zinger in her arms. Zinger had on a ruby-red fleece jacket with a fake white-fur collar. Betty held Zinger's paw up and waved to everyone.

"Hey, girls," she yelled at them as she went by. "Merry Christmas!"

A tall young man, one of the shelter volunteers, sat beside her dressed up like an elf with a black lab at his side. The dog looked perfectly fine wearing green velvet antlers and a collar of bells.

Luke leaned down and whispered in Kyla's ear. "I feel like I'm in an old-fashioned movie."

"It's a Wonderful Life perhaps?" Kyla asked.

Luke hugged her. "Absolutely."

Elves in hats and curvy boots ran in front of them doing cart-wheels. Following them, the Basset Hound Club paraded across the street with ten stout hounds wearing glittery angel wings.

"And now for the angels," Jude said. "One of my favorite parts."

Ryan laughed. "Those bassets are darn cute. Wouldn't mind having one myself."

The noise level rose as people cheered on the high school band as they marched by blasting "Holy Jolly Christmas" slightly off-key on their trombones and trumpets.

"Look, Mom," a child shouted, "it's Frosty the Snowman."

Adults in various costumes held the hands of young pre-schoolers from the local Boys & Girls Club. Little angels, elves, and sprites skipped down the street, tossing candy canes as they went.

"Look at those cute costumes," Lily said.

Luke watched a little boy skip by wearing antlers and an obviously homemade reindeer costume. "Look at his red nose," he said as he waved at the boy.

"Adorable," Kyla said.

Luke longed for a family of his own. Maybe someday they would have children in the parade. He would be sure to be present with his kids and take the time with them his father never had with him. Kyla seemed much healthier lately, but still, maybe having a child would have to wait a little after they were married.

At the end of the parade, a Chamber of Commerce float boasted gift-wrapped baskets of donations from various businesses.

"The Chamber does great work around town," Kyla said. "Those baskets will be raffled off in the community center later in the evening after the tree-lighting ceremony and boat parade." Carolers followed singing in perfect harmony "Let it Snow." Bringing up the rear was a jolly Santa Claus joined by local equestrian club members riding beautiful Clydesdales. The mammoth horses snorted in the crisp air, making the bells around their necks jingle.

"Merry Christmas, everyone," Santa said. "Ho, ho, ho," were his last words as he marched out of sight.

The crowds cheered and clapped. Families and children filled the now-empty streets, greeting each other and huddling to stay warm.

Jude stepped up on the curb and yelled, "Free hot chocolate and spiced cider for all at Island Thyme Café."

"Free?" Luke asked Kyla.

"It's a holiday tradition," Kyla said. "Jude's way of saying thanks for a great year."

"Do you want to go in?" Luke asked.

Kyla shook her head. "It's going to be so crowded."

Luke put his hand in hers. "I have another idea. Let's go to my house and I'll make us a hot toddy."

"Perfect," she said.

As they walked back to Luke's car, carolers dressed in velvet capes and hats strolled the street carrying candlelit lanterns. Their lyrics filled the air: "Dashing through the snow…"

Kyla sang along. "In a one-horse open sleigh. O'er the hills we go."

Luke joined her, "Laughing all the way."

Some of the crowd joined them on the chorus of "Jingle Bells." Luke sang out, enjoying the moment.

When they reached the car, he drew Kyla into his arms. "Merry Christmas, my love," he said. He wrapped her in his arms and kissed her. "My happiest ever," he whispered in her ear.

She looked up into his eyes. "Mine, too."

Chapter Twenty-two

Kyla curled up on Luke's couch and watched him add logs and stoke the flames in his river rock fireplace. She pulled the plaid, wool blanket over her that he'd offered when they first arrived. The scent of winter pine drifted in the air from the green pillar candles. The room glowed in the firelight, and so did Luke. His hair picked up the golden hues as they fell across his face. She loved watching the fluid way his body moved. He turned and matched her stare with a penetrating gaze. Heat raced down her limbs, and a longing that was almost painful.

He sat down beside her and handed her a small box wrapped in gold paper. "An early gift," he said.

Kyla lifted the lid. Nestled in gold tissue paper was the beautiful golden eagle necklace she'd admired at the craft fair. "Thank you so much," she said. "Yours is coming Christmas Day."

"Let me put it on you," he said.

His delicate fingers brushed her neck as he hooked the clasp. "There you go."

Kyla fingered the eagle on her chest. She remembered her father saying his totem animal was the eagle. She had loved watching the majestic birds soar in the woods over his cabin when she was little. "My dad used to say that eagles come to you to inspire and bring courage for you to flyer higher than ever before."

"You never talk about your father," Luke said.

"He wasn't around much and he died when I was young."

"I'm sorry," Luke said. He pulled her close to him and ran his fingers through her hair, gently massaging her scalp. She felt her tension melt away as he rubbed her temples gently in a circular motion. Heat raced through her body as his lips trailed over her ear and down her neck. "You taste like the ocean," he whispered.

Kyla moaned as he brought her into his arms and his musky smell filled her with desire. His hands slipped under her sweater and with long, soothing strokes worked their way up her back.

"I could get used to this," she whispered.

His eyes, pupils large with longing, captured hers. "Forever and always?" he asked.

She nodded, affirming her answer with a soft kiss. His lips lingered on hers a moment longer and then he stood and walked over to the fire. Luke reached out his hand to her. "Come join me," he said.

She tossed the blanket aside and went over to him. A visible shudder moved down Luke's body as he stood facing her. Kyla held her breath. Like a knight before his queen, Luke knelt on the soft, furry rug. He reached out and took her hand.

"Kyla. My only love. I asked you once upon sand, but I ask you now on solid ground. Will you marry me?" Luke pulled a black satin box from his vest pocket. He raised the lid.

An exquisite Irish claddagh wedding ring sparkled back at her with its emeralds surrounding a diamond heart.

She could barely catch her breath, making it impossible to speak. She wanted him more than life itself. But…

Luke squeezed her hand. "Be my wife, Kyla. Let's not let another minute pass by that is not shared. We can live our dreams together here on Madrona Island."

Kyla looked at the man kneeling in front of her. Life was offering her another chance. "I will marry you, Luke."

He placed the ring on her left hand, with the tip of the heart facing up toward her fingertips, signifying an engaged woman. Then he rose and pressed his warm, strong body into hers. The space between them melted and disappeared. Luke lifted her chin and kissed her gently.

"I will not break," she whispered to him. Kyla pulled his lips to hers, deepening the kiss. She ran her fingers through his hair, pulling him in close. She raised her gaze to his. His eyes were dark with passion, but still he looked to her for permission.

"Are you okay? Can we…?" he stuttered.

Kyla took his hand and started for the steps to the loft bedroom. Luke pulled her around, swept her into his arms, and carried her up the stairs. At the top, moonlight shone through the skylights, bathing the bed with a silver glow, creating a place of magic for their love.

Chapter twenty-three

The Captain's Cove oak-paneled dining room was crowded and bursting with noise. "Maybe we should have picked somewhere else for brunch." Kyla asked Luke.

"Oh, come on," he said. "What did you expect for New Year's Day? And look, there's Jude and Ryan waiting for us."

Luke waved, caught their attention, and started toward them. Kyla held his hand as they made their way through the crowd. It smelled like heaven on a plate. Everyone was dressed up island style. Jude had on a bright purple turtleneck with a matching fleece vest and velvet scarf. Even Ryan had on a button-down black shirt tucked in his jeans.

Jude threw her arms around Kyla. "Happy New Year!"

"Same to you." Kyla turned to Ryan, expecting a handshake, and was pleased by a big hug.

"Let's get you two a mimosa," Ryan said. He turned to the bar behind him and picked up two glasses. "Here you go."

Kyla reached for the glass and her new engagement ring sparkled in the overhead lighting.

Jude grabbed her hand and admired the ring. "Is this the news you promised us today?" she asked. "We've not seen you for a few days and lots has changed."

"It's a claddagh Irish engagement ring."

"I can see that," said Jude. "And just when did this new development happen?"

"Right before Christmas," Luke said. "We've been hiding out at my place since the parade, so now it's out. I asked Kyla to marry me and she said yes."

"Congratulations to you both," Ryan said, shaking Luke's hand. He stepped back and put his arm around Jude.

Kyla caught the glance between them. Love was at work there, she was sure.

"When's the big day?" Jude asked.

Lily, wearing a bulky red sweater, slipped between Jude and Ryan. "Big day for what?" she asked.

Jude held up Kyla's hand. "Seems another wedding is in the making."

"Another wedding?" Ian said, joining the party. "Nice ring. I've seen some like that in Ireland."

Kyla held her hand up, admiring the ring herself. But it was more than a gorgeous piece of jewelry; it represented the bond between her and Luke and his acceptance and embracing of her Irish lineage.

"The big day is set for some time in June at the winery," Luke said. "We'll let you know more soon."

"This calls for a toast," Jude said. "But first, let's eat. I'm starving."

Ian spoke up. "I'm going to get a drink and get Lily some orange juice. You all go find a table and we'll join you in a minute."

Luke scanned the room. "There's a big table by the window that just opened up. I'll go grab it."

Kyla and her friends followed behind him, saying their hellos to neighbors and friends along the way. She waved at

Audrey across the room, who was sitting with that rowdy book group she led. Empty champagne bottles were scattered across their table. Kyla wondered if they realized they were sitting under the mistletoe.

The waitress was clearing off their table while Luke stood and kept guard over it. Kyla admired the gold candles surrounded by a fresh holly centerpiece on the polished old mahogany table. Harp music played softly in the background. She looked out the window at the cove. A winter's mix of snow-flaked rain drifted toward the ground, laced the trees with white, and danced on the surface of the water before dissolving. A lone deer stood under a glossy-leafed Madrona tree. The smooth red wood with its delicate peeling bark made the tree most enchanting.

"You can have a seat now," the waitress said. "It's a buffet, so you can help yourself whenever you're ready. Can I get you all coffee first?"

"That would be great," Kyla said. "There are six of us."

"Forget sitting, let's get in line," Jude said. She steered Ryan toward the tables of food.

"Are you ready?" Luke asked Kyla.

Her stomach growled. "Actually, I'm pretty hungry."

Kyla swooned at the smell of crisp bacon and cinnamon coffee cake as she retrieved a plate and followed along in line. Her first addition was a still-warm piece of pumpkin-cranberry coffee cake, followed by a generous slice of Italian brunch torte filled with creamy egg, spinach, and tomato. Luke followed close behind her, repeating her choices in larger portions.

"And what is that called?" Luke asked the chef behind the hot chafing dishes.

The chef grinned. "I call it twice-baked potato casserole. Bacon, cheese, sour cream, and all the fixings."

Kyla lifted her plate for a portion, beating Luke to the draw. "Ladies first," she said, smiling back at him.

Luke grumbled and held his plate high. "Just leave some for me."

After completing her plate with chicken apple sausage and a small piece of loganberry French toast, Kyla continued back to the table past the blazing fireplace covered with an antique metal screen. They hardly needed the heat with all the people that had turned out, but it was barely forty degrees outside.

Kyla and Luke placed their plates down on the table and took a seat across from each other. The other couples soon joined them. The food tasted as good as it looked, and Kyla made fast work of it. Luke wasn't wasting any time either.

"Some champagne here?" the waitress asked.

Jude held up her now-empty mimosa glass. "Why not? We have plenty to celebrate."

The waitress poured champagne in everyone's glass. Lily held her hand over her glass, still filled with fresh-squeezed orange juice. "None for me," she said, smiling sweetly at Ian.

Those two, Kyla thought. Would she and Luke be like that as newlyweds?

Ryan held up his glass and clinked it gently with his butter knife. "I have been informed by my boss," he said, winking at Jude, "that it is time for multiple toasts."

Jude hit him in the arm. "Hey. When out of the restaurant, please refer to me as your…" Jude hesitated and looked askance at Ryan.

Kyla watched for Ryan's reaction.

He sat there and let her squirm for a minute. "My girl-friend?" he said grinning.

Jude's smile lit her whole face. "That will do," she said.

Ian held up his glass. "The tradition on Madrona Island, as I have been told by my grandpa—who is graciously babysitting this morning—is to go around the table and each make a toast for the new year. So, if no one minds, I'll start." He turned to Lily. "To the new little addition to our family and the most perfect mother, Lily, who brings her or him into this world."

Everyone clinked their glasses and repeated the toast.

Lily went next. "And to my husband and father-to-be, Ian."

The toast continued around the table with Kyla toasting Luke's new winery and Luke toasting their engagement. Jude surprised no one toasting to love and friendship that would last always.

Ryan held up his glass last and looked at each of them. "To my new home and the friends that make it the best place I've ever lived."

Kyla sighed at the sweetness of his toast and clinked her glass with everyone's. It was the best New Year's Day she could remember. But something about Ryan's words made her uneasy. His secrets had still not been revealed. Somewhere in that man's background were the other places he'd known that were not his heaven on earth. She looked at Jude and prayed that, when they did surface, Jude's hopes and heart would not be shattered.

Chapter Twenty-Four

Luke paced the cement floor of the tasting room, trying to calm his tightly wound nerves. His brother Stefan had been in town since late yesterday and was due at the winery any minute. In the pit of his stomach, Luke wondered if he'd made a mistake inviting his half-brother here. But the phone call last week had been so unexpected.

Luke had been in a deep sleep when the sound of his ringing cell phone woke him from a dream. He'd sat up in bed and stared at the caller ID. Stefan. Luke's heart pounded. Why was Stefan calling from New York at 5:00 a.m.? He hoped nothing was wrong.

Luke cleared his throat. "Hello, Stefan."

"Morning. You sound like you just woke up. Life in the country making you soft?"

It was just like Stefan to spin an insult into his greeting. Luke gritted his teeth. "It's five o'clock in the morning here. There is a west coast you know."

Stefan laughed into the phone. "Right. I've been up for hours here. I remember you as an early riser."

Luke used to wake before dawn when his life was in full throttle in New York. "Here in the Pacific Northwest in January, the sun does not come up until close to eight."

"Whoa," Stefan said. "Half a day missed."

After two years of not hearing from his half-brother, the last thing Luke wanted to talk about with him was the weather.

"So, what's up? Mom and Dad doing okay?" Luke asked.

"They're fine. In fact, Mom told me she talked to you the other day and you had some news for the family."

So that was it, Luke thought. "That we did. It had been a while." Luke held his breath.

Stefan continued. "I think it's time we did some catching up. Mom said you bought a little winery. Congratulations."

"Thanks," Luke said cautiously. "It's an amazing place. Twenty-two acres. Barns, vineyards, and a log house."

"Nice," Stefan said, his tone conveying a completely different word.

Luke tried to be civil. "I hear congratulations are in order for you."

"You mean my engagement with Lizbeth. We're both very happy. I hope there's no hard feelings on your part."

"None whatsoever," Luke said. "All I've ever wanted was for you to be happy. And Lizbeth. I think you make a fine match." Luke rolled his eyes. Actually, they really did suit each other. His father must be more than pleased.

"Thank you. I'll tell her that," Stefan said. "It'll make her very happy."

Luke felt off-balance. Did Stefan actually sound sincere?

"How would you feel about a visit from your long-lost brother?" Stefan asked. "I could come out, get a hotel room, come over and see the vineyards, and toast to your new venture."

Luke hesitated. Was Stefan reaching out? Trying to end the ridiculous sibling rivalry that had been going on since as far back as Luke could remember? "You don't need to stay in a hotel. I have a big house."

"I wouldn't dream of putting you out. I understand there are some fine inns there."

"Do you remember the artist Ian McPherson?" Luke asked. "He and his new wife own Madrona Island Bed & Breakfast. I stayed there a few days myself. They'd take fine care of you."

"Madrona Island B&B it is then. Would early next week suit you?"

Luke looked at the calendar on his phone. Chocolate tastings for the new Valentine truffles were scheduled and a few other meetings. If the weather were decent, he could start early pruning. "That works for me."

"I'll send you my itinerary," Stefan said. "And hey, sorry I woke you."

Luke laid the cell phone back on his nightstand. Was Stefan really sorry or was it a tactic to catch Luke off-guard? Stefan hadn't wasted any time booking a flight. The call had barely been a week ago and he was already on the island.

Luke stood in the cozy tasting room by the woodstove and stared out the window, waiting for his brother. Luke thought of Kyla. She'd met Stefan for the first time at a glamorous party in New York City. He'd kissed her hand and winked at Luke. Stefan thought her a good catch back then. But not marriage material. What would he think now? Luke would find out soon enough.

Through the window, Luke saw a silver Land Rover stir up the dirt as it made a quick stop in front of the winery. Stefan had arrived. He must have rented the Land Rover at the airport, expecting Luke to live in the middle of the wilderness.

Luke opened the door and stood on the front step. Stefan stepped out dressed like he'd just finished skiing in the Alps: black ski jacket, leather boots, and cashmere gloves. Luke recognized that gleaming white smile. The one Stefan used when zeroing in on unsuspecting prey.

"Good afternoon," Stefan said. "Nice place you got here."

Luke invited him in and offered Stefan a glass of his best Pinot Noir.

Stefan accepted. He twirled the wine then breathed in its scent. After swirling a sip in his mouth he said, "Not bad." His half-slatted eyes scanned the walls, the awards, the pictures, and the Madrona Winery T-shirts. He lifted bottles off the shelf and read the labels. "Are all of these made here?"

"Yes they are," Luke said. "But not all of the grapes are grown on my land. We grow mostly the reds and pick up the whites from Red Mountain and other regions to the east."

Stefan sipped the wine and then laid the glass back down on the counter. "You have a nice little hobby going here."

Don't take the bait, Luke told himself. "How are your accommodations at the inn?" he asked.

Stefan shrugged. "It's very….cozy," he said, his tone strained. "Clean. Nice enough people. Are they close friends?"

Always probing and looking for an angle, Luke thought. "We know each other and do some business together."

"They speak highly of you and Kyla. It is Kyla now, not Darcy, right?"

"Right," Luke said between clenched teeth. He already regretted this little get-together.

Stefan stared out the window. "Why don't you show me around?"

Luke put on his coat and took his brother on a tour of the property. "We have three areas right now where we grow wine." He pointed out the fields lined with stakes and dormant vines. They walked by the pond bordered with large boulders and barren trees and over to the chicken coop with its painted red door and metal roof. "The hens and roosters make their home here, and the vegetable garden is out in the pasture past the oaks."

"The property looks valuable," Stefan said. "What's the home, about 3,000 square feet?"

Always checking the assets. His brother had not changed at all. "The 4,000-square-foot log house was built a few years ago by the former owners," Luke said. He walked up the path to the front door, let them both in, and flipped on some track lights on the wood beams above. The fire was still burning from the morning, and the smell of espresso lingered behind.

Stefan removed his coat and gloves and handed them to Luke. His eyes circled the room then looked up at the wood-beam ceilings. "Does everything on this island look like it's right out of Country Living Magazine?"

"I know you didn't come to appraise the property or set up a photo shoot, so why don't we sit down and discuss why you're here." Luke took the couch and waited.

Stefan chose the leather armchair and settled in. "I'm just a bit surprised to see you living out in the middle of the woods. But I guess love will do that to a man."

"What exactly do you mean?" Luke asked. He could feel his blood sizzle the way it used to whenever they were in the same room together.

"You know, make him leave his home and family and chase the woman across the country."

The smirk on Stefan's face made Luke's stomach turn.

Luke slowed his breath. "I did not chase her. I found her."

He ran his fingers through his hair. As much as he wanted to tell his brother the truth, it wasn't fair to Kyla until she was ready.

Stefan was relentless. "It probably didn't set well with you that Kyla was the only woman who didn't want you back."

"Maybe years ago that might have been true. If a woman played hard-to-get, I enjoyed the challenge. But Kyla had a very good reason to run, and when she is ready to share it, you and everyone else will know it."

Stefan raised an eyebrow. "Should the family be worried?"

"We love each other and that's all you need to know," Luke said.

"You always did get what you wanted." Stefan laughed. "But do you really plan on marrying her?"

"Why do you care?" Luke asked. "It has nothing to do with you."

"Oh yes it does," Stefan snapped. "How do you think Lizbeth's family will respond if they hear my long-lost half-brother is marrying an ex-model with a shady past? Will they still accept me as their daughter's fiancé?"

Luke sprang up from his seat. "So that's why you came. To make sure I didn't do anything to embarrass you."

Stefan's expression hardened. "Or Dad. Or yourself. And don't think just because Mom's all friendly with you now that you can walk back into the family and take over."

"And just what is it you think I want?" Luke asked. He forced himself to sit back down.

"Money maybe?" Stefan said with a maddening grin. "To keep your little venture going?"

Luke glared at him. "You're wrong. You've always thought the worst of me and never took the time to know me. When we were kids, all I ever wanted was for my big brother to like me. Can you believe that?"

"Hardly," Stefan spit back. "From the minute you were born, everything changed. Little Luke, with the golden hair, who could do no wrong. They never even noticed I was there. Have you ever watched any of the family home videos?"

Luke shook his head.

"You don't know what you're missing, little brother. Every shot is focused on you. Your sports games, your trophies, your school honors, your conquests. I am a dark shadow in the background. That is, until two years ago, when you mercifully left New York. Our father had no choice but to turn to me. And I did not disappoint him." Stefan's black eyes radiated triumph.

"That's not how I wanted it to be," Luke said.

"Of course not." Stefan's face reddened. "Nothing was ever your fault. You'd pout and cry like a baby and I always got the blame."

Luke shook his head. "I was just a kid. You always seemed like you hated me."

"For good reason," Stefan said.

"Then why come here now?" Luke asked. "You have everything you ever wanted. Dad, the business, Lizbeth. I'm not ever coming back. It's all yours with my blessing."

Stefan stood. His hollow voice echoed in the room. "You think for one minute I believe you?"

Luke stood and faced his brother. "Believe it or not. I'm tired of trying to prove anything to you. You can't see the truth through your hate. I can't help that."

"And you, Luke. You had it all and where did it get you? Holed up on this remote island chasing after a woman who dumped you years ago?"

Rage burned like fire on Luke's skin. For a split second he wanted to take Stefan by the neck and slam him against the wall. It was probably just what his brother wanted him to do. He stared at the man before him. Dark hair cut razor sharp. A black tailored shirt under a steel-grey cashmere sweater. And a prominently worn Rolex watch worth more than Luke's two cars together. But all Luke saw was his sad, big brother whom he'd always wanted to love him. Damn, he didn't want to feel sorry for Stefan. Every word out of Stefan's mouth was barbed and targeted for Luke's jugular. What a waste.

"You're wrong, brother," Luke said. "It's only now that I have it all." Luke waved his hand around the house and pointed toward the grounds. "This was always my dream. Not climbing the corporate ladder in our father's company. That was his idea."

Stefan narrowed his eyes. "Really?"

Luke nodded. "It must be hard for you to believe, but I'm doing what I love and with the only woman I love."

"Why here?" Stefan said.

"It's beautiful. Look around at the untouched woods, and clean water teeming with life. Air I can breathe, and fertile soil that produces pristine grapes that I can make into wine with my own hands."

Stefan turned and walked toward the front door. "Beauty is only skin deep, they say. And with that profound statement, I'm out of here. I need my coat. I have a ferry to catch."

"Have you heard a word I've said?" Luke asked.

"I've heard every word."

Luke tossed his brother his coat and gloves.

"I wouldn't be too sure your happy ending is going to turn out just the way you've planned it this time," Stefan said. He pulled on his coat and slipped his hands into the leather gloves.

"What did you do, Stefan?" Luke blocked the door with his body. "Tell me."

Stefan cocked his head. "This morning I paid Kyla a little visit in that charming shop of hers. I'm pretty sure she's not quite so anxious to marry you any time soon."

"I should wipe this floor with you." Luke grabbed him by the collar. "You have no idea the damage you may have done."

Stefan brushed Luke's hands off of his coat. "Can't be that great of a relationship if you're afraid she'll run off and leave you again."

Luke pinned Stefan with his glare. His body shuddered. Each word bit the air as it left his lips. "You're right, but not the way you think. Kyla's ill. That's why she left New York. Are you happy now, big brother?"

Luke opened the front door.

"Now get out."

Chapter Twenty-Five

As Stefan raced out of his driveway, Luke dialed Kyla's cell phone. No answer. Dread washed over him. He pulled on his coat, jumped into the truck, and raced into town. He parked directly in front of Tea & Comfort and jumped out.

Relief was his first emotion when he saw the "open" sign on the shop door. But when he walked in, he saw only Becca behind the counter and his muscles tensed.

"Kyla around?" he asked, trying to sound normal.

Becca shrugged. "She had a headache and went back into her cottage to lie down."

"Thanks," Luke said. He bet it was one doozy of a headache after Stefan's visit. He left the shop and jogged along the path to Kyla's house. The curtains were drawn and he couldn't see any lights on. He exhaled and shook out the tension in his shoulders. He needed to remain calm.

Luke knocked softly. No response. A cold sweat dripped down his back, propelled by the dark thoughts flashing through his mind. Would he find her passed out inside like Jude had found her last year? He pounded the door a bit louder.

"Kyla," he shouted. "It's Luke."

Finally, the door cracked open. Luke caught his breath. Kyla's eyes were swollen and red. She looked right past him as if he weren't there.

"Luke," she said. "What is it?"

He stepped closer to the door in case she tried to close it. "Can I come in?"

She leaned on the doorframe. "I don't think so."

"My love," he whispered, making her look up. "I know my brother was here and I know the damage he can do."

Her sigh tore at his heart. "It doesn't matter, Luke," she said. "I'm tired of fighting everyone and everything. Please go away and let me sleep."

She tried to shut the door, but Luke caught it with his hand. "You're not rid of me that easily. I'll wait on the couch while you sleep. Whenever you're ready, we'll talk."

Kyla looked up. Her emerald eyes reflected back a deep hurt. Luke could kill Stefan. He reached his arms out and she fell into them. He stroked her hair and held her close.

"Let's go inside," he said. Luke walked her into the bedroom and helped her into bed. "Take a little nap and you'll feel better soon." He tucked her in and kissed her on the forehead.

"Can I get you anything?" he asked.

She shook her head. "Thanks, Luke."

"Just close your eyes now," he said. "I'll be right here when you wake up."

Luke watched as Kyla curled into a ball and shut her eyes. Her breath slowed and her face finally softened. At least for the moment she was peaceful.

Kyla opened her eyes. Why was she in bed in the middle of the day? Then it all came back to her. Stefan's slick smile and cutting words. He knew just where to shoot his arrows and do the most damage. Kyla thought she'd finally accepted her past and put it behind her with all the fears and insecurities that went with it. She'd clawed her way to the top for the power, success, money, and acceptance only to find it empty up there, as shallow as the airbrushed images of her on the slick magazine covers.

Finding love in Luke's eyes when they first met only made her fears deepen. He would never love her if he knew who she really was.

Stefan had cleverly reminded her of that this morning. He'd stalked into the shop while she was working and circled her like a shark going in for the kill.

"I never would have recognized you," he said. "You've really let yourself go."

His malignant energy shot at her like a harpoon. Kyla's hand flew to her throat. She was underwater, unable to breathe.

He stepped closer and leaned over her. Kyla caught a whiff of whiskey on his breath. The smell burnt her nose and her mind flashed back to being in the cabin with her father when she was young. Her dad was passed out on the sofa, bottles all over the floor, and she was alone there with him in the middle of the woods. She'd hid in her small bed under piles of covers, trying to get warm while her stomach screamed for food.

There'd been no one to rescue her then and no one now. She steadied her breath and pulled protective light around her body. Kyla stepped around him. "I see you look just the same."

His laugh grated against her nerves. She retreated behind the counter to put a barrier between them.

"You obviously belong in this quaint little place," he said. "But do you really think you're going to pull my brother into this sweet dream with you?"

"I'm not pulling your brother anywhere he doesn't want to go."

Stefan leaned on the counter. "With your past, do you really think you'll ever fit in with our family? Do you think my father will ever give Luke his inheritance if he marries you? And with no father, who will walk you down the aisle?"

The shaking had started in her legs, working up until her whole body trembled. Her father's death still haunted her. Some distant family from his Iroquois tribe took away the remains. It was not a story her family ever repeated. She looked at Stefan with his dark aura. Nothing was sacred to him. His calculated words had hit their mark, and Kyla had shown him to the door and then run and collapsed into her bed.

Was that only this morning? It had been so easy to fall into old patterns. She sat up in bed and reminded herself she was not the seventeen-year-old girl who ran away from home anymore. And she was not alone. Tea & Comfort was a solid business that she loved running, and it financially supported her. Kyla looked at the hand-painted silk scroll on the wall beside her bed. She'd bought it last year at the summer crafts festival because it had one her favorite quotes pasted on it from the mystic Meister Eckhart. Kyla whispered the words aloud: "If the only prayer you said in your life was thank you, that would suffice."

Gratitude shed light on the dark corners of her fear and chased it from her mind and heart. She had so much to be grateful for. Luke. How many women lost and found their soulmate and had the chance to live their dream with him? She had her amazing friends and a family that loved her. A home and thriving business. The list grew and grew and with it so did her mood. Stefan was but a blip in a peaceful stream.

She heard Luke rustling through some magazines in her living room. He had waited while she slept. That was the true reality in her life. Kyla slipped out of bed and splashed water on her face in the bathroom.

"How you feeling?" Luke asked.

Kyla turned to see Luke watching her from the doorway. "Much better."

Luke's smile brightened her heart. "How about some tea?" she suggested.

The ritual of making tea always comforted her. She poured the boiling water in her favorite dragonfly teapot and placed a calming mixture of chamomile, rose buds, lemon balm, and lavender into the pot. The sweet, flowery smell filled the room. Kyla placed the teapot and iridescent porcelain mugs on the oak dining table.

"Join me," she said with a smile.

"Anytime and anywhere," Luke replied.

As they sipped their tea, everything came back into focus. Kyla had let Stefan's words pierce deep into her heart and soul, and she could expel them just as easily. Every setback had its lessons.

"Do you want to talk about my brother's visit?" Luke asked.

"I do," she said. "Some of what he said made sense, and I want to get some clarity between us before I put it all behind me."

"Sounds like a good idea," Luke said. "I'm pretty sure Stefan's reality and ours are very far apart. He left the island and is out of our lives."

"But he's still your brother," she said. "And he is so lost."

Luke sighed. "I know."

"One thing Stefan said is that you'll lose your inheritance if you marry me. Is that true?"

Luke placed his hand over hers. "Absolutely not. I have no interest in my family's money and all the strings that go with it. I made that clear to them when I left New York. The trust my grandmother's left for me is what I used to buy the winery, and it is more than enough for the lifestyle I plan here with you."

"It isn't just the money, Luke. Those tabloids can spin my background any way they want and blow our marriage up into a big scandal that affects your family. What if your winery business is damaged? I couldn't stand that."

Luke leaned over and held a finger to his lips. "What other people think is not going to affect us unless we let it."

Kyla knew he was right. All the darkness swirling around Stefan came from his own fears. And she knew all about that. She had vowed to turn her life around, and now was the time to take action. "If we decide to put the truth out first, neither Stefan nor anyone else can threaten us with it ever again. It's time to stop running…for both of our sakes."

"You're right," he said.

"Every word Stefan said to me cut to the core," Kyla said. "I want to tell you everything about my past so there will be no surprises in the future."

"You don't have to, Kyla."

"There are things I don't want you finding out from Stefan or in some tabloid."

Luke took a few sips of tea then laid the cup back on the table. "I know more than you think. My father had you investigated when we first got engaged. I tore up the report without reading a page, but he taunted me with its contents."

Heat rushed though Kyla's veins. Of course her tracks were not that well-covered. Large amounts of money and persistence could reveal her past if someone really wanted to know. She was lucky Luke's father hadn't made it public. That probably would have been his next move if Kyla hadn't conveniently disappeared.

"Do you think he put Stefan up to this visit?" she asked.

Luke shook his head. "No, Stefan is quite capable of doing this all on his own." He placed his hand over hers. "I'm sorry about my family."

"And I'm sorry about mine," Kyla said.

They looked at each other and laughed.

Kyla squeezed his hand. "Mostly I'm sorry I hid them from you. I can see now, like most teenagers, I blamed my family for everything. I was ashamed of where I came from. But even after I ran away to Europe, changed my name, and my lifestyle, I still never felt like I fit in."

"We came from complete opposite upbringings," Luke said, "yet I felt just the same. I never fit into that mansion with those people, and certainly not Harvard. And the harder I tried to fit in somewhere, the more depressed I got." His gaze was sincere. "Until I met you. You looked right through me, saw everything I am, and still loved me."

A tear fell down Kyla's cheek and she wiped it away. "When we first met, I saw a golden boy from a wealthy family.

Everyone at that shoot was posing in designer wear, a glass of fine wine in hand, yet they all seemed so vacant...except you. Our eyes met and it took my breath away. I recognized a fellow runner and realized we'd always been running toward each other."

Luke pulled her into his strong arms. She laid her head on his shoulder and breathed in his musky scent.

"Kyla," he whispered into her hair. He lifted her face to his and kissed her deeply. "Thank you for finding me."

"I almost ran, you know."

"That first night we met?"

She nodded.

"What made you stay?" he asked.

"I never felt totally safe as Darcy Devereau. Exposure seemed always just around the corner. And there you were, the son of the upper crust, part of a family that would never, ever want their son with a woman like me. Being with you was the ultimate risk, but your eyes said, 'Save me,' and I knew you would save me too."

"You're always safe with me," he said.

Kyla threw up her hands. "Let's throw safety to the wind."

"Your smile looks almost witchy. In a good sort of way," Luke said. "I love watching your mind work. Tell me your diabolical plan."

She leaned forward. "We'll beat him at his own game and get the news out first, exactly where and how we want it. I'll call my agent and tell her it's a go with Celebrity Magazine and to follow up with the Lupus Society."

"Are you up to this?" Luke asked.

Kyla jumped out of her seat. "More than up to it. I feel better than I have in a long time. We could talk about my illness and my running away. About how our love was lost and how we found love again. Maybe we could get in the Valentine's issue."

Luke stood and faced her. "Are you sure you want to do this?"

"Absolutely," she said. "And you?"

She heard Luke take a deep breath. "Once everything is out, there would be no more speculating, nothing more to run from. Those who love us will accept everything and no one else matters."

"You're so right," she said.

"How do we start?" Luke asked.

Kyla clapped her hands. "Leave it to me. Arlene's daughter is one of their top reporters."

"In that case," he said, "I've got some work waiting for me at the winery. How about I pick you up later for dinner?"

She was so lost in thought she didn't even realize he'd said anything.

"Kyla?" he said.

She focused her gaze on him from a very faraway place. Visions filled her mind and she was ready to make them come true.

"Dinner it is, Luke. I'll make my roasted chicken with herbs and we'll eat in. Just the two of us."

"Good choice," he said.

Luke opened the door to leave. She noticed her words stopped him momentarily.

"I'll finally be free," she said softly.

Luke parked his truck near the house. The barren vineyards were beautiful in the afternoon light. He walked along the muddy paths, assessing if it was time to start cane pruning. He let the conversation with Kyla run through his mind. Part of him was ecstatic that the truth would come out. They would never be in peace until it did. What worried him were his father and Stefan. How far would they go to spin this story in their favor? Luke was sure beyond a shadow of doubt that his marriage to Kyla would not tarnish the family name or business. If anything, there might be some morbid curiosity from the press, but it would pass quickly.

The shiny green tractor sat protected in the barn, waiting for spring when the fields would be bursting with color. The red wine lingered in oak barrels after it had fermented in bins. In the spring, the vines would fill in with wide leaves. Luke could imagine a couple of kids running through the field, chasing a big dog, and Kyla by his side. The house was more than large enough for a family. They had not discussed children yet. Luke did not want to add any more pressure to Kyla. He longed for kids of his own, but if Kyla's illness prevented it, so be it. A light drizzle moistened his cheeks. Acres of vineyards, trees, and fields lay before him. It was just as he'd always dreamt it. And soon Kyla would be his wife and the dream would be complete.

He could hear his father's voice in his head. "If it's too good to be true, it probably is. Life is about suffering. We don't always get what we want, Luke. It's time to grow up and be a man."

That had been his father's tactic when he wanted Luke to join him in the family business. Luke had wanted his father's approval, but not at the expense of his own soul. If his father saw how happy he was here on the island with Madrona Island Winery, would it make any difference? Dream on, Luke, he told himself. Dream on.

A cold wind rushed through the cedars, engulfing him in its force. Dark clouds billowed ominously in the sky. There would be no working outside today. In the distance, a dog howled. Luke hoped to heck the owner brought the dog inside on a day like this. He thought about Zinger, the dog Betty had adopted. He certainly was well-cared for. And smart. If the cutie wanted to be picked up, he leaped straight up until Betty caught him in mid-air. And he loved his tiny tennis balls and would retrieve them for hours. Luke's warm hearth was a perfect place for a dog to stretch out and nap. He could make a difference for one dog today. And he would.

Luke jumped in his truck and followed the main highway to MIAR. Madrona Island Animal Rescue, affectionately referred to as MIA by the locals. It was where Betty volunteered, and they'd had some good-looking dogs on their Christmas float.

He blew in through the doorway of the lobby and was greeted at the desk by a volunteer. "I'd like to see your dogs that are up for adoption," he said.

The man brought Luke back to the kennel area. Each dog had a cement area and a small sheltered portion to curl up in behind it. But the wind and rain could easily blow through the chain link fence exterior.

"How is the new shelter building coming along?" Luke asked.

The volunteer lit up. "Just great. We can always use more volunteers, though," he said with a hopeful smile. He put out his hand. "The name's Sean."

Luke shook his hand. "Luke. I own Madrona Island Winery. I'll certainly think about helping out here."

He walked along the covered path, looking inside each space. Some dogs just peeked out and would not make the effort to come see him. One big terrier rushed the fence, barking and jumping in the air.

"He's just a puppy," Sean said. "Lots of energy."

Luke continued on. It broke his heart to see some of the dogs' sad and desperate faces. At the end of the first row, sitting at attention, was what appeared to be a heeler mix. He was a mix between sun gold and strawberry blonde in color. His white markings were splattered along his back and muzzle, and a dark patch of hair circled his one blue eye. The other eye was a warm brown. Both eyes watched Luke carefully.

"Hello, boy," Luke said reaching out his hand.

"Bailey is very well-trained," Sean told him. "Just say, 'Come, boy,' and he'll come right up."

Bailey was a fitting name. Bailey's Irish Cream was a good description, and Luke knew one Irish woman who would love this dog as well as him.

"Come, Bailey," Luke said.

Never breaking eye contact, Bailey walked to the fence.

"Good boy. Can I pet you?" Luke put his fingers through the fence.

Bailey leaned forward to rub his furry head against Luke's hand.

The wind had died down a bit and the sun poked through the clouds. "Can I take him for a walk?" Luke asked.

"Of course."

Once Bailey was leashed, Luke walked him down the trail through the back woods behind the shelter. The dog's ears were the color of brandy and stood straight up. Luke picked up the pace, and Bailey followed right along. He'd make a great companion in the vineyards.

They stopped by the edge of a clearing. "Sit," Luke said.

Bailey obliged and cocked his head.

Luke kneeled down next to the dog. "Do you want to go home with me?" Luke asked.

Bailey licked his face.

Luke petted his head. "You're a smart boy, aren't you?"

Bailey barked in answer.

There was only one concern left. How would the dog get along with customers milling around his land and tasting room? And children? When they were back at the shelter, the volunteer slipped off the leash and placed Bailey back in his kennel. The dog's eyes widened as he looked to Luke.

"Don't worry, boy," Luke said. "I'll be right back."

Inside the office, Sean gave Luke a stack of paperwork to fill out. Was he a homeowner? Yes. Was there a fenced area? Most of the perimeter was fenced and Luke would make sure the rest was completed. He filled everything out and handed the papers back.

"One other question," Luke asked. "Do you know how Bailey is with strangers? Kids?"

Sean smiled. "He was raised in a daycare with lots of kids and parents coming and going. I think he's been pretty bored here."

"Why is he here?" Luke asked.

"Sandy owned the daycare. When her husband was transferred out of the country and they couldn't bring Bailey with them, it about broke her heart. I promised her Bailey would find a good home."

"Well, he'll have one now. I promise." Luke signed the final papers, paid the fee plus a generous donation, and waited for Bailey to join him on the journey to his new home.

As soon as they were secure in his truck, Luke called Kyla. He didn't want to disturb her busy day, but he just had to tell her.

"Tea & Comfort," she answered.

"Just a quick call," Luke said. "Do you mind if I bring a new friend to dinner tonight at your place?"

"A new friend?" she asked.

"His name is Bailey. He's three years old and he is an Australian cattle dog mix."

"Luke, you got a dog!" she said.

"He's a keeper for sure."

Chapter Twenty-Six

Kyla carried her laptop into the parlor and joined Lily—now sporting a baby bump under her shirt—and Jude, who waited at the dining room table. As usual when they met at Madrona Island B&B, Lily had coffee in a large thermos and scones waiting on silver platters. The warm air smelled of apples and cinnamon. There was no better place to meet and no better friends to help her with her quest.

"Thank you both for being here," Kyla said.

"With such a juicy plan in the making, I couldn't get here fast enough," Jude said.

Lily scoffed at Jude. "And of course we're always here for you, Kyla."

"Right," Jude said. "Now, what's the plan?"

Kyla almost laughed out loud. With these three incredible women putting their heads together, watch out anyone who got in their way.

"Coffee?" Lily asked.

"The sooner the better," Kyla answered.

Lily poured coffee into thick, handcrafted mugs. She took a seat across from Kyla and pulled out a legal pad of paper. "I'll take notes," she offered.

"Perfect," Kyla said. "I'll do research while we talk and I can type up the notes later." She opencd her laptop. "Password still the same?"

Lily nodded and leaned back into her chair.

Kyla typed in happy2Bhere and waited for it to connect. Living on the island, the signal was on-again/off-again. She looked up and all eyes were on her. "I'm still nervous about Luke and I sharing our everything, including my past."

"With us?" Jude asked.

"You and the rest of the country," Kyla said with a smile.

"Is that a wise idea?" Lily asked. "You'll lose your privacy, and Luke's family…how will they take this?"

"Don't worry, Lily," Kyla said. "If I keep running and hiding, how can I ever be happy? I'd always be looking over my shoulder and worrying. This way, the truth is out."

"And the truth shall set you free," Jude said triumphantly. "I get it. What can we do to help?"

Lily still looked concerned, or was it simply exhaustion that Kyla picked up on? Her translucent skin could be the winter white of Washington, but Kyla made a mental note to mix up some iron tonic and bring it over soon. A dark cloud crossed her vision, then vanished. This pregnancy was taking a toll on Lily, and Kyla needed to stay alert if she was to help her friend. She shook away the dark thoughts and spelled out her plan.

"First, I need your help to write up a short draft about Darcy Devereux. Who she really was and why she ran away. Then we can write a few paragraphs about meeting and falling in love with Luke in New York. But mostly the story will be about reunited lovers overcoming all obstacles to be together and follow their dreams to Madrona Island."

"That will be quite a story," Jude said. "You write it, and we'll read it and give our feedback."

"Of course," Lily said. "Who's going to publish the story?"

Kyla sat up straight, taking a model's pose. "I'm going to call my agent in New York and have her contact Celebrity Magazine. 'Darcy Devereux tells all.'" She winked at them.

"Celebrity Magazine? Will they come to the island?" Lily asked.

"That's my plan," Kyla said. "I'll make sure we get some shots here and at the café."

"Wait until I tell Ryan," Jude said. "What should I wear?"

Lily shook her head. "Jude, what we wear is not the problem. Kyla has a lot at stake here. She may not want Ryan to know."

Kyla sipped her coffee. "That's fine, just make sure he keeps it a secret until the article comes out in February. I want everything to come out. Luke's family will read the article, and whatever issues they have will be faced before the wedding." She made a mental note to call her family soon and let them know about the engagement and the article.

"Have you set the exact date yet?" Lily asked.

"June twenty-seventh, in the vineyards if it's sunny. And a reception in the barn. We were hoping you and Ryan would cater it, Jude. And, Lily, will you make the cake?"

Both women nodded enthusiastically.

"First Lily, then Shirley, and now you. Three weddings in less than a year." Jude frowned. "I better catch the bouquet this time."

"I'll see what I can do," Kyla said. She pointed out the window toward the porch. "I think we have company, ladies."

There was a knock at the door and a familiar voice said, "Anybody home?"

Grandpa John walked into the parlor. Lily rose and waved him over. "Come join us," she said. "I'll make fresh coffee."

"Don't go to any fuss for me."

Lily waved him to a seat. "We need the fuel ourselves."

"Morning," Kyla said. She watched him ease into a chair on her other side. "How are you today?"

His smile was warm and bright as always. "Doing fine. How about you ladies?"

"We're good," she said. "Just having one of our powwows."

"Well, don't let me disturb you."

Kyla placed her hand on his arm when he tried to rise. "You are the perfect person to join us. We could use some of your sagely advice."

His laugh reminded her of Santa Clause. "Me, wise? Happy to help if I can."

Lily entered with fresh coffee and placed a mug before Grandpa John. "Just the way you like it," she said. "One sugar and a splash of cream."

Ian poked his head in. "Mind if I stoke the fire a bit?" No one spoke as he added logs and adjusted them until the fire caught at the edges. "Don't mind me," he said.

"Why don't you join us?" Kyla offered. "I would never have come to Madrona Island if it wasn't for you."

"Don't mind if I do." Ian joined them at the table. He reached over, picked up a scone, and took a big bite. "So, what's up?"

"Kyla's going to tell Celebrity Magazine her and Luke's whole story," Jude burst out.

"Sounds like an interesting idea," Grandpa John said.

His warm gaze overflowed with love and filled her heart. "Secrets take a lot of energy to keep," he said.

Kyla took Grandpa John's hand. "That they do."

His warm fingers tightened on hers. "We'll all be here for you. No matter what."

"We will be," Ian echoed.

Tears filled her eyes. "I'm not afraid anymore," she said. "I'm even going to talk again with the Lupus Society and see how telling my story might help others."

"The best way out of your own troubles is to help somebody else with theirs," Grandpa John said. "Works every time."

Kyla wiped away her tears. All she had to do was look around the table at the people she loved, and any doubts she had about what she was planning vanished in the golden light of the fire.

As Kyla walked in the front door of her cottage after leaving the morning meeting, the phone was ringing. She looked at the caller ID—it was her mother. Perfect timing.

"Hi, Mom. Great to hear from you."

Her mother asked about her holidays. They'd talked briefly on Christmas Day about all the great food and baked goods her grandmother had made, but Kyla had not shared her news yet.

"We miss you so much," her mother said. "And…I have a little surprise for you."

Kyla used to love surprises. "As a matter of fact, Mom, I have a big surprise for you, too."

Her mother laughed. "Synchronicity. You tell yours first."

"Luke proposed to me. I'm engaged to be married."

"What wonderful news!"

Kyla could hear her grandmother in the background yelling, "What? What?"

"Go ahead and tell Grandma Mona," Kyla said.

Now they were both on the line. "Comhghairdeas," her grandmother said.

Kyla had not heard the Gaelic word for congratulations since she graduated high school. "Thank you, Grandma Mona," she said. "The wedding is all set for June twenty-seven. I hope you both will be there."

"And our surprise is…." her mother said making a noise like a drumroll, "we are coming out for a surprise visit in March to see you. And now we'll be able to help with the wedding plans." Her mother sounded ecstatic.

"That will be great," Kyla said. "We're trying to keep it simple. Not too many people or fuss."

"Of course, dear," her grandmother said. "And we'll help you do just that."

Kyla liked the idea of three generations of women all working together to plan the wedding. And this way, Luke would get to know and, hopefully, love her family. A shadow crossed before her as she remembered Stefan. Would he try to stop this wedding? And what about Luke's family? She shook the thoughts away.

"I have other news," her mother said. "My book on herbology is going to be published. I'll tell you all about it when we get there."

"While we're on the subject of surprises," Kyla said, "be sure to buy the Valentine's Day issue of Celebrity Magazine. I'm going public."

Kyla was relieved to tell her family everything and have their love and support promised every step of the way.

Before they hung up, Grandma Mona told Kyla to sit down, close her eyes, and let the words of this blessing she said fill her: "May you always have walls for the winds, a roof for the rain, tea beside the fire, laughter to cheer you, those you love near you, and all your heart might desire."

Chapter Twenty-Seven

The last few weeks had been a whirlwind of activity. The early afternoon sun trickled in, casting rainbows through the glass prism that hung in the window. The colors sparkled off her curtains and flashed on her walls. It was a rare sunny day for February and the temperature had jolted to fifty degrees outside. The cats sat in the front window, basking in the rays and giving each other a bath with their tongues.

Mondays were her day off, and she usually used them to get caught up on her paperwork. But not today. She walked around, gathering her coat and gloves, singing aloud the words to the Beatles' "Here Comes the Sun." She slipped her Keens on over heavy socks, zipped up her fleece coat, and went out to the car.

Where to go? she asked herself. The view from the cliff where the lighthouse stood would be spectacular today and she could walk the driftwood-filled beach afterwards. Kyla thought about calling Luke but then decided against it. She'd once been told that good relationships were built on each person having their own alone time, and that sounded wise. Today was hers to be with herself and clear her head. She did her best thinking alone and in nature.

There was almost no traffic as she drove across the island to the state park that used to be an old fort for the military during WWII. It covered almost 500 acres with green hills, forests, trails, and even had an old cannon that kids could crawl on topping one of the now-vacant bunkers. The old-fashioned lighthouse was now a museum and offered the best view of Madrona Island.

Kyla drove slowly toward the parking lot. Deer meandered across the narrow road. A young fawn stood right in front of her and stared into the car. "Go on with your mother, little one," Kyla said out the window. She waved it along. It scampered into the woods and Kyla cautiously drove on.

She parked and locked the car. She hiked up to highest point in the park, stood on top of the old bunker, and looked out to sea. The tip of Canada was visible to the north. Stretching along the peninsula across the water were the pristine, snow-peaked Olympic Mountains, glowing against the crystal blue sky. Next week the article would come out in Celebrity Magazine and Darcy Devereux would be revealed to the world once again. Many people would remember her face and even her name. Some would know her old persona well. But in the end, it was a passing story. That's all it would be. People could be cruel and kind. She did not want pity for her lupus, just understanding of the disease and how it affected others. Mostly, the readers would see her blissful reunion with Luke and sigh at the romantic ending to the story. Then they would move on to the next juicy story.

She and Luke would move on as well. Kyla cringed. She hoped people wouldn't treat her differently on the island. Or avoid her shop. Suddenly she was back as a little girl, playing in the herb gardens behind the house with her mom and grandma, singing songs and harvesting remedies. Kyla had been quick to learn and her grandma told her she was gifted. But that was not the gift she wanted back then. She wanted to be safe and she thought money would buy that. But it hadn't.

"Stop it," she commanded herself. It didn't really matter what others thought. Her real friends and family already knew the truth. And her old crowd? Friends, foes, or casual acquaintances, users and abusers, only those who fit with her new life would remain. And maybe now she could do some good for other people with the disease, especially those who tried to hide it like she'd done.

Kyla watched a couple walking down the beach with their two young boys. The man had his arm around the woman's shoulder. The tallest boy threw a stick for the lumbering dog that chased after it. The dog retrieved the stick and ran off with the boy running after him and yelling to stop. What a cute family.

Seagulls dove overhead, their cries filling the air, their white wings flashing against the sky. Kyla looked up into the massive wingspan of a red-tailed hawk. Her Native American father had believed in totems. She hadn't spent a lot of time with him, but she remembered some of their walks together in the woods of upstate New York. "Hawk is a messenger," he had told her.

"What is the message?" she'd asked.

Kyla remembered the essence of his answer. "Free yourself of your limitations, soar high above, and see the world as it really is."

She closed her eyes and imagined letting go, letting her life flow and trusting her wings would be filled. Her worries drifted away on the light breeze. Everything began to fall into perspective. The island was her home. Her roots would grow into the fertile soil and here she would stay. With Luke. She could see them together, walking through the fragrant vineyards, Bailey frolicking at their side. A dog barked in the distance. She opened her eyes and watched a wave wash to shore. Everything was just as it was supposed to be. She filled her lungs with the clean, salty air and blessed the day she'd met Ian and heard of Madrona Island.

A ferry horn blasted as it left the dock. She turned and followed the trail down to the water. The white, three-story ferry moved steadily across the water heading for the cute old towns on the peninsula. Kyla walked out on the rocky beach and held her hand up to her eyes to block the sun. Her eyes searched the water. Whales. A pod of the incredibly beautiful orca whales were heading out to sea. She ran down the shore alongside a young family. Their little boy was skipping along the shore shouting in excitement, "Whales!"

Kyla fought the urge to run into the water and join the whales. The freezing sound was not a place to be swimming, especially in winter. She remembered that orcas' offspring remained with their mothers their entire lives. Family.

Gracefully the majestic mammals moved along in the water, a few lingering as if saying hello. A black and white giant broke the surface with a full breach in the air. Kyla caught her breath at the magnificent sight. As if peeking out to say hello, another orca lifted its head above the surface, looking right at them. Her heart burst with joy as she felt contact with this amazing creature. In complete awe, she watched as the pod splashed and glided by.

A day of signs. A day of blessings.

Chapter Twenty-Eight

"C'mon, boy," Luke yelled to the dog, "let's go check out the chickens and get some eggs for breakfast."

Bailey had a real fascination for the chickens, so Luke made sure their coop was sturdy and dog-proof. The fields were covered in a light frost that glistened in the pink morning light. His breath came out like miniature clouds. Together they walked across the icy paths between the vines. He'd had to lime the vineyard because of all the rains, but in a few months they would dry and fill with sunlight.

Luke looked up at the sound of the mail truck making its way down the dirt drive. He'd ordered a copy of Celebrity Magazine special delivery. This was the day it had been promised to arrive and would also hit the stands. He walked back to the tasting room and waved.

"Package for you," the mailwoman said. She handed Luke a stack of letters. "And here's your larger mail for today. Save you a trip up the drive."

Luke took the package and thanked her. His heart thumped in his chest as he brought the mail inside. He held the slick-covered issue in his hand.

The headline read: "Lovers Reunited—Mystery Solved."

Luke rolled his eyes and prayed that when he opened the magazine the article would be favorable. Celebrity Magazine had a good reputation, and their best reporter, Jean Gates, had been excited and supportive when she'd interviewed them. The cover featured other couples as well and an insert picture of Kyla at the top of her modeling career. Underneath, it said, "What happened to Darcy Devereux?"

His stomach knotted as he opened the magazine and found the article. He scanned it and let a relieved smile cross his face.

"Darcy Devereux gave up a lucrative modeling career to do what so many women find difficult...take care of themselves. She was willing to do whatever it required to deal with her diagnosis of lupus and find the path to remission." There was even an insert with symptoms of lupus listed and websites to go to for help.

Luke released a long breath. Well-handled, he thought. The picture of him and Kyla holding hands in front of her shop made him smile. "Love Lost—Love Found," it said. The article went on to mention their engagement and planned wedding at the winery. It was a beautiful piece and he was sure Kyla would be pleased with it. Luke made a mental note to send a thank you note to Jean. She was a gem.

He picked up his cell phone and called Kyla at her shop.

"Did you read it?" she asked. "It's sitting here but I have not had the guts to look at it yet."

"I did and the article is great. How about I pick you up for lunch and we can go celebrate at Island Thyme?"

Luke listened as Kyla asked Becca to cover for her. "How about noon?" Kyla said. "I'll read it then meet you at Jude's place."

"Will do," he said.

He picked up the pile of mail he'd placed on the counter and took it over to his desk. The bills went in one pile, the ads in recycle, and the rest was carefully screened. A cream-colored embossed envelope stood out. Luke looked at the return address. It was from Lizbeth. For a moment, he considered adding it to the recycle pile, but caution won out. What if something was terribly wrong with his brother? Why would she write him? Was it a wedding invitation?

He tore open the envelope, pulled out the personalized stationery, and let the words sink in.

Luke,

As always, I hope you are well. We were friends once, and I hope to be counted as one still. Your family called a meeting that Stefan and I attended to discuss an early copy of the magazine article they had procured. Forewarned or forearmed or something like that. I am telling you this because we were greatly moved by Kyla's struggle. Your brother has always been difficult, but, Luke, he actually admitted to me that his actions during his visit to you were less than appropriate. And that's saying a lot for Stefan. The truth of the article touched your mother's and my hearts. We stood up to your father and told him we were supporting your marriage to Kyla. Stefan was silent, but he did not take your father's side either. Perhaps someday he will tell you all of this himself. This year there will be two weddings and new families forming. My greatest hope is that we will be welcome at your wedding to celebrate your union and that you will feel welcome at our marriage to celebrate ours.

Much love to you and Kyla,

Lizbeth

Luke dropped the letter on the desk. It was the last thing he'd expected when he opened it. He'd hoped his mother would understand, but Stefan…that he never could have imagined. There was a heart in there after all, it seemed.

Perhaps this was a year to start believing in miracles. And this letter was surely one of them.

Kyla stopped at Grandview Bank to make a deposit on her way to meet Luke. The teller acted like Kyla was a celebrity. After reading the article, Kyla figured people might treat her that way for a while. Most people in town did not know about her modeling career. Or her illness.

Everything was out in the open now, and Kyla felt a bit exposed as she walked toward the café. She never tired of the quiet waterfront town with the historical buildings lining Front Street. The new sign was up for the bookstore— Nooks, Books & Coffee it read now. She had to admit Marco's lattes had their own kind of magic. Kyla admired the new window display at the thrift shop. Maybe later she would stop in. People smiled as she walked by. Don't be paranoid, she told herself. People being friendly was nothing new in Grandview.

She held her head high and walked into Island Thyme Café. Luke was right inside waiting for her. It was packed for lunchtime. There was one table in the corner by the window open, but it had a reserved sign on it.

"Looks like we might have to eat somewhere else," Kyla said.

Jude swooped in, menus in hand. "Right this way, your table's waiting," she sang to them with a twinkle in her eyes.

Kyla looked up at Luke.

He shrugged. "I called ahead and let them know we were coming in."

Kyla followed him to the table. "And, Jude, trying to make me feel supported, probably called the whole town to let them know, too."

Luke waved his hand for her to take a seat. "Ladies first." His smile was contagious.

Jude placed the menus before them. "All week, in honor of Valentine's Day coming up, we have lovers' specials for two."

"Is that why it's so crowded?" Kyla asked. She looked around the room and spotted Ian and Lily waving at her across the room. They were sharing a table with Grandpa John, Shirley, Betty, and Ron. At the next table was Audrey, who brought with her half the library staff. All of them had their heads buried in a copy of Celebrity Magazine. Marco and Frank were sitting at the bar and toasted her by holding up a mug of beer.

Kyla narrowed her eyes at Jude. "What's going on?"

Jude beamed back at her. "Just a lunch gathering for the celebrity couple."

"I see," Kyla said.

"Are we going to get special treatment today?" Luke asked with a grin.

Kyla hit him in the arm.

"As a matter of fact, Ryan baked up a few of his seven-layer chocolate cakes with buttercream caramel icing." Jude turned around so everyone could hear, "After lunch, dessert is on us for the whole place."

A few cheers went up.

"And for lunch?" Luke asked.

"Lunch for two includes an appetizer of mussels in wine sauce, your choice of handmade gnocchi in pesto sauce or roasted chicken with apple stuffing, and creamy garlic soup."

Kyla watched Jude walk back toward the kitchen. Her eyes wandered slowly around the room. She nodded to some of her neighbors and customers who were scattered around in the restaurant. Some whispering was going on and she could imagine the shock some must be feeling. Except for her closest friends, no one knew she was a former model or that she had lupus. She turned to Luke.

"Do you think the news about my illness will affect my business?" she asked.

Luke looked surprised. "Why would it? If anything, when they see all you've been through and how healthy you are now, they'll flock the store for herbs and potions."

"I guess so," she said. "The celebrity status will probably bring in some curiosity seekers and tourists as well."

Luke sipped some water. "I hadn't thought of that. I bet the winery business will pick up. Good for business."

"So you're fine with all of this coming out?" Kyla asked. "No regrets?"

He kissed her forehead. "No regrets."

Ryan, in his black chef coat, approached the table with the appetizers and small plate entrees and set them on the table. "That was quite a piece in the magazine," he said. "It took guts for both of you to come forward with the truth."

Kyla watched a shadow cross Ryan's face. He was nervous about something. His own discovery maybe? "I was tired of running," Kyla said. She looked deep into Ryan's eyes. Fear and sorrow lurked there just below the surface.

"Running gets old," Ryan said. His shoulders dropped as his focus drifted from them.

So he, too, was running. Kyla wondered how far and how long.

He turned back to the table. "I hope you enjoy your lunch," he said mechanically before striding back to the kitchen.

"Something is wrong there," Kyla said, her eyes on Ryan.

Luke squeezed her hand. "We all have our skeletons."

All during lunch, people stopped by the table to greet them and mention the article. Shirley even asked them to autograph her copy of the magazine. So far everyone was very encouraging.

Jude brought a cart around with plates of giant pieces of chocolate layer cake. She placed two in front of them. "Enjoy. Compliments of the chef."

Jude leaned down and whispered in Kyla's ear. "Ryan brought me flowers for Valentine's Day."

Kyla winked. "And what did you get him?"

"That's coming later," Jude said grinning. "Anything else I can get you two?"

They both shook their heads and Jude flitted off to another table.

As they finished the last bite of the huge piece of cake they were sharing, Cherise, the owner of Raven Art Gallery in town, walked over to the table. She'd always been a bit of a mystery herself, impeccably dressed and self-contained. Ian showed his work there and Kyla had been to a few openings, but she'd never really spoken to the woman except for a moment in the bookstore. Cherise had never made it to the store.

"Good afternoon," Cherise said. She stared intently at Kyla. "Would it be possible for me to make an appointment with you at your shop soon to discuss…some matters?"

"Of course," Kyla said. "I'd be happy to book a specific time for you."

Cherise nodded. "Would later today work?"

Kyla was taken aback. "Name your time."

"Four o'clock?"

"I'll see you then," Kyla answered.

The woman turned and hurried out the front door. Kyla could feel the urgency in her request. "I wonder what that's about," she said.

"The article is out a day and already you have a new client," Luke said.

Perhaps he was right. Now that she'd come out and exposed her secrets, others would come to her to share theirs.

Kyla brewed her T&C store blend tea and let the sweet smell of rose, chamomile, and lavender fill her senses.

Cherise was due in and she wanted to have something warm and comforting ready to share with her during their talk. She brought the porcelain tea set out on a tray with a plate of warm cinnamon apple muffles and set them on a table by the window. An exotic bouquet of red Chinese witch hazel flowers in a glass vase sat in the center. Kyla often used the flower in creams to combat stings and bites.

At promptly four, Cherise blew in the front door grasping a soaked-wet, full-length raincoat around her. She pulled it off and hung it on the coat rack by the door.

"Good afternoon," she said, untying her scarf and taking off her gloves. "Not the prettiest of them."

Kyla pointed to the cozy table. "Come warm yourself over here. I'm glad you came." She poured the tea and sat down to join her. Cherise was avoiding eye contact and Kyla suspected she was nervous about sharing what, up until now, had been her own secret to bear.

"Delicious tea," Cherise murmured.

"I'd be happy to send you home with some as a gift," Kyla said.

When her guest looked up, Kyla saw deep pain in her eyes. "Thank you for your kindness," Cherise said. "It took a lot of courage for you to share your story, and it showed me it was time I stopped hiding my lupus diagnosis as well."

"There is no shame in being sick," Kyla said. She sipped her tea. "But I know how you feel. I ran away from my whole life rather than tell anyone."

"I used to have a gallery in Carmel-by-the-Sea. It was a very different lifestyle in sunny California, where everyone was beautiful, rich, and bought expensive art like most people buy groceries."

"How long have you been on the island?" Kyla asked.

Cherise placed her cup on the saucer and adjusted the napkin in her lap. "I met Ian at an opening in Monterey five years ago, and he told me about the island. I'd just gone through extensive treatment and was exhausted. He offered me his work exclusively in the Pacific Northwest if I opened a gallery on Madrona Island. I decided to relocate in the hope of a quieter life and a more peaceful place."

"We have a lot in common," Kyla said. "That Ian is a good guy."

"Who knew?" Cherise said. A smile lit up her face. "Would you be willing to share what has helped you with lupus?"

Kyla leaned forward. "I have no magical potions, but I can tell you what worked for me. It's been a long road to realizing my beauty was not exclusively on the outside and that it was really okay to take care of myself."

Cherise's polished demeanor started to crumble as her lower lip trembled. "Thank you for reminding me."

Kyla patted Cherise's hand. "Any time." She rose from the table. "I'll go make you a list of some of the herbs that helped me and the foods that seem to work best. But you will have to listen closely to your own body and see what makes you feel good. Rest is so very important, and lots of water."

"I'm so grateful my twists and turns brought me here to the island and to you," Cherise said. She stood at the counter and waited for Kyla to finish her list.

"So am I." Kyla handed her a bag of T&C tea and a printed list of herbs, foods, and other ideas that had helped her get and stay in remission. "I don't have to tell you to keep the stress down," Kyla said.

They both laughed. "I wish it were that easy," Cherise said.

Kyla walked her to the front door. "Come back anytime."

She watched the beautiful, raven-haired woman walk down the sidewalk. How hard we all were on ourselves. It was so obvious to Kyla that Cherise deserved love, care, and kindness. And that meant she herself did, too.

Chapter Twenty-Nine

The buds were bursting on the vines. The shoots had grown rapidly and Luke would have to do some thinning soon. The apple trees were sprouting tiny leaves, and the plum trees were covered in delicate pink blossoms, brightening the warming March day.

Luke walked over to the pond and watched the large koi glide around the water. He hoped they liked their new habitat. The Japanese bathhouse with the hot tub that overlooked the pond had been his and Kyla's favorite place all winter. He looked forward to sitting there with the doors open to the pond now that spring was here.

The morning was probably the last moment of calm he would have for the next week. Dread sat heavily on his shoulders and had filtered into his dreams. His mother and father were arriving today, and Kyla's relatives were already here. It would be quite interesting to watch two such different families together on the same island, except for the fact that he and Kyla were hosting them. He'd never met Kyla's family and he hoped they liked him. Kyla had assured him they already did. He knew his mother would be gracious, but his father… Luke shook his head. He was grateful Stefan wasn't joining them. The note from Lizbeth had indicated a peace offering might be coming from Stefan, but none had been received yet. There was no sense worrying about the inevitable. Nothing was going to stop the wedding. They were both ready.

Luke glanced at his watch. Time to get ready. His parents' shuttle arrived in less than an hour, and he would be picking them up and bringing them to Madrona Island Bed & Breakfast for their stay. Luke's father had asked if they needed to hire a driver while they were there, but Luke had suggested they take the shuttle. Luke had arranged for a rental car to be waiting at the inn for them for convenience. Kyla's mother and grandmother had arrived late last night and were already settled there. Lily had offered to serve afternoon coffee and baked goods this afternoon for everyone to meet and get acquainted. It was going to take more than coffee to smooth out that meeting. Luke grabbed a couple of bottles of his best wine as he walked out the door to the car.

Luke drove over to the local pick-up location at the gas station and waited. The rain had stopped, and patches of blue sky lit up the day. Within minutes, the Madrona Airport Shuttle pulled in. Luke took a deep breath. He hadn't seen his parents in almost two years. And the last farewell had been a bit of a screaming match. It ended with him slamming the front door of his parents' house and leaving town. Not the best move in his life, but it was what he'd needed then. But it was not how he wanted their visit to go now. He'd made a promise to himself to keep calm and stay focused on their wedding plans going smoothly.

His mother walked gracefully down the stairs of the shuttle, wrapped in a full-length cashmere coat with a Prada bag slung across her shoulder. Right behind her stood his father, wearing a steel-grey herringbone overcoat and perfectly matched scarf and gloves. Both of them wore Italian leather boots that looked like they'd never stepped on concrete before. They looked so out of place here on Madrona Island, it seemed as though royalty had arrived.

"Luke," his mother said. She waved and hurried toward him, arms wide. Her hug was tight and long and felt wonderful.

"Son," his father said. He reached out his hand to shake Luke's.

"Father."

The brief handshake was a sharp contrast to his mother's loving embrace. Luke picked up their suitcases from the back of the shuttle van and carried them to his car.

"How was your trip?" he asked.

"Long, but beautiful," his mother said. "Your island is magnificent. I can see why you settled here."

Luke laughed. "It's not exactly my island, but I'll be glad to show you both around if you'd like."

His mother sat in the front seat, leaving the back for his father. Just as well, his father was used to being chauffeured around and would feel comfortable there.

As they drove toward the inn, his mother barraged him with questions. His father stared out the window as if he weren't there.

"And when will we meet Kyla?" she asked.

In the rearview mirror, Luke saw his father tilt his head to listen.

"Kyla's mother and Grandma Mona arrived late last night, so they will be at the B&B waiting for us with her. Lily and Ian, the proprietors where you're staying, have arranged an afternoon coffee time for us all to get acquainted."

"I understand coffee is big business here in Seattle," his father said. His father must have researched the area before they arrived.

"You can get an espresso on almost every corner in the city," Luke joked, "and several places on the island."

Luke pulled the car into the driveway of the inn. Afternoon sun filtered through the clouds and sparkled on the sound, lighting up the snowcapped mountains in the distance.

"What a magnificent sight," his mother said. She turned to the back seat. "Alex, this reminds of that lovely place we stayed in Switzerland last year."

Only his mother called him Alex. He and Stefan called him Father or Dad, his peers Alexander, and the rest Mr. Bradford.

A shiny, top-of-the-line, silver Lexus was parked next to them. Luke motioned to his father that the car was at their disposal during their visit.

They exited the car and moved along the path and up the front steps. Lily stood on the porch holding open the door. "Welcome," she said. "I'm Lily. Come on in."

Luke watched his parents quickly assess their surroundings. He could hear Kyla's voice in the parlor.

"It's nice to meet you, Lily. I'm Grace Bradford, Luke's mom."

"Welcome," Lily said. Her hand rested on her stomach.

Grace smiled. "It looks like you'll be welcoming a little one soon."

"Yes, in May."

Ian moved in next to Lily. "Ian McPherson," he said, holding out his hand to Luke's dad.

"Alexander Bradford. Nice to meet you, Ian." He smiled at Lily. "You have a very fine place here."

"I hope you'll both be comfortable. Mary will take your bags to the Honeymoon Suite. It's our largest room and has a private entrance. She'll be here if you need anything during your stay."

Luke turned to his mother. "It's where I stayed when I first moved here. Very elegant."

"Very good," she said. "But first things first. Where is Kyla?"

"Of course," Lily said, leading them into the parlor.

A spread of beverages and pastries was beautifully displayed on china plates on the coffee tables in front of the matching antique satin sofas. Kyla sat between her mother and Grandma Mona. They'd been laughing and talking all afternoon. Lily had given her family the Rose Room upstairs. They were thrilled with the inn, its proprietors, and the lush grounds that surrounded it. Time sped by as they laughed and caught up with each other's lives.

Kyla glanced up to see her soon-to-be in-laws enter the room. Her breath stopped. She'd seen them only at a distance before, and they looked exactly as she remembered them. Flawless. Their families were two sides of the same coin, but one was heads and the other tails. Her mother's bright periwinkle sweater and her grandmother's silver-white hair against her fringed shawl were a striking contrast to the greys and winter ivory of the cashmeres and wools worn by Luke's parents. The old shame nipped at her heart, but one look into Luke's reassuring eyes and it vanished.

She stood and walked over to greet them. "Mr. and Mrs. Bradford. How nice to meet you," she said.

Luke's mother pulled her into her arms with a brisk hug. "Call me Grace," she said. "You're family now."

Kyla turned toward Luke's father and held out her hand to shake his. He nodded and shook hers. She detected amusement in his eyes. Just what exactly was he enjoying so much? She noticed he did not say to call him Alexander. Mr. Bradford it would stay then. Certainly never Father.

Everyone was introduced. Grace warmly shook hands with Kyla's mother, Alana, and Grandmother Mona before sitting down next to Luke and her husband. Kyla sat in a wingback chair and poured some coffee.

"Can I get anyone anything else before I leave you to get acquainted?" Lily asked.

"We're fine," Kyla said. "Thank you."

No one spoke at first. Kyla glanced at Grandma Mona and she winked back.

"I hope you both had a good trip out here," Kyla finally said. She looked up at Luke, wishing he would get the conversation going.

Grace put her cup down on the saucer. "Very nice," she said. "And, Alana, when did you and Mona arrive?"

"Late last night," Alana said. "We are very excited to see the rest of the island and, of course, Luke's winery."

Mr. Bradford cleared his throat. "We have a lot of ground to cover planning the wedding and I can only stay a couple of days. Do we know what the itinerary is for tomorrow?"

"We're all aware that your time is limited here," Luke said. "So we thought we would start tomorrow with viewing our venue, Madrona Island Winery. We can have breakfast at my home, tour the grounds, and go over all the necessary details."

Luke's tone was formal and distant. Kyla hoped the chill she felt in the air was from the wind picking up outside.

"That sounds perfect," his father said. He looked directly at Kyla's mother. "And how long are you staying on this visit?

"About a week. We haven't seen Kyla in almost two years and there is so much to talk about. We'll be back for the wedding, of course."

"We haven't seen our son for a few years either. So we know exactly how you feel," Mr. Bradford said.

Luke's mother quickly changed the subject. "Alex, do you remember that gorgeous Vera Wang gown your niece wore last year at her wedding in the Hamptons? Wouldn't Kyla look lovely in one like that?"

Mr. Bradford smiled politely. "Perhaps the bride has other ideas for her gown."

Very politely said, but it still made Kyla uncomfortable. "I hadn't thought that much about the dress yet," she said. "So far all we've planned is that Chef Ryan at Island Thyme Café is going to cater the reception and Lily is going to bake the cake."

"Chef Ryan?" Luke's mother asked. "Have I heard of him before?"

Kyla groaned inside. "He's cooked for the finest restaurants in San Francisco and a James Beard Award-winning restaurant in Seattle."

His mother looked surprised. "Aren't you lucky to have him here on the island then."

"We can always pitch in anywhere you need us," Alana said.

"Thanks, Mom." Kyla couldn't imagine Grace in the kitchen at all.

The women chatted for a while about wedding gowns and menus while the men smiled and nodded appropriately. Everyone had different ideas, from her mother's idea for vegan fair to Grace's gourmet, six-course dinner suggestion. She and Luke had been hoping for a small ceremony and reception, but the numbers of "have to be invited" kept climbing. Kyla's head spun. She needed some time alone with Luke to make their own plans before the meeting tomorrow or everything they wanted would be derailed.

Finally Luke asked if anyone would like a glass of the Pinot Noir he grew on the vineyard. The complete consensus of "yes" was the first and probably the last thing they would all agree on. After two rounds of toasts to the engagement and the bride-and-groom-to-be, Luke's parents finally retired to their room.

Kyla was grateful that her mother and Grace, both excited over planning their children's wedding, seemed to bond pretty quickly. Grandma Mona was quiet and watchful.

"You two must be tired after a long day," Kyla said. "Why don't you go rest a bit and Luke and I will pick everyone up for dinner later."

"No need to go to any fuss for us," her mother said. "We can cook something up in the kitchen."

"Mom, I'm not sure Lily wants anyone in her kitchen. It's her private domain."

"Oh, I never thought of that," Alana said. "Maybe take-out? Or whatever works."

"We'll give you a call in a few hours," Luke said. "Meanwhile, just enjoy yourselves."

Kyla helped her grandmother off the sofa and gave her a hug.

"Go rest yourself, dear," Mona said. She kissed Kyla on the cheek.

As soon as they left the room, Kyla fell into Luke's arms. "Let's get out of here."

"Where do you want to go?" he asked.

"Anywhere. Just drive."

The sun was low on the horizon and would set soon. Luke drove down the back road toward the bluff overlooking the water to catch the last of the sunset. They jumped out of the car and walked through the wind-blown trees toward the edge. The water and sky were tinted the color of tangerines, lined by dark purple clouds. Luke put his arm around her and she snuggled against him. Seagulls screamed overhead, diving toward the water.

"We got through today," Luke said.

Kyla looked up at him. His lips curled up suggestively with his devilish smile. Very kissable. His hair was sun-drenched caramel in this light. The warmth of his body radiated into hers, melting away any leftover tension.

"It went better than I thought," she said. "Your mother was wonderful and your dad polite."

"My father is nothing but polite in public. It's tomorrow when I meet with him alone that his true colors will come out."

Kyla formed a pose as if for a fashion shoot. "Can you imagine me walking down the aisle through the vineyard in a puffy Vera Wang wedding gown?"

Luke struck a pose himself. "And me in a custom-made tux by my father's European tailor?"

"Just as long as my mother doesn't do any of the sewing," Kyla said.

They both laughed.

She clasped his hands. "Luke, in my heart, we're already married. The ceremony is for our families. Let's listen tomorrow and see what would make them happy, okay?"

"Compromise is something I've done to accommodate my family for most of my life."

"This is not about accommodating, it's about healing and putting the past behind us. A small gesture could go a long way."

Luke closed his eyes, tossed his head back in the breeze, then he gazed back at Kyla. "You're right. I'll give it a try. I'm sure they'll get their hearts' desires with Stefan's wedding."

The stood silently and watched nature's art show before them. A lavender hue radiated across the water as the sun dipped behind the Olympics. The beauty was spellbinding. Kyla reached up and stroked Luke's cheek then pressed her lips to his. His fingers ran through her hair as he pulled her closer to deepen the kiss.

"Let's go back to my place," he whispered in her ear.

She giggled. "Do we have time before dinner?"

He snatched her hand and hurried back to the car.

"Dinner will be late tonight," he said.

Chapter Thirty

$\mathcal{L}$uke and his father walked over to the tasting room and left the women behind in the house sitting by the fire sipping tea. It had been a long day of wedding plans, going over flower choices, seating arrangements, and music choices. But it wasn't over yet. Luke's father wanted to have some man-to-man time alone to talk before he left at the break of dawn tomorrow morning.

"Have a seat. The leather chairs are comfortable," Luke said. "I'll bring over some glasses and a bottle of wine."

"Do you have anything stronger?" his father asked.

Luke unlocked a cabinet under the bar. "As a matter of fact, I have a bottle of barrel-aged gin distilled right here on Madrona Island."

"Aged?"

Luke opened the bottle and poured a little in each glass. "They age it for a few months in oak barrels with a curl of Madrona bark. It's excellent."

His father raised his glass to Luke. "To your new venture and its future success."

Luke sat in the chair next to his father and let the unique-tasting gin warm his insides. After a few minutes of uncomfortable silence, his father finally spoke.

"You have an impressive place here. I'm glad I got to see it."

"Thanks. I'm glad you got to see it, too." Luke shifted in his chair. He wasn't used to compliments from him. His father's face was drawn and showing his age.

"Time seems to slip away sometimes, and with it, one's dreams." He looked over at Luke, his eyes soft and present. "I understand more than you know," his father said.

Luke had no idea what was coming next. He'd never seen his father like this before.

His father placed his glass down on the oak side table. "You may not believe it, but I do want you to be happy. It's obvious you are in love, but are you absolutely sure you want to go through with this marriage?"

"I'm very happy here and plan to settle on this island permanently. We love each other and that's all that matters." Luke gulped back some of the gin.

"You'll live on love until breakfast. Then what?"

Here it comes, Luke thought. "And what is that supposed to mean?"

"I'm concerned for both of your futures. What if Kyla changes her mind and wants to start modeling again? Have you considered that?"

Luke shook his head. "Tea & Comfort is her passion, and with her health concerns, a career with travel and pressure is the last thing she wants."

His father gave him his all-knowing glare. "Are you sure?"

"Yes, I am," Luke said. "And what would you know about marrying for love? Grace was your perfect partner socially and financially, but did you ever really love my mother?"

"How can you ask me that? Of course I love your mother, but I took my time and made sure it was the best possible match. I did not jump in heart-first like my previous marriage."

Luke stood and retrieved the bottle of gin. He poured them a refill and sat back down. He couldn't imagine his father ever making an impulsive decision, especially concerning love. "Was it different with your first marriage?"

"It might be hard to imagine, but I was young once," his father said. "I've made my own mistakes and I'd like to see you avoid doing the same thing."

"That's interesting," Luke said. "I've never heard you admit to making a mistake before."

His father rubbed his eyes. "I know I haven't been the greatest dad, but I am trying here, Luke. About seven years before I met your mother, I thought myself head over heels in love with a young, beautiful, and talented opera star. My father's private jet was at my disposal and wherever she went I followed. In every country I lavished her with gifts and begged her to marry me. My family thought it would just blow over and indulged me in my fantasy. But when I called and told them I had married her one fabulous weekend in Paris, their disappointment was palpable."

Luke reeled from this insight into his father. "So what happened?"

"My parents were cold and polite when I brought her home. Nine months later, Stefan was born. Ten months later, my wife started professionally singing again. Within a year she was never home. Stefan grew up with a nanny; his mother preferred her adoring fans. And I could barely look at the child whose black eyes and raven hair looked just like his mother's. At times I wondered if I were truly the father or a convenient husband to foot the bill."

"I'm sorry," Luke said. And he meant it. He thought of Stefan always trying to get their father's attention. How hard it must have been for the dark-eyed older son when Luke was born and received all the love Stefan had been denied.

"How did it end?" Luke asked.

"Not well. There were rumors of her cheating and my father always made sure I heard them...his stupid son who had married for love and been dazzled by beauty. The divorce was quiet and expensive. I retained full custody of Stefan, and every time I looked at the boy I was reminded of the fool I'd been."

Luke saw a sad, old man before him who was trying to reach out.

"It's not like that with me and Kyla. Dad, I never wanted to disappoint you and Mom, but you still haven't really given Kyla a chance. She's a wonderful woman who's been through a lot. With every cell of my body I know we are meant to be together. I'm asking you to trust me, Dad."

He saw the raging conflict in his father's eyes and prayed, just this once, he'd let down. With a reluctant nod, his father said, "If you think this will work, let's go back and join the women. We have a wedding to plan."

Chapter Thirty-One

Kyla stood at the counter with Becca and watched her mother, Grandma Mona, and Grace sip rose-colored tea in china cups. They chatted away at the front table nestled in the dormer window of Tea & Comfort. In the overhead light, Grace's hair looked like the color of fine champagne, contrasting her own mother's deep mahogany flowing locks. A pang of sadness pierced Kyla's heart. They would all be going home tomorrow. She would miss their quick humor, support, and having family nearby.

"They sure look like they're all getting along," Becca said.

"Pretty well, surprisingly."

Kyla joined the three women at their table. "Good morning, ladies."

"Good morning," her mother chimed back. "We were just discussing what we were going to write in that charming guestbook at the inn before we leave."

"It will all be glowing," Grace assured her.

Becca placed a silver tray of just-out-of-the-oven scones on the table before them. "Enjoy," she said.

"What is that divine smell?" her mother asked.

"One of our special recipes for lavender chocolate chip scones."

Her mother winked at her. "Do you share your recipes?"

Kyla sat beside her. "For family only," she said with a grin.

"The tea is delicious," Grace said. "What's in the mixture?"

Kyla looked to her grandma to see if she could guess.

Mona winked back at her. "I'd say there is chamomile, hibiscus, and a pinch of rosebuds."

"Exactly right," Kyla said. She warmed her hands on the porcelain china cup before her. Three generations of her family circled the table, as well as her new mother-in-law-to-be. As different as they all were, afternoon tea brought them together.

"How do you like my new purchase?" her mother asked. She held out the fringed ends of a sparkly purple scarf. "Feel how soft it is."

"Like velvet," Kyla said.

Grace pulled back her luxurious hair to reveal silver earrings inlaid with a blue heron in flight. "We did a little shopping in town today before we arrived. These earrings are handmade."

"I recognize them," Kyla said. "They're by the same artist that made Lily's necklace that Ian gave her for Christmas. And what did you get, Grandma?"

Her grandma looked striking in a black turtleneck with her long white hair pulled back in a knot at her neck. Mona pulled red and black embroidered gloves out of her purse.

"Toasty warm for my chilly hands. And look at this." She slipped her slim hands through the gloves and her fingertips popped out of the tops. "I can keep my old hands warm and still pick herbs on a chilly day."

"Shopping is so easy here after New York," her mother said. "Friendly sales people, no rush, no lines. What heaven. I even found socks made of bamboo." She held up a half-eaten scone. "And your baked goods are to die for."

"Quite delicious," Grace echoed. "The lavender lingers on the tongue."

Grandma Mona stared out the window.

"Jude calls this light rain and mist mixture 'mizzle,'" Kyla said.

Her grandma sighed. "This lush green island reminds me of Ireland some. The hills, fog, curving inlets of water…there's something magical about it."

"You're all welcome here anytime," Kyla said and realized she truly meant it. She and Luke were joining families by getting married. Once, she had feared Grace's disapproval, but not anymore. Grace wanted Luke happy and she'd sincerely extended friendship to Kyla.

"Alana has some news," Grandma Mona said.

"Yes I do," her mother said. "You know how I've been working on a book forever. Today, I received notice that my book, Herbs, Healing, and Love will be in the bookstores next week."

"Congratulations," Grace said. "We'll have a published author in the family."

"Great news, Mom," Kyla said.

Alana patted Grandma Mona on the back. "I couldn't have done it without your grandmother's help. Maybe you can all come when I have my first book signing next month."

Her family's business was going to be very public now, Kyla thought. Everything was coming to the surface and sometimes she still felt the urge to find a dark cave to hide in. But not today, she told herself.

"Have you checked on Lily lately?" Grandma Mona asked. "She looks so worn-out every day. I told her we can make our own breakfast and Mary is there, eager to help, but Lily insists on cooking for us herself."

Kyla realized that with the magazine article, wedding planning, and family visiting, she'd barely talked to Lily in the last month. "Not in the last few days," Kyla said. "She did ask us to hold off planning a baby shower until after the baby is born."

Grandma Mona's expression sent a chill down Kyla's spine. "I'll call her tomorrow."

Grace took one last sip of her tea. Her sleeve slipped back to reveal a reddened rash up her arm. Kyla watched her grandmother lightly touch Grace's hand.

"A rash. Is it bothering you?" Grandma Mona asked.

Grace pulled down her sleeve. "Why yes, it is," she said. "I've been to three doctors and nothing has worked."

"May I look at it?"

Grace's eyes flew to Kyla.

"My grandmother is very knowledgeable. Perhaps she can help," Kyla said.

"It's certainly been worrisome." Grace rolled up her sleeve and let Mona have a look at the splotchy red rash.

The word "worrisome" rang in Kyla's ears. Often the words people used to describe an ailment were a clue to the emotions contributing to the condition. She stared at Grace. As beautiful and put-together as she appeared, underneath she was just like everyone else: a mom worried about losing her son to a new bride.

"Kyla," Mona said, "do you have any medicinal honey and lavender oil?"

"I do." Kyla stood. "Come with me to the back and I'll get you anything you need."

Becca leaned over the counter. "Do you need any help?" she asked.

"Just hold down the store," Kyla answered as she guided her grandmother back to the workroom behind the curtains. "This is where I work."

Grandma Mona smiled. "Your shop is wonderful, Kyla. So many beautiful things and carefully-thought-out products."

Kyla hugged her grandma. "Thank you. I'm so glad you're here. I've missed you terribly and I'm very sorry it's been so long."

"We knew when you were ready you would come home." Grandma Mona touched Kyla's cheek, wiping away a tear. "And we will always be there for you. We love you."

"I love you, too."

Her grandmother looked right through her. "And what tonics are you taking?"

Kyla hesitated. "I have done my research and used my own sense of the plants."

"Tumeric? Red clover? Licorice?"

"Yes, Grandmother. And pine bark extract is quite helpful and reishi mushroom."

"No nightshades," Grandma Mona whispered.

"None. But plenty of eggs and fresh garlic."

Her grandmother nodded. "Good. Now let's get to work healing Grace's arm."

They gathered the supplies they needed and brought it back to the table. Mona explained to Grace how to put the honey on with a dressing before bed and use the lavender oil sparingly during the day.

"Thank you both," Grace said. "I'll let you know how it goes."

Kyla took Grace's hand. "I want you to know that you are always welcome here with me and Luke, and I hope you will visit often."

Grace's smile lit the room much the way Luke's always did. She opened her Fendi bag and brought out her iPad. "We really do have to make a few more wedding plans before we leave tomorrow. So let's bring this official meeting to order."

Everyone snapped to attention as Grace listed the areas where decisions still needed to be made. "First we'll need the head count and how many people each side of the family will be inviting."

"We really hope to keep it small if possible," Kyla said, probably for the hundredth time. "We have a dozen or so friends on the island, and my mother and grandmother, of course."

"Any other family?" Grace asked.

Kyla froze. It was a perfectly innocent-sounding question, but it was the one she'd dreaded having to answer.

"In this country our family is small. We have a few close friends who might be able to make it out to the island for the ceremony."

Grace stared at her, waiting to hear more.

"My father passed when I was young," Kyla said. She turned to her mother for support.

"My girl had a bit of a tough time growing up, but we are very proud of her and the person she's become," Alana said.

"And rightly so," Grace answered. "Luke had a lot of pressure on him when he was young, and I never thought I'd see him so happy." She turned to Kyla. "I'd love to help make this a dream wedding for you, whatever it is you both choose to do."

Kyla realized this was Grace's only son's wedding and it obviously meant a lot to her, too.

"That is a very generous offer," Kyla said. "I hope in June we can get a sunny day out on the vineyard. That would be blissful."

"Just in case," Grace continued, "how about I arrange for a large open tent outside with a crystal chandelier and tea lights where the tables can be set and perhaps a dance floor."

Kyla could see the dreamy tent sparkling in her mind. "Lovely idea."

Her mother could barely contain herself. "Your grandmother and I would be very pleased if you would let us provide the wedding cake," Alana gushed. "Just tell us what you want and we will arrange it."

"Just talk to Lily," Kyla said. "If she's up to it, she plans to bake one."

Weddings seemed to bring people together or tear them apart. With her and Luke, Kyla would be sure it brought everyone together.

Her grandmother's eyes twinkled. "And I would like to buy your wedding dress for you," she said.

Kyla laughed. "I'm not sure where I'm going to find one out here."

Grace cleared her throat. "That brings up another idea. The three of us have been conspiring the last few days and have a surprise for you. I hope you'll like it."

Take a deep breath, Kyla reminded herself. These are people who love you. "And what is it?"

"We want to throw you a bridal shower," her mother exclaimed.

"In New York," Grace said, "at the elegant Parisian Tea Room in Manhattan. That way we can spend a little time with the bride before the wedding."

"And do all the 'girl' stuff," her mother said.

New York. Kyla had not been there in two years, and the thought of going there sent a chill through her body.

"Would it be too much for you?" Grandma Mona asked.

Kyla saw the longing in all of their eyes. She had to go back sometime, and this was the best possible reason to. She could meet with her agent, Arlene, while she was there.

"I see you're all in on this," she said. "Let's do it. Give me the date and I'll book a ticket."

"We'll take care of everything. All you have to do is show up. One little thing: The only date we could get is April eighteenth," Grace said.

"Three weeks away," Kyla said. "I can do it."

They would be gone tomorrow. Kyla had been both relieved and sad at the thought of their parting. But with this new development she would see them all very soon.

A line was forming at the counter, and Becca looked like she could use some help. "I guess I better get back to work now," Kyla said. "Luke and I will bring dinner over later."

"We'll be there," her mother said.

Chapter Thirty-two

Kyla tightened the wool scarf around her neck to ward off the chilly March evening. A storm had blown in with high wind warnings. Luke had suggested picking up pizza for dinner so everyone would not have to bundle up and go out on a night like this. The scent of garlic and pesto from the back seat tantalized Kyla's taste buds. The wind off the sound howled through the swaying trees, causing branches to whip around ominously. The drive to the B&B only took ten minutes and she would be happy to be safely parked and inside.

When her cell phone lit up with a new text message, Kyla's heart skipped a beat. It was from Ian. *Won't make dinner. Lily fainted. The doctor is with her now at our house. Others waiting at inn for you. Will call with update soon.*

Kyla hesitated. She didn't want to bother them while the doctor was there, but worry curled up into her chest and made it hard to breathe. What if Lily lost the baby? She did not want to let her mind go there. It would devastate them all.

"What is it?" Luke asked.

"It was Ian. The doctor is with Lily at their house."

Luke glanced at her as he pulled the car into Sunshine Lane. "Is she all right?"

"I don't know. Ian said he'd call."

She clutched the phone in her hand and let her mind reach out and drift toward Lily. Kyla counted on her fingers. The baby was not due until late May. If Lily went into labor this early, the outcome could be… She forced her thoughts away from that darkness. She had to do something.

"Luke, you go to the inn and bring dinner with you. Let them know Lily is not doing well and I went over to see if I can help."

Luke turned the car down the driveway of Grandpa John's ranch-style house and drove around to the back where Ian had added on a master suite and sitting room. A golden light shone through the French glass doors.

As she stepped out of the car, the wind ripped through Kyla's hair and made it hard to traverse the stone path to their door. Rain bounced off her like small pebbles. Ian met her at the door. His face was drained of color.

"Come in," he said.

Gretel greeted her, wagging her tail ferociously. Ian reached out a shaky hand to help Kyla in.

His worried eyes met hers. "Thanks for coming."

Kyla gave Gretel a quick pet on the head and then peeled off her soaking wet coat. She could hear the doctor speaking softly to Lily in the next room.

"What happened?" she asked.

Ian motioned for Kyla to follow him through the door into the main kitchen. Jason, wearing a Seahawks jersey, sat in the corner desk working on his computer. He turned to wave.

"How's Mom?" he asked. Worry etched his face.

Ian forced a smile. "She's resting, but you can go see her after the doctor leaves."

Jason frowned. "Do I still have to finish my homework tonight?"

"Yes, you do, buddy," Ian said. He went over and gave Jason a hug. "Everything's going to be fine. Let's let the doctor do his work."

Grandpa John was making coffee and stopped to greet her.

"Good to see you," he said. "Coffee?"

"No thanks." She couldn't stomach anything right now.

Ian poured himself a cup. "I knew she wasn't feeling that well, but why didn't she tell me?"

Kyla watched him warm his hands on the mug and stare out to space. She walked over and patted his shoulder gently. "Tell you what?"

"She's been going to her appointments and said she was fine. But now the doctor told me her spotting had been progressively worse and a few hours ago she had painful contractions."

"Contractions," Kyla whispered. "Is she still having them?"

"I think they finally stopped. Before she fainted, Lily was doubled over, screaming in pain. The doctor finally arrived and gave her a shot. She's resting now."

Kyla forced herself to take deep breaths. She'd seen other women recover and have full-term babies even with this happening. The key was rest. Kyla felt a pang of guilt. Her family and Luke's had been staying at the inn, and even with Mary there as the live-in caretaker, Lily had been doing a lot of extra work.

"Did the doctor say anything else?" she asked.

"He said she's anemic and she was supposed to go home yesterday after her appointment, go to bed, and not get out."

"I didn't know," Kyla said. "I would have made her go to bed."

Grandpa John put one arm around her and the other around Ian. "Stop blaming yourselves. It won't do Lily any good. Now let's go back in there and cheer that lady up."

"Can I help?" Jason asked, joining them in the kitchen.

"Let me check on her first, son," Ian said. "I'll come right back and get you."

Kyla followed Luke back to the bedroom. The doctor was seated by a window writing up a prescription. Lily tilted her head and smiled, and then patted the bed beside her. "Looks like I'll be spending the next few months right here," Lily said.

Ian hurried to her side. "That's for sure. Don't you dare move."

"We can take turns keeping you company," Grandpa John said.

Lily giggled. "You mean keeping guard?"

"If we have to," Ian answered.

Kyla leaned over and kissed Lily on the forehead. It was clammy and cool. "I'll be here whenever you need me," she said.

"She's going to need complete rest," the doctor said. "And regular meals. But she's a tough one, and with everyone helping out, she'll be just fine."

Hopefully, Kyla thought. Her mind spun considering what types of teas might be calming and healing and gentle for mother and baby.

"Everyone in town will want to help," Grandpa John said. "The casseroles will probably be on the porch by morning."

The doctor chuckled. "I'll be going now, but you have my number if you need anything."

Ian walked the doctor to his car, closing the door tight behind them.

Grandpa John pulled a chair to the bedside and patted Lily's hand in his. "We're going to have some good times together. I'll rent some movies and even make popcorn."

Kyla knew Grandpa John would be Lily's rock. And after all, love and kindness was the best medicine of all.

Lily waved Kyla over. "Sorry about leaving your families over there without me."

"Don't be," Kyla said. "I'm sorry they were extra work for you. Lily, I wish you would have told me how bad you felt."

"Friends help friends," Lily said. "And I've grown to enjoy your mother and grandmother very much. And Grace."

"They'll probably want to come running over to help as soon as I tell them," Kyla said.

"Not today," Lily said with a yawn.

"You sleep now. I'll let them know they can come by tomorrow before they leave, but only if you are up to it."

Ian blew back in through the door and shook off the rain. Icy winds howled outside and crept between the windowsills and under the door, hissing along the wood floor.

"Any chance of giving me a ride over to the inn?" Kyla asked. "From the look of you, I don't think walking is an option."

"Of course," Ian said.

Kyla knew she would be back tomorrow with her family before she drove them to the airport shuttle. Lily's worry lines were deep, but her color was already coming back. With all the healers, friends, and prayers that would be coming Lily's way, she would be healthy and happy again in no time. And Kyla would do whatever was needed to be there for her friend and the new little one waiting to be born.

Chapter thirty-three

$\mathcal{L}$uke hung up the phone and tossed it onto the side table. Kyla had been in New York a week and it felt like a year. Between her work schedule and her helping to care for Lily, he'd barely seen her the last few weeks before she'd gone either. He sank into his favorite chair by the window overlooking the vineyard. Luke had planned to share with Kyla the amazing smell when the flowering, yellow pinot spikes bloomed. But she was in New York. Bailey curled up next to him and placed his large silky head on Luke's feet.

"Good boy," Luke said. He scratched behind the dog's ears. "Loyal and true is what you are." Bailey moaned as if agreeing and thumped his tail on the floor.

Kyla was not coming home tomorrow, even though it was two days later than originally planned. He shuffled in the chair, trying to get comfortable. His father's warning rang in his brain: "She'll take off to pursue her career and you'll never see her again."

He shook off the words that clenched his heart. Not Kyla. She'd be back. It was only a few days. She had meetings with her agent, and the Lupus Organization wanted her to do some photo shoots and interviews. It was a good cause after all,

Luke assured himself. It wasn't like she wanted to start model-ing again and traveling full time all over the world.

"I'm having a great time seeing old friends and everyone's been wonderful," Kyla had said. She'd been hesitant to go back to New York, but now she was so excited she'd barely said goodbye. His mother had called and gone on and on about how beautiful Kyla looked all dressed up and how the shower had gone. He had expected her home by now.

Luke sprang up and paced the floor. Head cocked, Bailey watched him with his doe-brown eyes. "And what are the things she needs to tell me when she gets home?" Now he was talking to dogs. He walked over and stared out the window. What was she hiding that had to wait? Maybe he should drop everything and fly out there to be with her. Kyla had told him there was no reason for him to drop his business and wait for her during the shower and meetings. Was that the only reason she didn't want him there?

He stopped himself short as he reached for his iPad to book a flight. Who was he kidding? Spying on her was his real motive, motivated by plain old fear. His father had planted mistrust, and he was watering it and helping it to grow. He had a winery to run and a wedding to plan for. Right here, right now he had to make a decision; he either loved and trusted Kyla or he didn't.

Out the picture window, the rows of woody vines stretched across the hills. Early morning sunlight cast a golden glow over the land. His land. They had decided Kyla would move here after their marriage and it would become their home. Happiness rose to the surface and beckoned. Then he realized the truth—he was afraid to be happy. His whole life, happiness had been just out of reach and not meant for him. Could it possibly be real this time?

On the evening before she'd left for New York, Luke had invited Kyla to spend the night. Luke closed his eyes. Baily had been stretched out in front of the blazing fire. They'd sat next to the dog, cuddled up on the rug by the stone fireplace, listening to the crackle and snap of burning logs as they sent sparks leaping in the air. They'd lingered over a glass of Pinot Noir as the sweet smell of cedar filled the room.

"Let's go upstairs," Kyla whispered.

He'd lost himself in her arms, her sweet scent and passionate kisses taking him to places he'd never been before. They fit together perfectly in every way. Their tender lovemaking brought an even greater intimacy between them. Luke had never loved her more than at the moment they'd become one. And in the morning, when they woke to the ringing alarm, he held her tightly to his bare chest and never wanted to let her leave.

"If you don't let go," Kyla laughed, "you'll make me late for the shuttle."

"I never want to let you go," he said. Her mussed hair framed her sculpted face and drifted down her shoulders. A goddess would be jealous of her beauty.

"It's only a few days, Luke. Believe me, I'd rather be here with you."

A few days sounded like an eternity. He'd never been needy before with any woman. It was his father's lingering words that stuck in his gut like a stone.

"Let's get you ready and out the door on time," he'd said, forcing a smile.

As her airport shuttle drove off, the heaviness in his chest intensified, squeezing like a vise. And it hadn't let go. Luke remembered Kyla blowing kisses from the shuttle window. How could he even doubt her for a moment? This was ridiculous. He needed to snap out of it. He was not his father and never would be.

"Come here, boy," he said to Bailey. He hugged the dog. "Would you like to get out of the house and go for a walk? Clear our heads?"

Luke leashed the dog, turned toward the door, and stopped. He picked up his cell phone and texted Kyla: *Missing you! I'll be waiting for you with open arms when you return. Love, Luke.* He sighed and put his phone back down.

Just need a little space to sort a few things out. Counting the minutes to be in your arms again. XOXOXO Kyla texted back.

Stay as long as you need, he answered.

She needed space. From him? Or maybe from being overwhelmed from so much happening in New York? That made sense.

Instead of moping around, Luke was going to plan something special for Kyla's return. He would think about it on his walk and come up with the perfect idea.

Chapter Thirty-Four

Kyla was glad to finally get off the plane. It had been a long week in New York and she was excited to get back to the island and to Luke. She'd gained three hours coming east to west, so it was only noon here in Seattle. Perhaps she'd grab a snack at the Starbucks stand before getting on the airport shuttle back to Madrona Island.

She flipped her carry-on bag over her shoulder, stepped onto the crowded escalator, and headed for the baggage claim area. As Kyla stepped off, a familiar and very handsome face greeted her.

"Welcome home," Luke said.

Luke's black wool sweater clung to his smooth, muscular shoulders as he handed her the biggest bouquet of red roses Kyla had ever seen.

"What are you doing here?" she asked, admiring the roses.

He put his arm around her shoulder and kissed her cheek. "I wanted to surprise you and save you the long ride home alone in the shuttle. You look beautiful."

Kyla laid her head on his chest and breathed in his woodsy scent. His lips brushed the top of her head with kisses. "Thank you," she said.

"My total pleasure." Luke took her carry-on and retrieved her bag from the carousel before they walked to the parking garage.

Kyla buckled her seatbelt in preparation for the long ride home.

"I hope you're hungry," Luke said.

His grin was contagious. A smile spread across Kyla's face. "For you? Absolutely."

"That will have to wait just a little while. Would lunch interest you first?"

"Of course," Kyla said. "It was a long flight."

She glanced out the window as they drove up I-5 North. Just what did Luke have planned? she wondered. It was a beautiful spring day. She could tell it had recently rained because the sunlight twinkled off the remaining droplets on leaves and foliage. After only a few exits, Luke exited the freeway and drove up a windy, heavily forested road. A few bright yellow daffodils were mixed in with lavender trillium and azalea bushes along the road. She rolled down the window and breathed in the fresh smell. Seattle was so different from New York.

"Are you going to give me any hints?" Kyla asked.

Luke turned off the road, and a sprawling, cedar-wood-and-glass hotel came into view. She'd heard of the Pine River Inn and had always wanted to see it. It was known for the best local cuisine in Washington.

"Will this work?" he asked.

"I've been wanting to see this place," she said. "They serve food right from their farm to the table."

Luke winked. "I remember hearing that." He pulled the car into the valet lane.

"Checking in?" the attendant asked when Luke exited the car.

"For the night, yes," Luke answered. Then he opened the door for Kyla. "Shall we?"

"Overnight?" she asked.

"Think of it as a preview honeymoon, and don't worry, I let Becca know she needed to stay an extra day with the cats."

As they walked into the lobby, Kyla didn't know where to look first. The massive wood ceilings towered above them and full wall windows revealed the view of forests and ponds. Striking paintings of Northwest settings lined the walls and the sounds of the soothing, misty waterfall completed the setting. While Luke checked in, Kyla took off her jacket and made herself comfortable on one of the luxurious sofas surrounded by plants and bronze sculptures.

Luke returned and reached out his hand. "The dining room awaits us."

They sat in plush leather chairs at a table by the window overlooking a garden. Kyla opened her menu. "How will I ever decide? Everything looks wonderful."

"Why don't we live dangerously and order a little of several things. We can create our own tasting menu."

The waiter brought over a chilled bottle of a Willamette Valley Chardonnay Luke had ordered special. He poured a taste for Luke and then filled their glasses.

After they ordered, Luke held up his glass. "To us," he said.

Kyla clinked her glass with his. "To us." The wine tasted like grapefruit and sunshine. She sipped it slowly, letting her eyes caress Luke with their gaze. Every cell in her body longed to be in his arms. The days away had only intensified her feelings for this man.

"How was New York?" he asked.

"It was exciting and very exhausting. The shower was elegant and a bit Bohemian thanks to the families' influence."

Luke's eye's reflected humor and understanding, and it settled Kyla's heart. She wondered if Grace had called her son and told him the shower was a disaster.

"My mother went on and on how it was perfect in every way," Luke said.

"Glad to hear it," she said. Kyla sipped the cool wine.

Sunlight poured in through the garden windows, casting rainbows on the crystal glass. In the corner, sitting at a polished baby grand piano, an elderly man in a dark suit played classical Bach. The start of a five o'clock shadow on Luke's face added a rugged and appealing quality to his already handsome face. She'd missed him more than she wanted to admit.

"And after the wedding," she said slyly, "you will see some of the silky lingerie I received as gifts."

"Do I have to wait until then?"

"I'll think about it," Kyla said. "But one thing you will be waiting to see is the wedding dress we picked out."

"Mission accomplished then?" he asked.

The waiter stopped at their table to pour more wine. "Can I get you anything else?" he asked.

"Everything is fine," Luke said. He looked back at Kyla expectantly.

"We—Grace, my mother, and, of course me—started at New York's finest bridal shop, Pronovias. The dressing room was as big as my cottage. And my mother insisted on paying for the gown."

Luke laughed aloud. "I've heard about that place."

"So had I. Maybe at one time I would have loved trying on five- and six-figure designer gowns, but not now. Somehow, they just didn't feel right for the winery setting."

He placed his hand on hers. "We could change the venue if it's not what you want."

Kyla shook her head. "Luke, I love the winery and there is nowhere else I'd rather marry you."

When he smiled, his whole face lit up, and so did Kyla's heart. "We ended up at a designer I've always admired, Carol Hannah. Her dresses are handmade and known for their draping and movement. When you walk, they glide in the breeze."

"Sounds like you found one you love."

"We all love the custom design she came up for me."

"And…?" he asked.

"You'll see when I walk down the aisle." Her heart leapt in her chest at the vision. Lovely in white and blush, all eyes on her, soft music playing, Luke waiting. Would it really come to pass? She wanted to tell Luke about her last day in New York, but she did not want to take a chance on ruining this perfect lunch. Later was fine. When the time was right.

The first course arrived, consisting of fresh pea and mint soup finished with garlic oil and beet salad with saffron pears and warm chèvre cheese. Warm, crusty bread and soft aromatic butter were placed in the middle of the table.

"Everything looks too pretty to eat," she said.

"Or good enough to eat," Luke answered, taking a bite of the salad.

The warm, herby bread coupled with the creamy soup melted in Kyla's mouth. They'd barely finished one course when the next arrived. Luke claimed the Dungeness crab BLT and Kyla the delicate ricotta gnocchi in sage butter with baby radish greens.

"These gnocchi taste like I'm eating clouds," Kyla said.

Between bites, Luke offered her a taste of his sandwich. "Try it."

She wrapped her mouth around the delicacy and took a big bite. Flavors of bacon, crab, and a spicy aioli burst in her mouth. "Amazing."

"I've done some thinking about the wedding day," Luke said. "We can line the path with oak wine barrels topped with colorful flower arrangements."

"We'll have to talk to a florist about colors and themes," Kyla said.

He wiped his mouth with his napkin. "Whatever you like. We'll have an outdoor and indoor area for guests in case of rain. Perhaps you could divine a sunny day?"

"I'll try," Kyla said. She laid her fork down and sighed with contentment.

The waiter came over, cleared their plates away, and then came and presented them with a daily dessert menu. Kyla frowned. "I don't think I could eat even one more bite."

Luke gave her his evil grin. "Not even a bittersweet chocolate torte with a salted caramel sauce?"

Kyla rolled her eyes. "Why don't you order it to go for later?"

"Of course," Luke said. "How about we go take a walk in their gardens?" He patted his stomach. "Walk a little of this off."

The stone paths were laced with bright green Irish moss in a checkerboard pattern. The woodland garden contained lush ferns that moved gently in the breeze, dwarfed by towering evergreens that smelt like Christmas. They walked up the stone rockery steps and stood by a small reflection pond. Lily pads floated the surface, and the crimson-colored rhododendron blossoms from overhanging bushes and flowering trees reflected in the water.

Luke pointed to a bench nestled under a vine-covered gazebo across the water. "Shall we sit?"

Kyla nodded. She sat down and cuddled up next to him. Luke put his arm around her and squeezed her tight. A small bird picked at twigs at their feet.

"It looks like a fairy garden," she said. Being here with Luke, she lost all track of time except each moment together. Guilt played at the edge of her conscience. She had some confessions to make. She hadn't told Luke she'd stayed an extra day in New York to see her old doctor, or the reason why. And she wasn't ready to. She hated keeping anything from Luke, but she needed time to process everything she'd learned. But seeing Stefan needed to be discussed.

"And we're finally alone," he said. Luke's eyes traced her lips, then he pulled her into his arms. His warm mouth met hers with a luscious kiss. "My love," he whispered as his kisses trailed down her neck.

As tempted as she was, Kyla gently pushed Luke back. Confusion registered in his face. She stroked his cheek, longing to throw her cares away and be in his arms.

"I don't want to spoil a perfect day, but I have something important to tell you."

"Now?" Luke asked.

"It's weighing on my mind and I don't want you to think I withheld anything from you."

Luke crossed his arms across his chest and looked weary. "What is it?"

"Lizbeth invited me to dinner my last night there with her and Stefan."

Luke started to speak but Kyla held her fingers to his lips. "Wait," she said. "It went very well. Stefan was a perfect gentleman. He said he hoped I could accept your family even with an impolite and ignorant brother like himself."

"And you believed him?" Luke asked.

"It seems Lizbeth had tamed him some. They are obviously so in love. She couldn't have been more welcoming to me. I think he was sincere."

"And I'm supposed to just forgive all the things he's done and said?"

Kyla knew she had to tread lightly. "He doesn't expect it from you or me. But he did make an effort. I wanted you to know."

"Thank you for telling me," he said. "I just don't know what to think."

"Then don't," she said. Kyla put her arms around his neck and let her lips skim his.

Luke wrapped her tightly in his arms and intensified the kiss. His hands slipped under her jacket and stroked her back. Heat raced up her spine, causing her to moan.

"Perhaps we should go to our room," she said.

Kyla looked up and there was that darn cute grin of his again. Luke looked at his watch. "And we're right on time."

"For what?" she asked.

"You'll see. Let's go."

Kyla was touched by how much time Luke had put into planning this romantic getaway. He only needed to show up and that was more than enough for her, but this extra caring really touched her heart.

Luke unlocked the door to the suite and they stepped inside. Prominent glass windows overlooked the sparkling pond. Natural wood floors, walls, and ceiling made it feel like a tree-house but even bigger than Kyla's whole cottage. Next to a quaint stone fireplace was a king-sized bed covered in luxury linens. Two white terrycloth robes were laid out for them. Facing the deck was an oversized plush sofa with satin throw pillows.

She turned and gave Luke a big hug. "It's lovely."

Luke handed her a robe from the bed. "Would you like to get more comfortable before your next surprise?"

He took her hand and led her to the master bath. The Jacuzzi tub was surrounded by flickering candles. A bottle of chilled champagne waited on the windowsill next to a silver tray of dark-chocolate-covered strawberries. Deep red rose petals floated in the sudsy water.

Luke stood in the doorway. "If you'd like, you could soak first and shake off the jet lag. Then I could join you for a glass of champagne."

A wave of disappointment flashed through Kyla's mind. Why didn't he just tear off her clothes and carry her to the tub? She looked deep into his eyes and saw blazing passion. Then she realized, that was probably exactly what he wanted to do. But he was giving her space, putting her needs first.

Kyla snatched the terrycloth robe from his hand and pushed him out the door. "I'll soak a little and when I'm all warm, silky, and relaxed, I'll call for you."

"Oh, okay," he said, skirting out the door.

She contained a giggle and shut the door behind him. It felt good to take off her travel clothes and slip into the delicious, rose-scented bath. She laid her head against the built-in pillow and let her body float in this luxury. He'd given her everything she always wanted. Could she give him what he wanted?

Her thoughts slipped back to the doctor's appointment in New York. Why hadn't she told Luke she was going? When was she going to discuss the risks pregnancy would involve with her condition? Would he still want to marry her after she made it clear that having children may be difficult? She put her wet hands over her ears as if they could block out her thoughts. They needed to talk. But not now, not here, not after all the work that went into making this the perfect romantic getaway.

There was a light knock at the door.

"How's it going in there?" Luke called through the door.

"Pretty good," she answered.

He cracked open the door. "Only pretty good?"

"It could be better," she said.

"How?"

Kyla motioned for him to come in. He stepped through the door wearing only the bathrobe loosely tied in the front.

"With you by my side," she said.

Luke walked over and poured two glasses of champagne then set them on the ridge of the bath. His eyes washed over her glistening body.

"Are you coming in or not?" she said.

When he tossed his robe off and flung it over the chair, Kyla caught her breath at the sight of his lean, hard body in the candlelight. He hurried into the water and nestled down in the bubbles next to her.

She laid her head on his bare shoulder. "Now it's perfect," she said.

His arm wrapped around her wet, slippery back as he turned her toward him. His lips covered hers, his tongue danced over his lips.. Kyla slipped along the side of the bath, and Luke moved quickly to keep her head from going completely under the water.

She came up sputtering, and the horrified look on his face made her burst out laughing. "It was not your fault," she said. "Your kiss made me lose balance."

Kyla leaned forward and rubbed noses with him in a playful way.

"But we could try again."

Luke lay propped on his side in bed, his eyes adjusting to the early morning sunlit room. Next to him Kyla slept soundly. Her mussed hair draped over the pillow into her eyes. With his fingertip, he slid a patch of hair aside, exposing the face of the woman he loved. She twitched for a moment and called out in her sleep, then turned over, still very deep in dreamland. Something was bothering her. He was sure of it. You can't be this close to a person and not know when something is off. Silently he wished she would finally trust him enough to tell him everything. There was not a dark secret or skeleton in her past that he could not and would not accept. She'd seen his darkest side and accepted him completely. He'd learned what love was from her and that was what he would give back.

"Luke." Kyla wiped sleep out of her dazzling green eyes.

He watched her stretch her long, creamy arms and yawn. "Shall I order coffee? Breakfast?" he asked.

Just out of sleep and far from her worries, Kyla looked peaceful and happy. "Coffee, yes. More strawberries and whatever you want," she said.

Luke kissed her cheek. "I'll order a tray. We'll have breakfast in bed."

He slid out from under of the blankets and reached for his robe.

"You don't need to put that on until they arrive," Lily said.

After calling down for room service, Luke slipped back into the bed. Lost in her arms, he almost didn't hear room service knock. He jumped up, wrapped the robe around him, and retrieved the tray from the waiter. When he turned around, Kyla, looking cozy in her robe, was sitting at the small table facing the pond.

"Let's eat here. The birds are having breakfast at the feeder and we can watch them," she said.

Luke set out the coffee service and plates of pastries and fruit and took the seat opposite her.

"I wish we could stay here forever," she said wistfully. She popped a strawberry in her mouth and then another. "Just the two of us."

"Don't you want to go home?" he asked. Luke watched her turn within herself, and the familiar mask come across her face. Gone was the playful mermaid from last evening's bath.

"I love the island and my shop. It's just…"

"What, Kyla? Are the wedding plans too much for you?"

She forced a smile. "Of course not. I know it will be beautiful. Maybe I'm just tired from traveling."

"Maybe," he said, searching her face for clues. "One less worry for you is Lily. She's back to normal and the doctor said the baby is fine. In a week or two they'll welcome their new little one."

"I'm happy for them," Kyla said. She set down her fork and stared out the window.

"She thinks it's a girl," Luke said. "Maybe someday…"

"And maybe not," she said with a start.

Kyla suddenly paled and Luke realized, even though he'd been trying to cheer her up, he'd hit a sore spot. He looked down at the breakfast that no longer appealed to his clenched stomach. This conversation needed to be continued, but judging from her reaction, this was not the time.

He stood up. "I'm going to take a shower."

"Okay," she said.

He'd hoped she'd ask to join him. Disappointed, Luke turned on his heel and headed for the massive bathroom. Would it always be like this with Kyla? He just needed to give her time.

Chapter Thirty-Five

"Lily's in labor," Jude said, breathless.

"Hang on." Kyla ran into Luke's kitchen, tapped him on the shoulder, and switched on her speakerphone. "How is she doing?"

"She and Ian are on the way to the hospital, and Ryan and I are meeting them there."

"We're on our way," Kyla said. "What's her status?"

"Contractions fast and often."

"See you there."

Luke had the keys in his hand. "Ready when you are."

They hurried out to the car and Luke sped into town. The island hospital was known for its efficient care. There were no nicer nurses or more competent doctors anywhere, Kyla reassured herself. She'd been so busy with the wedding plans the last few weeks, she'd barely seen Lily. The baby would be a little early. It should be fine. Kyla forced herself to breathe into her abdomen. No sense bringing her own stress to the hospital with her.

The maternity waiting area was brightly lit and scattered with people. On a small leather couch, Grandpa John sat next to Jason, who was holding a bouquet of flowers. Lily's mother,

Katherine, who had already been there visiting a few days, was in the chair next to them.

"Any word?" Kyla asked, sitting down next to them.

Grandpa John's smile was contagious. "Just the normal waiting. Ian's in with her and the doctor's been out to tell us she is doing perfectly."

Luke exhaled with relief. "Can I get anyone anything?"

Katherine shook her head. "Thanks, but Jude and Ryan just made a coffee run and should be back soon."

"Sit down, Luke," Kyla said. "You're making me nervous." Her eyes scanned the bright yellow walls filled with pictures of smiling mothers cradling their babies in their arms.

He smiled sheepishly and took a chair next to her. "I'm so jumpy you'd think we were having the baby."

A weight dropped in Kyla's stomach. Her hands were clammy. She looked up, seeing all the love and concern in the room. It would be there for her, too, when her time came. It was time to tell Luke her fears about having children and put her past evasive behavior behind her.

Jude and Ryan turned the corner with cardboard trays of Styrofoam coffee cups and offered some to everyone.

"And hot chocolate for you, my man," Ryan said. He handed the fragrant drink to Jason. "So, how do you feel about being a big brother soon?" he asked.

Jason puffed up his shoulders. "Mom says I can hold the baby myself and help take care of her."

"You'll be a great helper for her," Kyla said. "And having your grandmother here must be special."

Jason grinned. "She made pancakes for me this morning. With strawberries on top."

"Yum." Luke rubbed his belly.

All heads perked up as the door to the delivery room opened and the doctor stepped out.

He announced with a bright smile, "It's a very vocal and completely healthy girl!"

A cheer rose up. Kyla reached out and hugged Jason and then Grandpa John. "Congratulations," she said.

Luke pulled her into his arms. "I'm so happy for them," he said. His dreamy gaze spoke volumes.

"Me, too," Kyla said. Relief flooded through her. As it receded, a palpable longing for a child clung to her.

The doctor cleared her throat. "We'll get them settled and you can go into the birthing suite."

Katherine rose from her seat. "I'm her mother. Can I come with you now?"

"Sure thing," the doctor said.

A few minutes later, a nurse came out and guided the rest of them down a shiny hall to the birthing room. Wood floors, fluffy curtains, and a bed framed by a large headboard made the room look more like a hotel suite. A balloon bouquet in shades of pink floated in the air announcing, "It's a Girl."

With Jason in hand, Grandpa John hurried over to Lily. "Congratulations, honey," he said.

Lily, face flushed, gazed down at the little swaddled bundle nestled in her arms. "It's a girl," she said, fingering the pink knit cap on the baby's head.

"We heard," Grandpa John said. He winked at Jason. "Couldn't be happier."

Jason leaned over to get a good look. "She's so little."

Ian put his hand on his son's shoulder. "That's how they come. You were that little once."

Jason looked unconvinced.

Kyla approached the bed, looking carefully at the mother and sleeping child. A golden light radiated from them, creating a healthy glow. All would be well now. "Congratulations, Lily, Ian. She's a beautiful baby."

"Have you named her yet?" Jude asked.

Lily looked up at Ian. "We've decided to name her Guinevere. And Gwyn for short."

"Pretty," Jude said.

"It's Welsh," Kyla said. "From the royal court of Arthur, if I remember correctly."

Ian stood beside the bed, staring down at his girls. "It's also from an old David Crosby song that Lily and I both love."

"I remember it," Luke said. "Good choice."

Lily held the baby out to Kyla. "Do you want to hold her a minute?"

Kyla took the tightly wrapped bundle in her arms. The sweet smell of baby filled her senses with longing. The child opened her clear blue eyes as if to say hello and then slipped back to sleep. The connection was instant and it stunned Kyla.

"She's an old soul, this one," Kyla said, handing her back to her mother.

Ryan rushed into the room with a huge bouquet of flowers in his hands. "Sorry it took so long." He brought them to the table beside Lily. "May I take a peek?" he asked.

Lily pulled the blanket back to show him the sweet girl.

"She has a heart-shaped face," Ryan said.

"And a delicate golden curl on her forehead," Ian chimed in.

Kyla stepped quietly back from the bed and let the others have their turn. She sat down on the leather loveseat by the

window and watched everyone admire the baby and congratulate Lily.

Jude wandered over and dropped into the rocking chair
next to Kyla. "I'm so glad everything turned out so well. Lily
had me worried there for a while."

"I know what you mean."

Jude nudged Kyla. "Look how cute Luke is being with
the baby."

"I know," Kyla said.

"What's wrong?" Jude asked. "I mention Luke and your
face falls to the floor."

Kyla sighed. "It's everything. The wedding, a baby, moving
into his house."

Jude raised her eyebrows. "Sounds pretty good to me."
She stared off longingly toward Ryan, who stood at Luke's
side. "Have you talked to Luke about it?" Jude asked.

"Not yet."

"Well, what are you waiting for, girl? After the wedding?"

Kyla watched Luke make a fuss over the baby. He looked
so happy. "What if I can't have a child? It's not fair to Luke."

Jude lowered her voice. "What if you can? Aren't you the
one who said attitude makes a big difference in healing?"

"Right," Kyla said. "Sometimes doubts just linger. And
with the wedding so close…"

"Wedding jitters. Don't worry," Jude said. "Luke is steady
in one direction, right toward you! I wish Ryan felt like that
about me. You're lucky to have a guy like that."

"Right. Thanks for reminding me, Jude."

"That's what friends are for. Now, can we talk about
important matters?"

Kyla nodded.

"Can we do a shower for Lily now?" Jude asked.

Lily had not wanted a shower until the baby was born. Somehow she felt, with all her health issues, it might be bad luck. Kyla had understood.

"Why don't we plan one for when she gets home?" Kyla said. "A special one with tea and cookies and lots of gifts."

Jude leaned forward and whispered, "I'll get it all arranged."

Luke whistled on their way home from visiting Ian, Lily, and the new baby. He glanced over toward Kyla again, but she was still staring out the window. Her red hair caught the light breeze from the open window. He'd seen the joy in her eyes when she'd held tiny Gwyn, but sorrow had rippled through her as well. Luke turned down Main Street to drive Kyla home.

"You're pretty quiet," he said.

"Just thinking. Jude and I are planning a quick baby shower for Lily when she gets home in a couple of days."

"Count me in," Luke said. "If men are invited, of course."

"You're in," Kyla said.

"They sure had a beautiful baby girl," Luke said.

"Very," Kyla answered.

Luke kept driving and gave up on the conversation. He turned down her gravel drive and parked in front of the house.

"Can you come inside so we can talk?" she asked.

"Of course," Luke's hands gripped the wheel. Don't expect the worse, he reminded himself.

Chapter Thirty-Six

Kyla turned on the light in her cottage and greeted the cats. The scent of lemon verbena lingered in the air from the creams she had made the day before.

"Take a seat." Kyla motioned Luke toward the oak dining table. "I'll make us some tea."

She turned her back to him to collect her thoughts. The conversation with Jude echoed in her mind as she boiled water and brought down her favorite tea blend. If she really wanted to move forward toward the life she longed for, she had to stop letting her fears get in the way.

At seventy degrees out, it was amazingly warm for May. "Would you like it iced?" she asked.

"Sure. That's fine."

Kyla brought over the clear glass teapot filled with the golden mixture to steep a bit before pouring. She sat down next to Luke. Even as he smiled at her, she could see the weariness in his eyes. She'd put him through enough.

"I know I haven't been the easiest to figure out lately, and I'm sorry." Kyla put her hand on his. "It's not because I don't love you, Luke, it's because I do."

She saw his face lighten. "And I you," he said.

"A good marriage is based on honesty and trust, and I know we've had a bumpy road in that area at times."

"We have at that." Luke's crooked smile touched her heart. "But I hope that's behind us now."

Kyla poured some tea into the iced glasses.

He looked questioningly at her.

"I've lived with a lot of secrets. It's always been especially hard for me to talk about my family."

"You don't have to tell me if you don't want to," Luke said.

"But I do. If I don't get it all out, it will always stand between us."

His long, beautiful fingers wrapped around the glass of tea and brought it to his mouth. He sipped slowly, his eyes never leaving hers.

Kyla fidgeted in her chair. "There were a few other reasons I stayed in New York longer than expected."

Luke's eyes widened and the fear lurking behind them became apparent. "I figured you'd tell me when you were ready."

"After the shower in New York, your mother asked me again about my father. There was no sense avoiding the subject any longer. I told her I remember very little and that he was never spoken of after he stopped coming by the house. I was only eight then. My father and I would romp through the woods by his cabin, his long, dark hair flowing in the wind. We'd stop and sit on a boulder overlooking a river and he would play his flute. He taught me about his culture and about the signs in nature and the spirit world. My father was Iroquois."

Luke caressed her cheekbone with the back of his hand. "You can thank him for these beautiful cheekbones," he said. "Why have you not talked about him with me before?"

"It wasn't exactly a childhood of the highest social register. And it left me damaged in its wake." Kyla remembered how her mother had drilled into her brain not to trust men and to make sure she relied only on herself.

"You know I don't care what my parents and society think," Luke said.

"I've never trusted anyone," she said slowly. "Until now."

Luke stared at her for a full minute. "Are you sure?"

"Completely," she said.

"You never saw your father again?" Luke asked.

"According to my mother, my father was a professional musician and played with bands at big festivals. But his career was waning when they met in the 1980s at a concert in the park. She called him an old hippie."

"Sex, love, and rock 'n' roll?" Luke said.

"And free love it seems." Kyla sighed. Was any love free? she wondered. "What I mostly remember was my mother laughing more when he was around and the bedroom door was shut a lot. And the yelling. Then he'd stomp out and leave for days at a time. Not even close to the childhood you had."

"I'm sorry," Luke said. "My dad wasn't around much, but he was there. Unfortunately, most of his focus was either telling me what to do or what I was doing wrong."

"At least he cared," Kyla said. She cleared off the table and brought the dishes to the kitchen. "My dad always bragged he was a distant relation to Crazy Horse. He seemed to value his freedom more than his family. I used to look around at the other kids' dads at school functions and wish they were mine."

Luke stood behind her and put his hands on her shoulders. His strong fingers worked out the knots in her shoulders. "You have me now," he whispered in her ear.

She turned and let the years of buried tears surface. "I made my mother tell me the whole truth while I was home. She'd kept it from me all these years. My father was found dead and alone by a neighbor covered in his own vomit, whiskey bottles strewn everywhere."

Luke held her close and stroked her hair. "Shhhh, it's okay," he said. He turned her around. "None of that was your fault."

"I know," Kyla said. She reached for some tissue on the sink and wiped her eyes. "It was just one more thing hidden."

"The good news is," Luke said forcing a smile, "we'll both be much better parents than our own."

Kyla froze. "If we get a chance to be parents."

"What do you mean, Kyla? What else haven't you told me?"

She turned, walked over to the couch, and plopped down. "I see how much you trust me."

Luke stood over her. "That's not fair. What am I supposed to think? You're still holding things back."

She forced herself to look him in the eye. "I went to see my old physician in New York. The one who diagnosed me with lupus. I'm feeling fine now, but I had to find out about getting pregnant."

"Don't you think we should have discussed that together?" Luke said. "I would have flown out and gone to the appointment with you."

"You kept talking about having a child and I know how much it means to you."

Luke let out a long sigh. "Give me some credit, Kyla. I know all about lupus and was well aware it could affect pregnancy. I thought we would cross that bridge together when we were ready."

"You're right," she said. "I was just afraid you'd marry me and if I couldn't have children you would…"

Luke pulled her off the couch and drew her up to him. "Either we face our fears together or we let them drive us apart. Which is it going to be, Kyla?"

Her body shook uncontrollably. In a split second, everything that mattered could be gone. Fear bit at her heels and doubt reared its ugly voice, but love spoke loudest of all.

"Together," she said. Kyla reached out to him with open arms. She could feel his body trembling and pulled him close.

He tipped her chin up to meet his gaze. "Together," he said. Luke put an arm around Kyla's waist and brought her to the couch. "Tell me about the doctor visit."

She sat down next to him, relief flooding every cell. Her secrets were out, and here she was sitting next to the man she loved, ready to discuss their future together. "The good news is if we wait to get pregnant until I have been in remission for at least six months, the doctor said having a healthy, full-term baby is very possible."

Luke looked visibly relieved. "Whatever it takes," he said.

"I will need to be closely monitored by a specialist in Seattle during pregnancy to avoid possible issues."

"We can do that," he said. "Ferry over to Seattle, go to Pike Place Market after your visit, make a day out of it." He was staying upbeat and supportive and she knew he'd be there no matter what.

"There are risks," Kyla said. "Luckily, there is a very small chance of the child having lupus. But there is also an increased chance of miscarriage and premature delivery. There are many things we can do to prevent it."

Worry was written on his face, but his spirit was strong. "Just name it," Luke said.

"I'll need to eat healthy, relax, get lots of sleep, and stay out of direct sun."

Luke laughed, "Not much sun here to worry about."

She scowled at him before laughing.

"No, seriously," Luke said. "Once we're married and living together at the winery, you'll have all the help you need. Becca can work in your herb fields in the summer. I can bring you breakfast in bed and…"

"I won't be an invalid," Kyla said. "I'll need to stay active. Becca will manage the shop, but I'll keep working and hire another part-time person and go in fewer hours. The more immediate focus is finalizing our wedding plans and picking out some baby gifts for Ian and Lily."

"Shall we go shopping?" Luke asked. He glanced at his watch. "If we leave now, we can get off island to the Babyland shop before they close."

Kyla retrieved her purse and followed him to the car. "A man who likes to shop? How did I get so lucky?"

Chapter thirty-Seven

Grandpa John's living room was filled with pink balloons and a bright banner announcing, "It's a Girl!"

Luke took the giant, stuffed dog he'd picked out and laid it next to the handmade cradle the baby rested in. "For the little one," he said.

Lily laughed. "It's bigger than her. Thank you."

Ian rocked the cradle gently. He held a finger to his lips and whispered, "Shh."

"Honey," Lily said. "They've all come to see Gwyn. Let's give them a viewing."

Kyla and Luke leaned in close as Lily lifted the blanket.

"She's a beauty," Luke said.

"And she has your little turned-up nose," Kyla said to Lily.

Out of the corner of her eye, Kyla noticed Ian checking to see if the comment was correct.

The baby stirred and opened her eyes. "Look at that," Kyla said. "She has her father's eyes."

"Yes, she does," Ian said. "She quiets right down when I hold her."

Katherine joined the conversation. "I think she's a bit of a daddy's girl from what I've seen." She smiled at her own daughter, Lily.

Ian all but gloated. "Yes you are, little one," he said to the baby.

"No wonder," Lily said. "Except for feeding time, Ian barely lets me see the baby."

"I didn't mean…" Ian stammered.

Lily took Ian's hand. "I'm just kidding. You are the best dad any baby could ever want."

Luke put his arm around Kyla's waist. "Let's go put your gift down and give some of the others a chance to see Gwyn."

As planned, Jude and Ryan had come over earlier and arranged a table with fresh flowers and various appetizers. Shirley would be bringing the cake. Kyla walked over to the counter already overflowing with gifts, placed their cellophane-wrapped basket on the table, and admired its contents. Healthy Baby soaps, creams, and shampoos rested on top of a soft, hooded bath towel and washcloth set. Tied in a satin ribbon was a hand-carved comb and brush set with pink and purple hearts on it.

"It's lovely," Jude said, looking over Kyla's shoulder. She pointed to a package. "We got her a dozen receiving blankets with bunnies and kitties on them. You can never have too many of those."

Kyla nodded. Jude had more experience in these areas, since she had a daughter. Although she hardly ever spoke of her and Kyla had not met her yet.

Ryan leaned over the table and pointed. "And I picked out some TinyTot tableware with a coordinating melamine ladybug plate, bowl, and spoon set for her."

"A budding chef perhaps?" Kyla asked.

Ian approached them. "What a bounty of gifts," he said. "Thank you all. Now, what can I get you all to drink?" He looked sleepy, but his wide grin said it all.

"We'll help ourselves," Jude said. "You go be with your wife."

Kyla turned and saw Luke admiring the baby now in Ian's arms next to them.

"She's sleeping," Luke whispered. "So peaceful."

"Wait until you hear her cry," Katherine said with a yawn.

At those words, Gywn's eyes burst open and a hungry wail filled the room. Lily started to get up, but Ian insisted she sit down and he'd bring the baby to her.

"Daddy's angel," he said. He patted the baby's back with his artist's hands. "It's okay, little one," he cooed at the baby. "Mommy's here." Gwyn was swaddled in a light blanket, wearing a tiny knit cap. Ian carried his precious bundle over to her mother.

Lily held the baby to her chest and wrapped a blanket around them both as she nursed the infant.

Katherine sat at her side. "I remember when I nursed you at your grandmother's house next door."

Lily looked up at her. "Three generations now."

Kyla imagined nursing her own child with her grand-mother and mother at her side. It would be four generations for her.

The front door burst open and Shirley and Ron arrived, followed by Betty. "The cake is here," Shirley called out. She put the pink, buttercream-iced sheet cake on the table.

"Sorry we're late," Betty said. "Shirley had us all putting on the final touches at the last minute."

"Well worth it," Grandpa John said, admiring the masterpiece.

Kyla agreed. She loved how they'd decorated the plate around the cake with little rattles, beaded baby bracelets, and plastic safety pins.

"My sweetie is quite the baker," Ron said, beaming at Shirley.

Lily handed the baby back to Ian. He placed a towel over his shoulder and patted her back for a soft burp. Together they walked over to admire the cake.

"How cute," Lily said. "It's shaped like a onesie. And I love the little elephant design." She turned and hugged Shirley, then Betty. "You two are the best neighbors ever."

Betty pointed to a package on the table. "I got you a gift that will last Gwyn's lifetime," she said.

Kyla watch Lily slip off the ribbon and paper and hold up an elegant, pale pink baby book. On the front, behind a sheet of plastic, was a picture of Gwyn on her first day of life.

Lily held it to her chest. "It's like my grandmother's guest-book, only for babies."

"My sister does come up with some good ideas once in a while," Shirley said.

"If you're up to it," Ian said, "let's open our gifts from these wonderful people."

Lily sat at the head of the table.

"I'll hold the baby, if you want," Katherine said. "You've already opened mine."

Lily held up a plastic fishing tackle box and opened the top. "Look what my mother gave me."

Kyla leaned in close to see. "Very clever," she said. "Look, Luke."

She pointed to the drawers stocked full of every supply from baby Tylenol to aloe wipes, creams, salves, and even baby Band-Aids.

"A helpful thing to have on hand," Luke said with a nod toward Katherine.

Katherine smiled and sat down in the rocker with the baby and sang her a soft lullaby.

Lily held up a set of pink, blue, and yellow stuffed ducks. "She'll certainly have enough stuffed animals to fill her room."

Ian petted the head of the massive stuffed dog from Luke. "And a guard dog."

Kyla watched Lily hold up tiny T-shirts, hair bows, and booties. Grandpa John gave them a little red wagon painted to say, "Welcome Wagon." It was filled with diapers and other supplies and wrapped in a big red bow. Lily passed the gifts around for all to see.

Kyla was swept right into the sweet scene. Everyone around the table was smiling, all worries forgotten and the joy of the new baby filling everyone's soul.

As Luke snapped pictures with his cell phone, Kyla posed holding a Sweet Dreams mobile in the air. Cute little animals circled the rainbow-colored base as it played a lullaby. Luke moved in next to her and snapped a selfie of them together.

He showed the picture to Kyla. "A glimpse of your future," he said.

In a flashing vision, Kyla knew his words were the truth.

Chapter Thirty-Eight

*L*uke carried the multi-colored, handwoven basket as Kyla scouted Saturday's local farmers' market for her next purchase. Booths lined the grassy park, covered with white awnings and filled with everything from food to crafts. The buttery smell of fresh kettle corn filled the air. The wedding was only a week away, so they had a long list of items to buy and people to meet with for final planning. Luke adjusted the heavy shopping basket in his hand. Island Thyme Café was catering the wedding, but they needed to stock up the house with appetizers to serve the company as they arrived this week.

"Looks like half the island is here today," Kyla said, waving to Audrey, who was walking with Frank and Marco from Books, Nooks & Coffee.

Luke was glad he'd worn a T-shirt, as the early summer sun beat down on his shoulders. He'd had to dig up his sunglasses for the day.

"Let's go over to the Happy Goat Pastures booth. We can get some of these herbed spreads to go with Brett's crusty bread."

Kyla counted out the money and piled the cartons of cheese in the basket next to four boxes of local eggs, jars of local preserves and honey, bags of fresh greens, and an over-flowing bunch of garlic shoots. "I don't think the basket will hold much more," Luke said. He set it on the ground and shook out his hand. "Why don't I go empty everything into boxes in the car and meet you at Brett's Bread?"

"Good idea," Kyla said.

"Hi, you two." Jude approached with Ryan at her side.

"Need any help with that?" Ryan asked Luke.

"I'm taking our loot back to the car. Be right back."

Luke often ran into Ryan at the market buying produce for Island Thyme Café, but today he supposed they were shopping for his and Kyla's upcoming wedding.

On his way to the parking lot, Luke passed the perpetu-ally tanned woman with the fish trailer covered in pictures of mermaids. Her husband caught king salmon in Alaska, flash froze it on the boat, and packaged it to sell. Luke had never tasted better. He added a few fillets to his load to make for dinner. He emptied the basket into boxes in the back seat of the car. He was parked right by the post office, so he ran in to see if any last-minute RSVPs had come in.

Luke leafed through the mail. Nothing from Stefan. He'd hoped, after his brother's peace offering to Kyla, he would rise above their differences and come to the wedding after all. He still didn't know for sure if his father was coming. Luke told himself it didn't matter, but deep down he knew it did. And he wanted everyone there for Kyla, to support their union and new life together. A now-empty basket in hand, he hurried across the parking lot and located Kyla. She was talking to Kelly, the local reporter, with Jude and Ryan near the Friends of the Library book sale. She held a large bag with breads looming over the top.

"Here, I'll take that." Luke placed the bag in his basket.

"Thanks," Kyla said. "Kelly was just filling us in some more on the movie being filmed next month in Grandview. The producers wanted a seaside town, and they picked ours because of the Victorian architecture and protected harbor."

Kelly continued. "It's called *Murder Most Magic*. I hear it is a cozy mystery and romance with a twist."

"You know they've asked if they can paint all our shops white for a few weeks," Kyla said, "but then we can get any color we want done after they leave."

"Nice way to get a free paint job," Ryan said as he scanned the piles of used books for sale. "It should bring in a lot of business while they're here."

"That's what I was thinking."

"Me, too," Marco said, joining the conversation. His arms were filled with books. "I expect they'll drink lots of coffee."

"And tea," Luke said, winking at Kyla.

"Becca around?" Marco asked.

"She's minding the shop," Kyla said. "But I'm sure she wouldn't mind some company."

Luke noticed Marco blush. Another budding romance. Then Ryan slipped in close to Jude and took her hand. He looked up and saw Kyla notice as well. She winked at him. Another wedding in the works, he wondered?

"I'm off to shop," Kelly said, turning to go. "Oh, and one other thing. Guess who is playing the lead role? Peyton Chandler!"

The gasp from Ryan was just loud enough for all of them to hear. He covered his mouth with his hand as his face went white as pure marble.

Jude stared at him. "Are you all right?"

Luke's eyes met Kyla's. The same concern registered in her as Luke felt. Something was not right, not right at all.

"Ryan." Jude shook his shoulder gently.

"I'm fine," he said.

Ryan's voice was flat and distant. Luke got the distinct impression that Ryan wished he were alone. "Kyla," Luke said. "We need to go pick out the flowers today. Let's head over there."

Kyla nodded and took Luke's arm. "See you soon. Call if you need anything," she yelled back at her friends.

They walked across the grass to the floral booth. He glanced back and saw Jude standing there alone and Ryan walking back toward town. "That was strange."

"I'm worried about Jude," Kyla said. "Did you see the way he dropped her hand and froze?"

"Something tells me having the infamous Peyton Chandler in town is going to make some big waves," Luke said.

Kyla stopped a few feet from the flowers and looked up at him. "More like a tsunami, I would say."

Luke leaned over the top of Kyla's head. "Let's hope this time your knack for foreseeing things is wrong."

"It does happen," she said with a smile. "Now let's go choose some flowers."

They waited for the line at the flower stall to thin so they could get to the front. Kyla held up a bunch of light pink peonies. "Aren't these gorgeous?" she asked him.

"Absolutely," Luke said.

"We'll order the blush-colored peonies, creamy roses, white oriental poppies, and ballet slipper pink ranunculus for the wedding bouquet," Kyla said. "And for the centerpieces and bridesmaids, add in the daisies, and the sweet alyssum and fragrant sweet peas with stalks of flowering rosemary." Kyla held the fragrant flowers close and lost herself in their scent. "It's going to be a beautiful wedding."

Luke smiled. "That it is."

While Luke carried in groceries from the car, Kyla put every-thing away in the stainless steel refrigerator in Luke's kitchen. It was soon to be "their" kitchen, she reminded herself. She'd already brought most of her things over, and Luke had been very accommodating, changing and moving anything she wanted. They'd gone shopping for new linens and bedding and a few items to add a woman's touch to the house. Kyla would leave most of her furniture at the cottage that Becca would now rent from her while she managed Tea & Comfort. Bailey wagged his tail and danced around the kitchen floor in anticipation of a treat.

Kyla petted the stocky dog. She loved the patch across his eye. "Good boy. Let me see what I can find for you."

"This is the last of it," Luke said. He set the box of pro-duce on the granite countertop. "Let's get this put away and take a break."

Kyla opened the refrigerator door. "I'm not sure I can stuff one more thing in here."

Luke reached in and adjusted a few items on the top shelf. "Plenty of room," he said.

"No fair, you're so much taller."

Luke scooped her up and held her in the air.

"Put me down." She wriggled around, trying not to laugh.

"I will for a kiss." He puckered out his lips.

Kyla leaned in for a quick kiss, but Luke held her close. She wrapped her legs around his waist and lost herself in the sensation of his moist lips on hers. The ringing of Luke's cell phone broke the moment and he slid her gently to the ground.

"I better get it," he said.

He answered the phone but remained silent for a few moments. Kyla watched on in concern.

"I'm glad to hear that," Luke said. "Thursday will be fine. We'll see you then."

Luke hung up the phone and stared at Kyla with a dazed expression. "It was my brother, Stefan. He was wondering if it was too late to RSVP for the wedding for him and Lisbeth. He apologized profusely for the late response."

"What did you tell him?"

"I hope it's okay with you, Kyla. I told them to come."

Kyla hugged him. "It's more than okay. It makes me so happy to know your whole family is going to be there for you."

"For us," Luke said. "But my dad has still not let us know if he's coming for sure."

"I know. I'm sorry," Kyla said. "Maybe he'll surprise us."

Luke shrugged. He'd thought he and his dad had made progress when he was out here visiting, but he'd not heard from him since. "Let's go sit outside on the deck. It's a beautiful day and just the two of us. And, of course, Bailey. C'mon, boy."

Kyla sat down next to him on the wooden bench and rested her head against his chest. His steady heart pattered in her ear. Bailey plopped down at their feet.

"I hope the weather holds for the wedding next Saturday," she said. "Guests will start arriving in a few days and everything is going to get pretty crazy."

Kyla wouldn't have it any other way. Her mother and grandmother would be here early to help out and her agent, Arlene, was coming on Friday. Luke's family and some old friends from college were attending, and most of the island was invited.

"Not too crazy, I hope," Luke said. He pointed to the grassy area. "If it's sunny, we can serve lunch on tables in the vineyard and under the flowering dogwood trees."

"Shirley wouldn't let me see the cake," Kyla said. "She wants it to be a surprise. All I know is that she wants to match each layer to the flowers we picked out."

"I thought Lily was making the cake."

"Shirley is in charge of the major baking. But Lily is making cupcakes with lavender icing and a grape vine motif on top."

Luke laughed. "We're in good hands."

Kyla squeezed Luke's hand. "So am I. The oak wine barrels with flower arrangements on top will look beautiful out there in the garden. That was a great idea, Luke. I'm sure Ryan will take care of everything else."

"He knows his stuff," Luke said. "I wonder what the issue was at the market with Ryan and the movie news."

"I don't have a good feeling about it. I'll give Jude a call tomorrow and see if there is anything I can do."

Luke stared out over the vineyard. Kyla felt sadness radiating off him. Panic stuck in her throat. Was he doubting...no! Of course not. And she would not let herself either. She held his hand and waited for him to speak.

"I hope my father shows up," Luke said.

Kyla stroked his face. He looked like a sweet, little boy. "How could he not? He loves you."

Hope lit Luke's face like a ray of sun. "Thank you."

"There are chocolate truffles in the refrigerator," Kyla said, tempting him.

"That reminds me," Luke said. "Ian finished the design for Madrona Winery's new blend we worked on together."

"I can't wait to see it. My spicy chocolate blended with your bold red wine is amazing."

"A magical blend," Luke said with a playful kiss. "Just like us."

Kyla looked out over the pastoral property. A deep peace and contentment washed over her. And gratitude. She imagined the cats stretched out in the sun and her tending the gardens and helping Luke with the vineyard. Very soon her lavender field would be blooming, interspersed with Chinese red poppies and golden sunflowers. Already her chives were coming up and the perennials were doing well. She'd planted nasturtium seeds that would bloom in all colors and go well in salads, and a new addition, chocolate flower seeds from a local nursery.

Luke caressed her face. "I feel like I'm dreaming sometimes." He waved his hand out toward the vineyard. "That I found this place and I found you."

Kyla placed her hand on his. "It's real, Luke. We found each other."

Chapter Thirty-Nine

The Madrona trees, their smooth red bark, slick leaves, and white fairy flowers beckoned Kyla outside the silky tent. The guests were nestled in the vineyard in wooden chairs. Notes of "Pachelbel's Canon" drifted through the air as Siri's string quartet began playing the song.

The bridal party proceeded ahead with Jude and Lily in their pearl-colored gowns, bouquets in hand, walking down the aisle arm in arm with the groomsmen, Ian, and Ryan. They took their place on the stage on each side of Luke. Kyla's heart skipped a beat. He looked so handsome standing there in his silver-grey tuxedo and creamy rose boutonniere waiting for her. She stood by the door watching the flower girl skip down the aisle tossing rose pedals in the air with glee. Following her, dressed in a doggie tuxedo, was Bailey. In his mouth he carried a small basket with the wedding rings tucked inside. Friendly faces turned and encouraged them.

Kyla's mother stood beside her and squeezed her hand. "Are you ready?" she asked.

Kyla admired her exquisite pearl-white- and blush-colored tulle dress with the cap sleeves. The iridescent pearl applique trickled down the full-length skirt in a floral pattern.

She touched the antique necklace her grandmother had placed around her neck for her "something old." It was time.

She stepped into the light of the gloriously sunny day and glided past the rows of family and friends. As she walked by, Betty and Mary waved, and a grinning Shirley shot her a wink. Familiar faces blurred as they moved toward the stage. Grandpa John, sitting right up front with Jason, nodded with an affirming smile. The sound of violins rose in the air as Kyla approached the grape vine arbor covered in flowers and twinkling lights.

Luke's eyes met hers. His face softened as his bride came into view, then a beaming smile burst across his face. Kyla could hardly move up the steps to join him. Luke nodded slightly toward the front row of seats. Kyla glanced over, and alongside Stefan and Lizbeth was Alexander, Luke's father, sitting beside Grace. Everyone was here.

But at this moment, only one person had Kyla's complete attention and all of her heart. She stepped up on the oak platform and took her place beside Luke. Tears of joy welled up inside her. The music stopped and Kyla turned to face the man she would happily spend the rest of her life with. All of her running had led her right here to this perfect moment.

The story continues in the Madrona Island Series...

Book One – *The Guestbook*
Everyone Remembers Their First Love...
But Sometimes it's the Second Love that Lasts *Evocative and heartfelt, The Guestbook is the profound story of one woman's journey toward hope, renewal and a second chance at love on a lush Pacific Northwest island. Curl up with your favorite cup of cocoa and enjoy.* ~Anjali Banerjee - author of Imaginary Men and Haunting Jasmine said about this women's fiction romance

Fleeing her picture-perfect marriage among the privileged set of Brentwood and the wreckage of a failed marriage, Lily Parkins decides to move to the only place that still holds happy memories, her grandmother's old farmhouse. The lush and majestic setting of the Pacific Northwest calls to her and offers a place of refuge and perhaps renewal. Her grandmother has passed away, leaving the Madrona Island Bed & Breakfast Inn to Lily. Left with only an old guestbook as her guide– a curious book full of letters, recipes, and glimpses into her family history–Lily is determined to embrace her newfound independence and recreate herself, one page at a time. With the help of the quirky island residents she has befriended, she slowly finds the strength to seek out happiness on her own terms. But as soon as she has sworn off men and is standing on her own two feet, Lily meets Ian, the alluring artist who lives next door, and her new life is suddenly thrown off course. The last thing she wants to do right now is to open her heart to another man. Ultimately, Lily must decide if it's worth giving up her soul for security or risking everything to follow her heart in this romantic love story.

Book Two – *Tea & Comfort*

Book Three – *Island Thyme Café*
The third book features the vivacious and loving, Jude Simon, owner of the popular Island Thyme Café. After Kyla's wedding festivities are over, Jude must face the dark secret from her past. Years ago, she'd found out her husband was cheating on her in an article in the local paper. Left a single mother of an infant daughter, Jude went on to make a success of her café, but still hides her broken heart behind her radiant smile. At almost 40 years old, she finds herself falling hard for her new chef, Ryan. Her feelings are returned, and just when she thinks she has found love at last, Ryan's own dark secret returns in the form of a seductive ex-lover who is determined to have him back. With the help of Kyla and Lily, Jude decides to fight for what she wants most and find the happy ending she has always longed for.

Don't miss Andrea's women's fiction book, *Always with You.*

Recipes

Kyla's Chocolate & Spice Cheesecake
Created by Andrea Hurst

Preheat oven to 375°

Crust:

1½ package of chocolate graham crackers crushed

1¼ stick of butter melted

2 tsp. honey

Sprinkle of cinnamon

Pinch of culinary lavender

Add honey, cinnamon, and lavender to butter mixture.

Mix butter mixture with graham crackers and line glass cheesecake dish.

Filling:

2 packages of soft cream cheese

2 eggs beaten

2/3 cup of honey

1 tsp. pure vanilla

1½ tsp. cinnamon

¼ tsp. culinary lavender

4 heaping Tbsp. pure cocoa powder

Mix until creamy

Pour over crust. Bake in the oven for 30 minutes. Do not over-bake.

Topping:

1 16-oz. carton sour cream

¼ tsp. culinary lavender

1/3 cup honey

1 tsp. vanilla

2 tsp. cinnamon

1 heaping Tbsp. of pure cocoa powder

Mix and spread over warm cheesecake just out from oven. Put back into the oven for five minutes. Remove. Cool and then chill in the refrigerator.

Decorate with a sprig of fresh lavender.

Biscotti with Lavender and Orange

Sarah Richardson–

Lavender Wind Farm http://www.lavenderwind.com/

Ingredients

½ cup sugar

3 Tbsp. butter

3 tsp. ground lavender

2 tsp. grated orange rind

½ tsp. vanilla

2 large egg whites

1½ cup all-purpose flour

¾ tsp. baking powder

1/8 tsp. salt

¼ cup toasted almonds

Optional: 3 oz. melted semi–sweet chocolate

Cooking spray

Preheat oven to 325°.

Beat the first 5 ingredients at medium speed of a mixer until well blended. Beat in egg whites. Lightly spoon the flour into dry measuring cups, and level with a knife. Combine the flour, baking powder, and salt; gradually add flour mixture to sugar mixture, beating until blended. Stir in almonds.

Turn biscotti dough out onto a floured board or other surface to work on. Spray a baking sheet with cooking spray; with lightly floured hands, shape the dough into two 5-inch-long rolls; move to the baking sheet and flatten the rolls to a 1-inch thickness.

Bake them at 325° for 30 minutes. Remove the rolls from the baking sheet, and cool for 10 minutes on a wire rack.

Cut each roll diagonally into 7 half-inch slices a good sharp knife. Place the slices on baking sheet. Bake the slices at 325° for 15 minutes (the cookies will be slightly soft in the center, but will harden as they cool.

Remove from baking sheet; cool completely on wire rack.

Watermelon Mint Salad

Sarah Richardson

Lavender Wind Farm http://www.lavenderwind.com/

At the farm we raise more than lavender! This year we have a good sized mint patch and so we're starting to cook with mint. For a potluck a couple of weeks ago I made this watermelon mint salad.

Watermelon Mint Salad

7-8 lb. seedless watermelon, chilled

1 red onion, chopped

½ cup extra virgin olive oil

3 Tbsp. balsamic vinegar

1 tsp. salt

1 cup fresh chopped mint leaves

¼ tsp. ground lavender

1 cup crumbled feta cheese

Cut the watermelon off of the peel and chop into bite sized bits. Put into a colander so the watermelon can drain as you are preparing the rest of the items. Chop up the red onion and the mint into small pieces. Crumble up the feta so it will make pea or bean sized pieces. Combine the olive oil, balsamic vinegar, lavender, and salt. Then put them all in a bowl and combine gently. Liquid will form at the bottom of the bowl, so you can serve it with a slotted spoon to avoid puddles on the plate.

Island Truffles
Michaelene McElroy

5 oz. 70% chocolate, chopped finely (Callebaut chocolate recommended)
3 Tbsp. Merlot (a fruit forward variety)
1 Tbsp. cream (preferably organic)
1/8 tsp. pure lavender extract
Cocoa powder (Cocoa Barry recommended)

Add first three ingredients to a double boiler set over gently simmering water. Do not let the bottom of the insert touch the water. After one minute, begin to gently whisk the mixture until the chocolate is completely melted. Take care not to let the liquid become too hot or the mixture will seize. Remove from the heat and gently whisk in the lavender extract. Remove truffle mixture to a bowl and let rest at room temperature until set, but still pliable enough to form into one-inch truffles. Refrigerate until firm. Once firm, roll the truffles in cocoa powder. Tap off excess. Truffles will last a week if refrigerated. Remove from refrigerator at least thirty minutes before serving.

Bouquet de Provence
Fines Herbes Culinaire

Cameron Chandler
2 Tbsp. Tarragon
1½ Tbsp. Savory
1 Tbsp. Sage
1 Tbsp. Thyme
1 Tbsp. Marjoram

1 Tbsp. Rosemary

1 Tbsp. Chervil

1 Tbsp. Borage

2 Tbsp. Rose buds and Petals

1 Tbsp. Lavender buds

1 Tbsp. Calendula (marigold)

1 Tbsp. Rose Mallow (hibiscus)

All ingredients should be dried organic or culinary grade herbs and spices. If necessary, remove any twigs, stems, flower pods, etc. If necessary, gently crush any larger pieces to coarse texture similar to the other spices. Combine all ingredients. Mix gently, bottle and label. For longer shelf life, store away from sunlight and heat.

A mixture of cooking herbs from France is commonly called *Herbes de Provence,* and it contains savory, marjoram, rosemary, thyme and oregano. More recently, when packaged for the American market, the blend would sometimes contain lavender leaves as well.

This recipe differs in several ways from traditional blends. First, tarragon replaces oregano because most people are more likely to associate oregano with Italian or Mexican food, whereas tarragon is a more elegant aromatic and is decidedly French. Building on the layers of flavor and complexity, chervil and borage are added. Both are commonly found in a French kitchen garden. To add the floral notes, lavender buds replace the lavender leaf; and rose petals, calendula (marigold) and rose mallow (hibiscus) are added. The result is a beautifully fragrant, colorful, and elegant blend that works well with roasted meats, fowl, fishes, soups and salads.

Bouquet de Provence can easily be made at home, although some of the ingredients are best bought in bulk from a spice supplier. Since this spice blend is so fragrant and colorful, it would make a lovely favor for a shower or wedding, or a home-crafted holiday gift, or a fundraiser item for sale.

Aknowledgements

It was a pleasure returning to Madrona Island while writing the second book in the series. I'd like to thank the many people that supported me on this writing journey and all the readers who kept encouraging to finish *Tea & Comfort*.

Special thanks to: Rebecca Berus for her expertise with plotting and for sharing brainstorming walks on the cliffs of Fort Casey while I worked out the storyline. Siri Bardarson for sharing her poetic visions and exquisite use of language and listening patiently as I read the chapters to her aloud. To Sean Fletcher for his encouragement during the dark moments of writer's block. To Jean Galiana, Barbara Scharf, Kelly Zupich, Arial Pakizer and to all the friends and interns who encouraged me along the way including Billee Escot for offering her island home for a writing retreat.

To Geneva Agnos for her encouragement and for helping with the new cover design. To Justin Hurst for cheering me on. And to my constant canine companions, Basil and Ferdie, thanks for all their love.

And last but not least, I want to thank myself for showing up and making my passion for writing a reality.

Beta readers:
Echo Yupan Lu, Natalie Carlisle, True Henderson, Tracy Munter, Joyce Lalacona,

A very special thanks to Karen and Jack Krug of Spoiled Dog Winery on Whidbey Island, for assisting with the book's research and generously providing a tour of their amazing winery. http://www.spoileddogwinery.com/index.html

Author Bio

When not visiting local farmers markets or indulging her love for chocolate, ANDREA HURST is an author, editor, and literary agent. Her passion for books drives her write stories that take readers on a journey to another place and leave them with an unforgettable impression. She is a developmental editor for publishers and authors, an instructor in creative writing at the Northwest Institute of Literary Arts, and a webinar presenter for Writers Digest. She lives with her dachshunds in the Pacific Northwest, on an island much like the fictional Madrona, with all of its natural beauty and small town charm.

Her published books include *The Guestbook, Always with You, The Lazy Dog's Guide to Enlightenment* and *Everybody's Natural Food Cookbook*, and she co-authored *A Book of Miracles*. To learn more about Andrea and her books, visit

http://www.AndreaHurst-Author.com
http://www.andreahurst.com

Made in the USA
Monee, IL
14 March 2021

62710318R20177